The Almond Picker

✕✕

The Almond Picker

Simonetta Agnello Hornby

✖✖

Translated from the Italian by Alastair McEwen

Farrar, Straus and Giroux

New York

Farrar, Straus and Giroux
19 Union Square West, New York 10003

Library of Congress Cataloging-in-Publication Data
Agnello Hornby, Simonetta.
    [Mennulara. English]
    The almond picker / Simonetta Agnello Hornby ; translated from
the Italian by Alastair McEwen.
        p.   cm.
    ISBN-13: 978-0-374-18234-2
    ISBN-10: 0-374-18234-5
    I. McEwen, Alastair.   II. Title.

PQ4861.G567M4613 2005
853'.92—dc22

                                                    2004053329

Designed by Jonathan D. Lippincott

www.fsgbooks.com

1   3   5   7   9   10   8   6   4   2

to British Airways

*I owe the "illumination" that led me to this novel to a delay in
the Palermo–London flight of 2 September 2000. For this
reason—and perhaps also for the aerial link that permits me to keep
up connections with both my countries—British Airways has a special
place in this book.*

Contents

Tuesday 24 September 1963

Wednesday 25 September 1963

Monday 23 September 1963

✗✗

1. Dr. Mendicò attends a dying patient

Dr. Mendicò suddenly felt exhausted, his legs stiff and his arms tingling. He had been in the same position for over an hour, Mennulara's hands clasped between his, ceaselessly caressing her fingers with a delicate circular movement. He lifted his right hand, leaving his left—in which the deceased's hands lay, still warm—palm up on the sheet.

It was a solemn moment, which he knew well and which always moved him: the final task of a doctor defeated by death. Delicately, he closed her eyes. Then he arranged her hands, interlacing her fingers, laid them carefully on her breast, smoothed out the sheet, and drew it up to cover her shoulders before, finally, getting up to inform the Alfallipe family that Mennulara was dead.

He stayed with them for as long as was necessary, gave Gianni Alfallipe the envelope containing the dead woman's last wishes, and hurried down the stairs of the small apartment block, coming across women neighbours on their way up to offer condolences. He had felt stifled in that flat; as soon as he went out the front door he walked off with small, slow steps, filling his lungs with the still-fresh morning air. The street was only a few dozen yards long but seemed longer because it was narrow and full of corners formed by the two-

and three-storey buildings that over the centuries had proliferated at random, piling up one on top of the other and engulfing the earlier houses until they merged into what were two almost contiguous uneven walls, pierced only by two arches, like a tunnel, through which passed one of the many meandering flights of steps that formed the street network of Roccacolomba, a typical inland town clinging to the side of a mountain.

All at once Dr. Mendicò remembered that he had not wound a rosary around the dead woman's fingers, as was the custom. In his mind's eye he revisited Mennulara's bedroom trying to work out how this oversight had occurred. It was an austere little room with only the basic necessities: a bed, a chair, a wardrobe, a lamp and a radio on the bedside table, and a narrow table that served as a writing desk, on which sat a metal tray holding pens, pencils, and a large eraser, arranged in perfect order. On the shelf were two photographs of her nephews and a rather faded shot of her parents, some notepads, and few books. The walls were bare, apart from a reproduction of Ferretti's *Madonna and Child* above the bed. Missing in the room were the feminine touches and the religious ingredients: the hodgepodge of holy images, statuettes of the Virgin and the local saints, and those bottles full of holy water brought home from far places that pile up on women's bedside tables; there wasn't even a rosary. Despite this, Mennulara's bedroom had given him the feeling of being permeated with a deep, almost monastic piety.

The strip of sky carved out by the irregular pointed roofs was dazzlingly bright, with only a hint of blue. The doctor stopped, took a deep breath, and looked up, staring intensely at the sky. "Who knows where her soul has flown? May God give her peace," he said softly before setting off again to take the steps that went down towards his house. The convent bell struck eleven. Dr. Mendicò thought he would have enough time before lunch to make the necessary telephone calls, have a coffee, and take a stroll: he needed to be on his own, to think. "Not even an old doctor like me gets used to death," he murmured to himself as he rang the doorbell of his home.

After seeing Dr. Mendicò to the door, Gianni went back into the living room. His sisters and mother were waiting for him in silence. Santa, the maid, did not dare go in, out of respect for the family and in accordance with Mennulara's orders. But she could not restrain her curiosity, and so she lingered in the corridor, leaning against the kitchen door, her face drawn and still wet with tears, her arms limp against her hips, and her ears cocked to pick up snatches of the conversation.

Signora Alfallipe was slumped in the armchair, her head thrown back, her eyes full of tears, her gaze vacant. Lilla was perched on the armrest, caressing her mother's forehead. Carmela was looking out from the balcony, waiting for her husband to arrive. "What did the doctor give you?" asked Lilla. Gianni showed her the envelope with his name written on it in Mennulara's large, untidy hand. At her sister's words Carmela turned to look at them. When she saw the letter, she rushed over, exclaiming, "It'll be the will. Don't open it; we must wait for Massimo," and, in an ever shriller voice, crying over and over, "We must wait for Massimo." Signora Alfallipe began to weep, feebly repeating, as if reciting a litany, "I knew Mennù would think of me; she really cared for me." Lilla and Gianni would have liked to open the envelope immediately, but they didn't dare, nor did they have time to argue with their sister, because Santa and the women neighbours burst into the room all at once, gesticulating and offering noisy condolences. The moment she saw them, signora Alfallipe dissolved into uncontrollable sobs and was instantly surrounded by the consoling women. "What will become of me? Mennù took good care of me. What shall I do now? Ill as I am . . ."

The Alfallipes were all hugged and kissed one by one, clasped in long embraces that left them smeared with the sweat of the women's armpits and the smell of the food they had been preparing: a blend of garlic, olive oil, tomato, parsley, and bread crumbs, an age-old odour that united the family in their disgust for the lower classes.

Lilla shuddered at the thought that, since her father's death, her mother had been living here in the same building as a fish merchant, the Alfallipe family's electrician, and some paper shuffler. She blessed the good fortune that had taken her to Rome, far from this vile town. Concealing her irritation, Lilla, after the last foul-smelling embrace, told the women that her mother was feeling ill and faint; luckily, Dr. Mendicò had given her some medicine and had prescribed bed rest. She and Carmela did not want to leave her alone, distraught as she was, and they would retire with her: the good ladies were welcome to go into the room where Mennulara was lying and to help Santa prepare the body, if they so wished, while the daughters would take care of their mother, who was so much in need of them at this distressing time.

Signora Alfallipe, by way of confirming these words—after all, being a doctor's wife, Lilla could speak with a certain authority about such things—slumped even lower into the chair, spreading out her arms and letting her hands dangle over the armrests, her head still lolling against the back. She started murmuring again, "I feel ill; I'm going to faint," whereupon the three children and Santa ran to her. At that point, they could not avoid the solicitous concern of the women, who bustled about dispensing advice. They carried signora Alfallipe to her bed, and each did her best to make the older woman comfortable: one brought a glass of water, another placed a damp towel on her forehead, another put a pillow behind her shoulders, and yet another took her pulse. Signora Alfallipe, gratified by their solicitude and worried lest any improvement might deprive her of the attention she was enjoying, increased her lamentations. It was then that her son-in-law arrived.

After Santa had telephoned that morning, waking them, to announce that Mennulara was dying, Massimo Leone had not dared accompany Carmela to the flat. He had opted to stay in Alfallipe House, a few minutes away, to await developments. Only when Carmela called him to say that the woman was in a coma did he feel he might be allowed to join her. Instinctively, he had complied with Mennulara's order: "I swear on my mother's soul that in my home, where I live, he shall not set foot"—an authentic excommunication. Massimo had been married to Carmela for seven years, and he was not even allowed to set foot in the entrance to the building or to call his wife when she was visiting her mother in Mennulara's flat. He had hated that damned Mennulara with a powerful hatred, and he hated her still. Now, finally, she was dead. Massimo felt liberated. He bounded up the stairs in a state of elation mixed with resentment: he would see her corpse, but he wouldn't be able to spit on it, as she deserved, because, judging by the chatter he could hear from the stairs, it was clear that people had already arrived to pay their respects.

The neighbours, who knew all about his banishment, gathered around him sympathetically and treated him as if he were a member of the deceased's family. Their condolences were studied: "Loved your wife like a daughter, she did." "She did everything for them." "A good woman she was, believe me." As soon as he could, Massimo detached himself from the women and went into his mother-in-law's bedroom, where the family anxiously awaited him.

They greeted one another briefly, dispensing with the usual hugs and kisses. Lilla asked Santa to leave them alone and not to let anyone in, taking care to close the door well, and then shot her brother an eloquent look. Gianni immediately opened the envelope he was holding, took out the note inside, and read it, frowning. His sisters and his brother-in-law stood silent and motionless around him. Gianni continued to read in silence. Lilla could restrain herself no longer: "Read it to all of us. What does it say?" Her brother showed it to her. "I just don't get it. You take a look." At Gianni's words, his mother, who seemed to have rallied rather quickly and who was following their conversation, slumped back on the pillows once more, moaning. This time, no one paid attention to her, because Gianni had begun to read:

This isn't a real will, because I have given you all that was due to you, and I have nothing of yours to give you, but I ask you to do as I say for the last time, and this will bring you wealth. I want a funeral in Roccacolomba, without any procession of orphans or nuns, and all you Alfallipes must be present, because I deserve it. I will be buried in the plot I purchased opposite your family's, as is right for one who, like me, was the servant of the Alfallipe family. I want my photograph and these words: "Here lies Maria Rosalia Inzerillo, known as Mennulara, who entered the Alfallipe household at the age of thirteen and served it and protected it as an upstanding domestic until her death." There is nothing for me to leave in Roccacolomba; the flat where I will die is in signora Adriana's name, if she wishes to continue living in it, but you must find her a good maid and pay her well, so that she will always be served until her death. Give the things in my room to Father Arena, if he can use them for the poor and the church. All the rest of the furniture goes to signora Adriana. I want you to place an announcement right away in the Giornale di Sicilia *as I write it here, word for word:*

TODAY, MARIA ROSALIA INZERILLO,
KNOWN AS MENNULARA,
ADMINISTRATOR AND MEMBER OF THE HOUSEHOLD STAFF OF
ALFALLIPE HOUSE,
PASSED AWAY AT 55 YEARS OF AGE.
WITH DEEP SORROW, THE ALFALLIPE FAMILY ANNOUNCES
ITS INCONSOLABLE AND ETERNAL LOSS.

This sad news is given by signora Adriana Mangiaracina, widow of counsellor Orazio Alfallipe; her son Gianni and his wife, Anna Chiovaro; her daughter Lilla and her husband, Dr. Gian Maria Bolla; and her daughter Carmela and her husband, Massimo Leone. From the age of thirteen she lived in Alfallipe House and honestly served the family, which, disconsolate, mourns her passing. The funeral will be held at 3:00 p.m. in the Church of the Addolorata on 24 September 1963 and the body will be taken to the cemetery of Roccacolomba for burial in the family plot.

Do not inform my nephews. I do not want them at my funeral. May my soul go to God and the property to those who deserve it.

The mother was the first to speak. "I told you Mennulara would see to everything. She's left me her flat . . . but which of you is going to look after me, now that I'm alone?" Huddled on the bed, she drew herself up from the pillows and looked around. Her children and her son-in-law, silent and furious, ignored her.

Massimo took the paper from Gianni's hands and scrutinised it at length. Then he began to curse, and his voice rose: "What kind of document is this! So where's the money, and who's she leaving it to? And I took shit from that whore because you, *you*," he yelled, pointing his finger at his wife, "you told me she would respect us when she died! You idiot!" Carmela burst into tears and went to take refuge beside her mother on the bed while Gianni tried to calm his brother-in-law, reminding him that they were not in their own home and that there were visitors in the other room, more than ready to eavesdrop before going off to gossip in town.

Lilla had taken a seat to one side, where she concentrated on rereading the letter. Then she spoke softly, struggling to control the rage building inside her; she felt it welling up in her throat and mixing with the words. "She's organised everything; she's even chosen the hour of the funeral. And she must have got Dr. Mendicò to write the letter. You can see that it's someone else's handwriting. It's a perverse letter! She doesn't want her family—maybe they've fallen out; that shouldn't surprise any of us—but she wants—in fact, she commands us yet again—to pay the funeral expenses and put this absurd, humiliating, ungrammatical obituary, a bizarre thing for a maid—or *criata*, as she calls herself—in the *Giornale di Sicilia* no less, she who spent her entire life in this town and isn't known anywhere else. She didn't even think of putting it in a local paper like *La Sicilia*; no, she wanted the news of her death in the paper read all over Sicily. She's a megalomaniac, that's what she is. This text is just self-glorification, singing her own praises. I'd never have believed that she was so vain and irresponsible. This is the last imposition we'll have to put up with. What's more, she's laughing at us: while she claims to have nothing to leave, she declares that continuing obedience will bring us good fortune. The nerve . . ." Lilla was so angry she could not finish; the others gazed at her in amazement.

Meanwhile others were arriving to offer sympathy. The Alfallipes could hear effusive expressions of mourning coming from the living room. The shrill voice of a woman who seemed to be crying her wares in the market rose above them all: "A saint of a woman, she was! What a life of work and sacrifice! She didn't deserve to die!" The voice was drowned out by an unintelligible chorus, doubtless the women singing the praises of Mennulara. Rancorously, Lilla spoke up again: "It would serve her right if I opened the door and told them loud and clear that they shouldn't be grieving for this maid, this remorseless woman who is now making a laughingstock of us!" Massimo was standing, his hands clutching the back of a chair as if he were trying to break it. In a loud voice, as if he needed everyone in the building to hear, he said, "All she ever wanted to do was mortify us. This document is dripping with poison." Agitated, Gianni turned to Lilla and said, "You live in Rome, but I teach at the university and I bear the Alfallipe name. To place an obituary of this kind in the paper would be an unbearable disgrace for Anna and me. People will take us for incompetents and fools; everyone will laugh at me." Carmela began to wail: "At least you left home, but what about me? I'm the one who has to live in Roccacolomba. What will people say?" They were all talking at once, pacing about the room like caged beasts, angry and frustrated.

Slight and seeming almost adolescent as she huddled among the pillows on the big bed, signora Alfallipe was watching them, startled and dismayed, eyes watery with tears. She had to step in to prevent a scene, surprising herself and them with her firmness when she did so. She was not interested in the funeral arrangements, to which she had paid scant attention, but she was concerned for her children's inheritance, she said, and they ought to be thinking about that more than she, who, after all, was old and might die soon—she felt it in her bones. "A wicked temper and tricky, yes, but she was honest, and she served us all. It's right that we give her the funeral. Believe me, she'll give you what you're entitled to, I have no doubt. Perhaps this letter is only about the funeral arrangements. There must be a will. Maybe she organised things in order to avoid paying estate duty—Mennù didn't like paying taxes. For goodness' sake, calm down. There are strangers through there." And then she dissolved in tears, exhausted by her long tirade.

Carmela, too, was worried about the inheritance, but she clutched at a straw of hope: "We ought to remember one thing. Mennù always kept her word, and right up until yesterday evening she told me to do as she said and wealth would come our way. Maybe there's a will with the notary or someone else, or perhaps she has already made some deed of gift, or maybe she has opened bank accounts in our names that we don't know about . . . We must look through her drawers. She wasn't the kind to trust Dr. Mendicò, who's a half-wit. What do you say, Massimo?" she asked, seeking her husband's approval. Massimo was standing in front of the balcony, his back to all of them, and did not move. Carmela blanched and threw herself onto her mother's bed again, sobbing.

The women in the next room had heard the shouting and were dying to know what was going on. Now, Santa was knocking at the door, curious and worried, asking cautiously if the newcomers might come in and offer their condolences to signora Adriana. The room filled once more with a crowd and the family group broke up. Massimo slipped away without saying good-bye to anyone and wasn't seen again until late afternoon. There had never been so many people in that modest flat. The visits continued until lunchtime; apart from those of Mennulara's own class, some relatives and close friends of signora Adriana also came, and there were even some former employees of the Alfallipe family.

2. On the afternoon of the day of the death, the Alfallipes make some fateful decisions, and Gianni and his sisters spend the night going about their own business instead of holding a vigil

In the early afternoon, during a brief interval between the intolerable condolence visits, Lilla proposed a plan of action: "First of all, we have to organise the funeral, because the body can't stay here forever. Let's do as she says—that seems right to me. Afterwards, we'll go into her room and look for the will or any other written disposition. As soon as we can call Vazzano, the notary, we'll trace the bookkeeper or accountant who did her tax returns. We'll have to find out who he is. As for the obituary, I am totally against publishing it in any paper. She was a maid, after all."

Signora Alfallipe, fortified by the visits and the praises heaped on the deceased, objected with a determination that startled her children. She wanted the death notice at least to be posted in the town, written as Mennù had wished. She spoke at length in a strong voice. "After your father's death, my life was tolerable thanks solely to Mennù. You rightly have your own families and you live in your own homes, yet none of you offered to take me in or came to live with me in Alfallipe House." She paused and looked at Gianni, her son and favourite. "You all agreed that I should stay there alone. At nights the wind makes the shutters bang, all the windows rattle, and there are thousands of other noises. I am afraid. During the day the empty rooms and deserted corridors depress me; then there's the cold in winter and the maintenance costs. You didn't think about me; you only thought about what people might say. I need company. Mennù's proposal that I eat and sleep in her flat was the best thing. By day I was free to go home whenever I wished. I continued to receive guests and to use my rooms, which Mennù kept clean and tidy. She never left me alone here or in Alfallipe House—she knew I'd have died of fright. Mennù looked after me very well indeed, and she really deserves the funeral and the obituary."

Surprised by their mother's determined tone and sensitive to her veiled reproof, the children had to yield to her will. And so they settled on a compromise: the death notice would be only posted in the streets of the town, and the text would be revised. To their surprise, Massimo, whom Carmela telephoned immediately to report on these final decisions, offered to see to things personally, and everyone was grateful to him.

The rest of the day passed quickly. Affectionate phone calls from signora Alfallipe's friends and visitors kept her mind off things and comforted her. She never seemed to tire of repeating the details of Mennù's long illness, her agonising death throes, the distress caused by her sudden demise; in fact, she took comfort in self-pity, which this time was at least justified. She wanted Gianni to stay near her, and so she was less of a burden to her daughters, who were left free to devote themselves to the host of chores to be done, including the preparations for their mother's by-now-inevitable return to Alfallipe House, at least temporarily.

Gianni and Carmela, who knew the townsfolk better, were involved in the unrelenting round of phone calls and the visitors who came, one after another, to Mennulara's small flat. Lilla, who had left Roccacolomba after getting married and had kept in touch with only a very few people, was to give Santa instructions about preparations for the following day and about cleaning Alfallipe House. In the meantime she searched for the will. When she called the notary, Vazzano confessed with some embarrassment that he was holding no will or other disposition from Mennulara, and he suggested a careful search of her drawers. When there was no one around Lilla tried rummaging through the bureaus and the cupboards, but she didn't find much: photographs of Mennulara's nephews, bills and receipts, a small notebook full of figures and sums, shopping lists, notes, and even draft versions of an obituary. So she decided to make a more systematic search in Alfallipe House.

In the late afternoon Lilla returned to the family home. It felt strange, opening the street door with the big iron key and going alone into the house where she had lived as a girl with her parents and her grandmother. She headed for the servants' quarters, through places she hadn't seen for years: the room where the maids used to iron, the pantry, the big kitchen, which had never been modernised. Then she went up the narrow wooden stairway that led to the maids' rooms in the mezzanine once occupied by the numerous household staff, where Mennù had slept alone for years. Although there was dust everywhere, it was evident that the rooms had periodically been cleaned and tidied. The house looked as if it had been closed for the summer holiday: the beds were covered with old but clean cloths; the objects and furnishings had been stored away in cupboards to prevent their getting dusty; the bathrooms and washbasins were spotless. She found no trace of what she was looking for, except lists of the contents of the cupboards, written in block letters in Mennù's uncertain hand.

As dusk fell, Lilla became aware of the noises—the creaking and thumping of doors, the squeaking of hinges, the trees in the inner garden rustling in the wind, the beating of the wings of birds whose nests were hidden beneath the cornices—and, for the first time, she shared her mother's anxieties; she even took comfort in the thought that she would be sleeping in Mennulara's flat that night.

Gianni Alfallipe was a quiet man by nature, and he had been stunned by the events of the last few days. He led a serene and orderly life in Catania, with his beloved young wife, who, like him, was a university lecturer. Mennù had told him about the real nature of her illness at the beginning of September, but she hadn't given him the impression that she would die so soon. By a lucky coincidence, Lilla had arrived in Catania on business the previous Saturday—otherwise she would have made her usual visit to their mother at the end of the month, taking the first flight in the morning, then returning to Rome on the last plane—and while she was there Carmela had told them both about the deterioration in Mennulara's condition and asked them to come right away.

In the meantime, his sisters decided, at Carmela's suggestion, that they would not hold the traditional vigil. Only Lilla and their mother, who had refused to leave the body alone, would stay for a last night in Mennù's flat. Gianni intended to return the following morning, with his wife, in time for the funeral. They would reopen Alfallipe House and take their mother back to it—to their relief and to her immense anxiety—thus putting an end to that deplorable cohabitation in the maid's flat.

Only when he had left Roccacolomba behind him did Gianni manage to get the situation into focus. Mennù had been a part of his life until his adolescence, at first as a devoted and affectionate maid and baby-sitter, then as the maid-administrator of the family property. She had become steadily meaner, but she continued to be the linchpin of the Alfallipe household: she goaded him into studying, hectored him in a way he often didn't understand about the hazards of the modern world and the importance of their social position, and insisted that he live up to the name he bore. In the end, he had been glad to flee the oppressive atmosphere at home for boarding school in Catania, and after that he had grown apart emotionally from all the family, including his parents: he looked down on the self-pity and scant learning of his mother, who oppressed him with her egoistic and anxious attachment, while relations with his father gradually hardened into mutual incomprehension.

After his father's death Gianni had not hesitated to divest Mennulara of the administration of the family property. His sisters followed his example, and thus they destroyed the base of her power within the family. Mennù had not managed to win it back, even after his mother's unseemly decision to live with her, but then she had at least partly regained it through an expensive stratagem: with a view to obliging the three children to visit their mother regularly, she offered to pay them a kind of monthly allowance, provided they came to Roccacolomba to get it. If they failed to comply with her order, they forfeited the money. This happened rather seldom: it was no mean sum, and the money came in handy for each of them. Mennù's death thus marked the end of a phase in Gianni's life. Now he could concentrate on his career and on the family he hoped to make with his wife. This still left the enigma of Mennù's apparently immense wealth and the difficulties they might encounter in trying to come into possession of it—as well as the problem of looking after their mother—but he hoped these matters would resolve themselves in time.

Like his father, Gianni had a remarkable capacity for removing everything that worried him: as soon as the car passed the Roccacolomba intersection and the road began to descend towards the valley along a long, gentle slope, passing through the thick oak woods of the estate owned by the princes of Brogli, which his forefathers had managed for generations, he began to look forward to the pleasure of seeing his wife again, and he forgot about Roccacolomba and its inhabitants. But that evening he had severe heartburn, and that night he slept badly.

3. *Massimo Leone rashly celebrates Mennulara's death in his own fashion*

Without a doubt Massimo Leone had had a very satisfactory day. In the afternoon, he saw to the organisation of Mennulara's funeral. He composed the obituary, as agreed to by the family. He would have made it even shorter, but it was necessary to humour his mother-in-law, who was, in his view, an accomplished impostor, a woman capable of improvising hysterics and faking indispositions to get what she wanted. The funeral would be simple—no more than the social position of the deceased required—and Massimo was gratified and comforted by the sincere thanks of his brother- and sister-in-law, especially because he still felt embarrassed and ashamed at having lost control in front of everyone.

That evening they dined at home alone. Carmela was telling him about the day's visits when she suddenly broke off. "But what will happen on the twenty-fifth?"

"I thought about that this morning. Do you know where she withdrew the money?"

"She got it in the post, I think," replied Carmela, faltering.

"How do you know that?" demanded Massimo in his usual aggressive manner.

"She always said that she had to go to the post office on

the twenty-fifth because Little Saint Stipend would send her the cash."

"Then it'll arrive as it did before," concluded Massimo.

"And who's going to pick it up?" asked Carmela, her blue eyes darkening at the idea that this new assignment might fall to her.

"Listen, it's been a hard day. Let's think about this tomorrow."

And they quickly finished eating.

After dinner, Massimo went out to meet his friends at the bar in the square. Carmela was relieved, and once alone, she began making long telephone calls to her women friends—the ones she spoke to every day—to tell the few of them who still didn't know about Mennulara's death. She urged them not to trouble to come to the funeral, which was to be an affair for a few very close friends and at an unusual hour; to attend they would have to forgo their siesta, and there really was no need, seeing that it was only a matter of a maid, after all. Even now she couldn't keep from complaining about Mennù, and she ended every telephone call with a hint of malice: "It's not right to speak ill of the dead, true, but she was a difficult character and you needed the patience of a saint to put up with her . . . Massimo is an angel—he's gone through so much on her account. Even today he gave us a lot of help." She was too embarrassed to add that the family was going to post a death notice on the streets.

Walking to the square, Massimo was assailed by the usual despondent thoughts and fears. Whereas that afternoon he had been looking forward to meeting his friends and telling them all he had to tell, now he feared the future. There was no more guarantee of the income that, although halved, had enabled him to keep his creditors at bay following the failure of his business. His thoughts returned to the conversation with Carmela, who was not so stupid, after all. He had allowed himself to be convinced by his wife and his in-laws that the will would nominate the Alfallipes as beneficiaries. Now the possibility had arisen that the maid had never intended to make a will, and that her property would go to her nephews. Everything was quite clear to him—that was why she hadn't wanted them to attend the funeral. It was her last slight at the Alfallipes' expense: I got rich sponging off you. I'll make you pay for my funeral, too, and then I'll leave everything to my legitimate heirs—that must have been her plan. At the mere idea that this was the way things were, Massimo had a kind of bad turn, a chill, a tremor in his legs. He would have gone back home had he not felt a pat on his shoulder.

"You're quite a guy, Massimo. After a rough day with the Alfallipes, you're not giving up on your night out!"

He steeled himself, and together with his friend he went on to the bar, where he drank a lot and held the floor, talking almost constantly about Mennulara. For years he had wished her dead; he had suffered many wrongs at her hands, she was a thief, and she had bought her flat and goodness knows what else with money stolen from his wife and her brother and sister. Massimo said this to anyone who joined the company, repeating it obsessively, in search of consensus. "She pulled so many low tricks, she deserved to be killed. I could have done it myself, too, with my own hands, but in the end there was no need. Her own poison welled up from her guts and drowned her."

Comforted by drink, reanimated by the hope of claiming the inheritance, and encouraged by the malicious exuberance of his friends, Massimo shelved the doubts that had assailed him earlier, and as he looked forward to the wealth that would finally return to the Alfallipe family, he had no qualms about showing his pleasure. Amid the general high spirits, he wound up saying that he had sworn he would not reach forty with that bitch underfoot, and next year he would celebrate that momentous birthday in Taormina: his friends were all invited to the party—men only, of course.

It was already late when, staggering drunkenly home, Massimo had the distinct feeling that he had talked too much. And his demons returned. After all, Mennulara, wicked as she was, had had a certain sense of justice, and, despite her aversion to him, she had never treated Carmela any differently from her brother and sister, as he had feared at first she would. Truth to tell, since January that year, rather than give Carmela the entire sum agreed upon, Mennulara had established a system by which she paid Carmela's bills directly to the shopkeepers, giving her the remainder in cash.

Massimo's older sister had wanted to know if Mennulara's suspicions were well founded: had he, in fact, raised his hand against Carmela? He clumsily denied the accusation, maintaining that in any case it was a husband's right and duty to keep his wife in her place and to make her respect him, even by using his hands if necessary, but in this case there was no need, because he knew how to deal with Carmela. Mennulara was just a perfidious, lying woman who wanted to destroy their conjugal happiness.

After that conversation, Massimo avoided being alone with his sister, though he loved her, for she had always helped him when he was a child, protecting him from his father's beatings. But he knew what had aroused Mennulara's suspicions. During a row one New Year's Eve, perhaps because he had drunk too much, a punch aimed at Carmela's breast had landed on her neck, leaving her with a large bruise. Carmela had tried to conceal it with a scarf, and he had given her a fine silk foulard in the hope that she would forgive him, but that witch who saw and knew all had noticed it.

Since then, Massimo had learned to restrict himself to beating his wife when sober, so that he could strike parts concealed from the gaze of others. When he came home drunk, filled with an uncontrollable desire to make Carmela pay for the rage that was eating him alive and the sense of inadequacy that was tormenting him, rather than beating her he would take her with violence, voiding himself deep into her guts. Having expelled his hatred and resentment of the world, he managed to find repose, exhausted but sated alongside his dazed wife.

In reality, that ritual had become almost pleasurable for both of them. Carmela interpreted it as a revival of passion and a proof of love, despite the intense physical pain. They made love the same way that night, too.

4. *A conversation between brother and sister in the Mendicò home on the day of the death*

Dr. Mendicò had been living for three years with his sister Concetta, the widow Di Prima, in the old family home. They had both ended up widowed and alone, and Concetta had returned to Roccacolomba. All their children lived in other cities, even on the mainland. "This is the reward for mothers who bring up their children well. They study, get married, do well for themselves, and then they go," Concetta would often repeat, "and we old people are left at home, sad and alone." The truth was that the brother and sister lived together most agreeably.

They revived an old custom of their youth: they would play piano duets almost every evening. Three times a year, they went to visit their respective children and grandchildren, and they took part in the social life of Roccacolomba with assiduous pleasure, even though they were both over seventy. Signora Di Prima had renewed old friendships, and the doctor no longer practised full-time; he made house calls in the late morning and in the afternoons, receiving patients only every other day in his consulting room at home, as his father and grandfather had done before him.

Both of them enjoyed the human contact that is so much a part of a doctor's life—not just with patients but also with entire families, which, in a town like Roccacolomba, often grew into fond friendships. And so Dr. Mendicò carried on treating a multitude of loyal and devoted patients, arousing the envy of the new generation of doctors in Roccacolomba. When her brother was not available, signora Di Prima dispensed advice and sometimes even went so far as to suggest remedies, to the patients' great satisfaction. Young mothers almost preferred to consult her when their children had influenza or caught colds.

Sitting on the balcony with his aperitif in the warm autumn sunshine, the doctor was telling his sister about the scene in Mennulara's flat. "In almost fifty years as a doctor, I've never had to be alone with a dying patient, as I was today. None of the Alfallipes, not even signora Adriana, had the sense of duty or the decency to comfort or stay with that poor soul, who was suffering so badly. After—think of *this*— after I told them she was dead, apart from the signora and Santa, the children didn't shed a tear. No one asked me anything—how she had died, if she had suffered, if they might go in to see her. Nothing, understand? As if a dog had died. Gianni Alfallipe was the first to speak to me, and what did he ask? He wanted to know if Mennù had given me something for them, a letter, a will."

The doctor had become heated, his cheeks purple. "Too much is too much . . . I didn't even look at him, and I asked all those fine folk, 'But first don't you want to see Mennù?' " He paused, not finding the words. He took a sip from his glass and looked around; his glance fell on the terra-cotta pots overflowing with geraniums that his sister so lovingly looked after. They were beautiful: the red and purple flowers stood out luxuriantly among leaves fleshy and rounded like fans. Then he spoke again. "Only Santa, who seemed to be waiting for the word, came with me right away into the room where Mennulara lay. The Alfallipes followed us in silence. They showed no emotion. They stood in front of the body like cabbages. They seemed embarrassed, almost irritated." The doctor broke off, ashamed of passing a judgement that was harsh and perhaps imprudent, certainly without compassion. After all, grief manifests itself in many ways, and perhaps the Alfallipes had been reserved and intimidated by his presence. He had been their family doctor for more than forty years, but by now there was no longer any intimacy with the children. Lilla and Gianni had been living elsewhere for some time, and Carmela had chosen another doctor after she married. He said out loud, "Maybe I was too hard on them, but I was fond of Mennulara." And he finished off his drink.

On Monday afternoons Dr. Mendicò did not receive patients, and so he decided to have a rest. He was tired, for the last few days he had been going to see Mennulara every morning and afternoon. He awoke reinvigorated from his nap and stayed in bed, listening to music on the radio. Idly, he picked up the book that some time before he had begun to read enthusiastically, but he couldn't concentrate; he wasn't interested in it any more. He closed his eyes, and in the slightly clammy warmth of the sheets the memory of his first meeting with Mennulara came to mind, buried and forgotten for half a century.

He was a young doctor. Shortly after he finished medical school his father had died prematurely, and now it was up to him to support his mother and his sisters. He liked the work and he had the energy of youth. The worthies of the town and his father's vast clientele took a liking to him. But he noticed that the rich families called him in only for minor ailments or to treat their servants, and he felt as if they were making him serve his apprenticeship with those poor souls. He didn't mind it, though, for it was a challenge to try to cure the complaints caused by inadequate nutrition and lack of hygiene, to provide the scant medicines he could afford to give away or the patients could afford to buy. And so he learned the physician's profession quickly and well, and that of the surgeon, too, when need arose.

The Minacapellis, a large and respected family in the province, were fond of him. One day, signora Carmela Minacapelli asked if he would call on the family of her daughter's favourite maid. The poor woman had left her job to get married, and since then all kinds of illnesses and misfortunes had befallen her.

The Inzerillos lived in a barn owned by the Minacapelli family, not far from their mansion, next to the stables that were still in use. The caretaker was reluctant to accompany him to the place, and after showing him to the door she vanished. Luigi Inzerillo was sitting by the door, coughing; the doctor thought that he was the patient, but he quickly learned that the wife was in even worse shape. Addoloratina, the little daughter, showed him in. The barn, which had no natural light or ventilation, was damp and stinking from the stalls where the goats and horses were kept. It wasn't dirty, but it wasn't clean, either.

Dr. Mendicò soon made the diagnosis: Nuruzza Inzerillo had pneumonia. For want of any other remedy for her high fever, it was necessary to bleed her. Hastily, before it got dark, he went home and returned with the necessary equipment. Under the anxious gaze of the husband and the frightened eyes of the daughter, he applied the leeches to her shoulders by the flickering light of a candle. He deftly detached the worms bloated with blood, put them back in the glass bottles, and replaced them with hungry ones, an unpleasant but effective operation.

He had an uneasy feeling, almost as if he were under surveillance. From the corner of his eye, he glanced at the two poor devils beside him, but it wasn't their worried and frightened expressions that were giving him this strange, disquieting feeling. Having reassured the sick woman, he put the leeches back in the container, closed his bag, and got to his feet. He heard a rustling coming from the wall in the back, and in the gloom he saw two big dark eyes trained on him. Luigi Inzerillo lifted the candle and the doctor managed to glimpse a face framed by thick dark curls. A little girl was emerging from the manger at the back of the barn. They looked at each other. "You did good," said a clear, high, ringing voice. The tone was approving, without shyness. Then the little head darted back into the hollow of the wall and vanished. Luigi Inzerillo said, "Mama's better, sleep now," and then, turning to the doctor, he explained in embarrassment: "She's my other daughter, Rosalia. You must excuse her, Doctor, not even four she is, she didn't mean you disrespect." That was his first encounter with Mennulara, and the first time that she surprised him.

After that, Dr. Mendicò often had to call on the Inzerillos and their elder daughter. Apart from Luigi's and Nuruzza's illnesses, all three suffered from tuberculosis, but miraculously the little one stayed healthy, and under his guidance she became an excellent nurse, quick to learn the herbal remedies that he, being unable to afford costly medicines, taught her to prepare and to dispense. She was a meticulous little girl, resourceful and cheerful, despite her troubles.

The doctor plumped up his pillow and dozed off again.

That afternoon, signora Di Prima received many telephone calls: her friends had word of Mennulara's sudden death and were avid for details. She couldn't answer all the questions as she would have liked, so she took advantage of dinner to return to the topic with her brother.

"Did you have the will? Did you give it to Gianni?"

"I had a letter to give him. I gave it to him, as she wished."

"Did you read it?"

"I had to."

"Why?"

"There was something missing."

"What?"

"That's none of your business, nosey parker." The brother and sister enjoyed sparring, the way they used to as children.

"Was it a will?"

"I don't think so."

"How ever could this maid have got so rich?"

"What's that to you, eh? You're getting worse than those gossiping women in town!"

"If she did, it must have been Alfallipe property, given or maybe pilfered. I can't believe that she could afford to buy a flat on the wages they paid her!"

"It's complicated to explain," said the doctor in big-brotherly tones. "You must understand and remember that

30

everything the Alfallipes possessed was given to them, and what Mennulara possessed was always hers, and that's that. She sweated blood to earn it."

"How do you know these things?"

"Never you mind. Don't forget that she may have been an extremely difficult patient, but she was a very fine person. We can go to the funeral together tomorrow, if you want."

The doctor hoped he had put an end to the conversation, and on this occasion he was right.

5. On the evening of Mennulara's death, people are discussing it in the porter's lodge of Palazzo Ceffalia

Don Paolino Annunziata had been in service as coachman and then chauffeur to three generations of Alfallipes. He would have served four had he not been made redundant prematurely, when the family fortunes began to wane after signora Lilla's death. He contented himself with a modest retirement bonus and their permission to continue living in the chauffeur's rooms, in the lower part of Alfallipe House, next to the garage, where he and his wife, donna Mimma, raised their children, now all married off and with good jobs. He was enjoying a pleasant old age, apart from the rheumatism in his legs and a lack of cash—there had never been any question of a pension, because the Alfallipes, miserly with their employees and generous with themselves by family tradition, had not wanted to regularise his position, even though he was entitled to this by right.

Every afternoon he would laboriously make his way

down the steps leading to Palazzo Ceffalia, on the square, where his sister-in-law, donna Enza, and her husband, don Vito Militello, were the porters. He would stay for a long time, chatting pleasantly and watching the world go by; he also made himself useful by keeping an eye on the porter's lodge when his relatives were busy elsewhere in the building.

Often, his wife would join them in the late afternoon. After finishing her duties in the big house, she would bring food she had cooked and then they would all eat together in the spacious rooms there or even, in the summer, in the storehouse courtyard, which was no longer used by the master's family and had become a part of the porter's lodge, complete with garden and chicken run.

In the porter's lodge of Palazzo Ceffalia, there was a great coming and going of people, at all hours, relatives and friends almost all of whom belonged to families in service with the worthies of Roccacolomba, who would stop to say hello and to chat and take a breather before going on their way. Since the fall of the ruling Bourbon dynasty the upper class of Roccacolomba had stood firm, enjoying more than a century of stability and well-being. The families that had served them for generations as domestics—coachmen, cooks, maids, wet nurses, porters—could boast an equally stable position and were by no means indigent, although they lived in poverty. Bound by ancient ties over generations—a blend of respect, resentment, and mutual affection—they had adopted their masters' values and models of behaviour. The families of the household staff looked down on the other poor people in town, who had no masters and scraped by, never sure of where their daily bread was going to come from. And in a certain sense they felt protected, but also threatened, depending on their masters' positions, by the other great component of their agrarian society: the mafia, which at that time was in a phase of rapid ascendancy and was poised to penetrate Sicily's eastern provinces.

Don Vito Militello's father had originally obtained the porter's job with Baron Ceffalia, an up-and-coming aristocrat in Roccacolomba's stratified society: the baron had installed him in the porter's lodge, the most sumptuous one on the square, with a carved wooden loggia, and had fitted him out in dark blue livery, as city aristocrats did. The lodge became a focal point where the domestics of the wealthy families would drop in for a gossip—a very useful source of information, which then reached the masters through the porter's wife, faster and more accurately than through the orthodox channels of conversation in the clubs and the salons. So this human traffic went on with the tacit acquiescence of the baron, who was not displeased that even the porter's lodge of Palazzo Ceffalia was bathed in reflected glory.

On the afternoon of 23 September, don Vito was sitting in the loggia, from where he kept an eye simultaneously on the entrance, the strollers in the square, and the activities of his family inside the lodge. Conversing agreeably with his brother-in-law, don Vito commented, "She died consumed by ambition and greed, an uncouth, rude woman she was. She cut herself off from her peers—wasn't our equal at all, born a farmhand's daughter—and gave herself all the Alfallipe airs, thought she was like one of them, she did. But she never was, and couldn't be. The master's children couldn't stand her, and she died alone, like a dog. Not even her nephews showed up."

Donna Enza was listening to her husband from inside as she cleaned the vegetables for dinner, and she came to the defence of Mennulara: "It's not like that. And don't speak ill of the dead when they aren't even buried yet. She worked hard for them, and signora Alfallipe was fond of her, so much so that she went to live in her flat after the master's death. Why would she have done that otherwise? Mennulara never let her do a stroke of work, and she served her right to the end."

"What's that got to do with what I'm saying? . . . A good servant maybe, but why did she have to look down on us? She never stopped in the lodge, she responded to a greeting as if it were an insult, and if someone did her a kindness, which didn't happen often, I never heard her say thanks. Her tongue would have dropped out of her mouth before she'd thank you," replied don Vito without looking at his wife. He shook his head, still keeping an eye on the entrance.

But don Paolino Annunziata agreed with his sister-in-law. "She always treated me with respect, even though I know she was behind the negotiations for my retirement bonus and never put in a word for me about a little pension, God rest her soul. It was hard for her, and for us on the Alfallipe family staff, to get used to her giving orders in the big house and on the estates. It was such a new situation, so different!"

"It was different all right. It was crazy," broke in donna Mimma, who didn't see eye-to-eye with her sister over this. "I'm old-fashioned, and things should be left as they always have been. These changes bring no good. That a woman should go off alone into the country, and what's more give orders to folk like her who work for the same masters, as if the land belonged to her, and stay there all night alone—that's crazy, and Mennulara lost her good name and caused a scandal. Alive or dead as she may be, Mennulara was a shameless hussy, that's what she was."

"There's something I never really understood. How did she end up looking after the estates?" asked donna Enza.

"You tell her, Paolino, seeing as you're an Alfallipe man," said don Vito, this time turning around to look inside. He fixed his gaze on him, reinforcing the request.

Don Paolino didn't wait to be asked twice, and he eagerly began his account, a glass of wine in his hand and a twinkle in his eye. "After the death of signora Lilla, who as a widow ran things with an iron hand, far better than her husband, God rest his soul, the two sons—the late counsellor Orazio and his brother, Vincenzo, an army captain, who lived on the mainland—they didn't know how to manage the land and began spending right and left. After the war, times were still hard, but that bunch spent money like water, buying themselves fine cars and all kinds of good things. They should have saved, but debts started eating them out of house and home, so much so that they had to sell off some big properties and dismiss some of the staff. A few years later—I swear I don't know how or why—Mennulara suddenly began to take charge of the estates. I remember as if it was yesterday the first time I drove her into the countryside on her own. She said to me, 'Don Paolino, get the car ready to go to Puleri.' I went down to the garage and did what I had to do. When she came along alone, I asked her if we'd have to wait a long time for the masters, but she told me no one else was coming, and she fixed me with eyes like burning embers. Had the look of command, she did. Then she got into the passenger seat and told me to get a move on. And after that we other servants understood that things had changed.

"But she had a tough time establishing her authority on the estates. It had rained all winter, and though the crop was good the harvest was still meagre, because the country folk stole a lot, more than was fair." He paused, giving his wife a reproving look. "The next year, Mennulara summoned the overseer of Terre Rosse and closeted herself in the office with him. I got the gist of what she was saying to him—I was even a bit scared, she was shouting so much. It was in the days of the agrarian reforms; the field hands were at loggerheads with the bosses, and there was fighting in the villages nearby, even a few deaths. So she was taking a big risk by playing the boss: even though she was a woman, that crowd didn't take any nonsense from anyone, and she could have got herself killed."

Don Paolino paused for breath, then carried on. "That's not all. At harvest time that year, she was seen in the fields almost every day—she didn't miss a single crop—while all the Alfallipes were off socialising or enjoying their holidays. At night she threw herself down to sleep on top of the crop, whether it was wheat or almonds—she put a blanket over it and there she slept in her clothes, without even a pillow for her head. After that, she could account for the whole harvest, and nothing was stolen. And then she began to collect the income from the estates, which was the Alfallipes' just due, and justly she paid the farmhands and country people the agreed sum, with no delays."

Donna Mimma interrupted again. "She was lucky someone didn't kill her, the way she behaved . . . She made a lot of enemies, and they also say that she used to lend money."

Without taking his eyes from the street, don Vito said, "She had guts all right . . . an unmarried girl spending all night outside, sleeping alone in the damp, under the stars . . ."

Aunt Carmelina Li Pira, the maiden aunt of donna Enza and donna Mimma, old and a bit senile, had been taken in by the Militellos. Her nieces could never understand if she was following a conversation or not. At this point, she broke in, exclaiming, "And who's going to marry a woman who spends the whole night outside!"

"Aunt Carmelì, no one would have taken her anyway, old hag like her," said don Vito. "No man would have wanted to go near her."

"Mennulara wasn't the marrying kind," commented donna Mimma.

"She didn't like men," added donna Enza with a smug smile, aware that she knew more than the others, thanks to the indiscretions of Baroness Ceffalia and her daughters, which she winkled out of them when she went up to the main floor to help them and to pass on news from the porter's lodge.

Don Paolino let them talk as he sipped at the wine left over from lunch. He chuckled. "I don't know if it's true that she didn't like men. When she gathered almonds on the estates, she knew what was what, and people don't change."

In the meantime, they were joined by donna Mimma's young cousin, Lia Criscuolo, a maid in the Pecorilla household, and don Luigi Speciale, formerly a chauffeur with the Fatta family and now a hire-car driver. It wasn't appropriate to talk so freely with outsiders about a woman who was dead and not yet buried, so the conversation shifted from the dead woman to death itself. Cancer—how many people in Roccacolomba had been carried off, still young, by this illness of modern times? Don Luigi was quick to realise he had interrupted a juicy chat. He tried to encourage don Paolino, who was particularly talkative that day and still had the wineglass in his hand, to come out with some indiscretion. "Say, Paolino, did something happen with master Alfallipe?"

This direct, disrespectful question displeased don Paolino. After all, he was still an Alfallipe man, and he answered warily. "When Mennulara went into service, she was a pretty girl, that's for sure, and when he was still a youngster, master Orazio had an eye for the ladies. This much I can say, because I know. I saw nothing with my own eyes in Alfallipe House, and so I can say nothing. Before Mennulara went into service, they said that some country fellow fancied her but that it didn't work out, and as a result she stopped working in the fields and signora Lilla took her as a maid. But she was a good looker, with a firm body and a pretty face, too. Later, as she got older, she went to seed."

Don Vito muttered, "The bitterness she had inside, and brought out in others, turned her ugly—simple as that."

Donna Mimma wanted to change the subject. Lia, still

unmarried, shouldn't be listening to this kind of thing. She joined the conversation: "Have you heard that her nephews aren't coming to the funeral, and that the masters are making the arrangements?"

"Who told you that?" Don Paolino was incredulous.

Raising her voice, donna Enza broke in before her sister could open her mouth. "Paolino, I know. This very day, upstairs, in front of me, signora Giovanna was telling the baroness that signora Lilla Alfallipe, the one who lives on the mainland, was shocked, too: Mennulara left a letter, written in her own hand, and in it she said that they weren't to let her nephews know she was dead, never mind invite them to the funeral! So the Alfallipes will pay all the expenses."

The conversation degenerated into hoary old tales about the Alfallipes' legendary miserliness. They all delighted in the way they were now being obliged to pay for the funeral. They speculated about the reasons for the appalling relationship between Mennulara and her only nephews—the children of her late sister—analysed yet again her dour character, speculated about the identity of her lover, and even made veiled allusions to signor Alfallipe.

Don Paolino followed in silence as the conversational threads wove in and out; at times they were all talking at once, gesticulating excitedly. Finally, he spoke again, this time in solemn tones. "I'm going to the funeral—first of all because I knew her well and I worked with her for many years, and second because it's important to have the Alfallipes understand: just as they respect a maid and pay for her funeral expenses, so do we appreciate their respect, and we expect the same treatment when our time comes." One by one, the others fell silent. Their serious, attentive eyes were trained on don Paolino as they listened with the deference that was his due.

"That's right, Paolino," said donna Enza to her brother-in-law, all contrite. "The Alfallipes must be fond of her, to give her the funeral, and I'll go tomorrow, too."

Don Vito looked at his wife disapprovingly, but he didn't dare try to stop her from going. "I have to work in the lodge," he said. "And even if I was free, I wouldn't go. But you do as you wish."

There was a lull in the conversation. Differences between spouses had to be glossed over without comment, and they all knew that the one who wore the trousers in that house was donna Enza.

At that point the company broke up, for it was time to close the lodge.

That evening, as don Paolino was kissing his sister-in-law on the cheek before leaving, donna Enza asked him point-blank, "Who was this boyfriend of Mennulara's, when she was a girl?"

Don Paolino looked her straight in the eye. "I can't say, not even to you, but I know," and he winked. Arching his eyebrows almost to his hairline and raising his wrinkled eyelids, he opened his eyes wide. Donna Enza understood and fell silent.

6. Lunch in Fatta House

Signora Fatta was busy embroidering, immersed in her thoughts. She knew that Mennulara was dying, and she was anxious to hear news from her cousin Adriana Alfallipe, but her well-known discretion kept her from the telephone, fearing she might upset her.

Lucia announced that lunch was ready. She had already called signor Fatta from his study. Husband and wife usually ate in silence in Fatta House, when there were no guests. Pietro Fatta, chairman of the Provincial Farmers' Association, was a man of few words. His wife, Margherita, respected his silences and had learned to hold conversations with herself when she needed company. But that day, the couple talked over lunch.

The husband took his place at the head of the table and his wife sat on his left, as always. Then Pietro said, "I got a call from Mimmo Mendicò: Mennulara died this morning, and she had asked him to inform me of her death, just like that. What an odd request!"

Margherita felt like admonishing her husband for not having told her the news right away, thus sparing her hours of worry and anxiety, but wisely she made no comment about his usual lack of sensitivity. She limited herself to asking, "Didn't he say anything about Adriana and the children?"

"No, we didn't talk about them. The funeral is tomorrow afternoon, at three, and I don't think he told me anything beyond that."

"I suppose her nephews will be coming from the mainland," commented his wife.

"I suppose they will," said Pietro, and he plunged into his thoughts, bringing a forkful of fried potatoes to his mouth.

After lunch, they usually took coffee on the terrace, weather permitting. That day, Lucia served them with special care. Eager to glean information about Mennulara's death, she bustled about, pretending to be busy. She straightened the chairs around the other cast-iron tables placed here and there on the wide terrace, moved the ashtrays, cleared the chairs of the wisteria leaves that were already beginning to fall from the pergola, and looked about for other tasks she could invent in order to stay there listening to her masters.

Signora Fatta was talking about the Alfallipes. "I'm worried about Adriana. She got very fond of Mennù after she went to live with her, and she'll miss her. I don't know if she's thinking of going back to Alfallipe House, but they'll have to do some work on it. There's no central heating, and there's also the problem of the housework—she'll need reliable staff, living there alone. Mennù did the work of three maids, not to mention her other skills . . . Just imagine, Adriana still had Mennù manage her dotal property. This death will be a great loss for her, and now she'll have to rely on the children. I'm really worried."

By now, her husband was listening attentively. "Do you know if the children are with Adriana?" he asked.

"Yes. By pure coincidence, they're all in Roccacolomba."

"I'd like to help them. Those Alfallipe children are inexperienced. I owe it to Orazio's memory. Find out as much as possible in town. If you get word that they need something, or are making rash decisions, tell me, and I'll do my best to try to guide them."

"All right, as you wish," said his wife. She was grateful for her husband's interest in her cousin's family, even though she found her assignment onerous. She was a shy woman, a housewife by nature, and didn't enjoy social life. Since her daughter-in-law, who lived on the floor below, had given her two fine grandchildren, she would find any excuse to avoid sticking her nose out of the house.

Judging this the right moment to make the request that she feared her husband would not grant, she added hesitantly, "Do you want me to go to the funeral tomorrow?"

Pietro Fatta was gazing into the distance. He turned in his seat and scrutinised her without speaking. He took a pull on his cigarette, inhaling with deliberate slowness, turned his gaze once more beyond the stone balustrade that gave on to the town, then looked her straight in the eye again and pronounced, "She was a first-class maid and served them honestly for decades, but she wanted to remain a servant and conducted herself accordingly. The fact that some incomprehensible logic prompted Adriana to move into her maid's flat does not change their relationship. I allowed you to visit her there because I saw no reason to break off an affectionate relationship between cousins. But I know that other relatives and friends in Roccacolomba took great care not to set foot in Mennulara's place. Certainly I didn't approve of Mennù's and Adriana's conduct, either."

He continued to observe his wife as he spoke to her, with her elegant pale green dress, her small, dainty hands, the neatness and composure of a real lady. "But you are my wife, you have an important social position in this town, and just as I would not normally go to the funeral of a maid of a relative or peer of mine, so I expect you not to do so, either. Naturally, you may visit Adriana before the funeral, and afterwards, too."

In his heart of hearts he sensed that Margherita agreed with this decision: appearances had to be kept up, especially in the case of the Alfallipes, who were not liked and had caused endless gossip because of their familiarity with and dependence on Mennulara. Yet he felt he'd been heavy-handed. Suddenly he wanted to be alone, and he sent her away, suggesting that she call Adriana. Then he moved over to the stone balustrade.

Fatta House was built on the highest part of Rocca-colomba, next to the Convent of the Addolorata and respectfully close to the imposing palace of the princes of Brogli, which now stood empty. The outer walls of the palace, the grandiose Baroque façade with its rounded balconies, perennially closed shutters, and great iron street door, were majestic and intact. The interior was hidden from the eyes of the townsfolk, but from the Fattas' terrace you could see the inner courtyards, which were luxuriant with trees and bushes growing wild; the windows shaken violently by the wind; the unkempt flower beds in a state of abandon—harbinger of the magnificent palace's imminent and accelerated metamorphosis into a ruin.

The view from the terrace was, in any season, a source of supreme enjoyment for Pietro Fatta. Leaning against the balustrade that jutted out beyond the outer walls, he felt he was hanging in the air, as if he were above the source of a dizzying torrent of tiles gushing below his feet to spread out all over the entire southern slope of the mountain. The roofs of curved tiles, each one slightly different from the next in shade, size, slant, and direction, looked like pieces of a subtly tinted terra-cotta mosaic made in several hues of the same colour and strewn about in a splendid harmony of tones. Here and there among the roofs sprouted the tall and graceful bell towers of the churches, built like the rest of the town of pinkish grey stone, which at twilight looked like a mirror of the sky, so readily did it absorb the ruddy glow of the setting sun. The dark ochre tower of the *chiesa madre*, the main church in town, stood out among the town-houses, its roof marked with rows of green and white tiles. Beside the *chiesa madre* could be seen the roof of the Palazzo delle Poste, the pompous title given to the round two-storey post office built during the fascist regime. With the passing years, this building, too, had become an integral part of Roccacolomba, as if it had always been there. Its cement roof, plastered in what had once been a bright pink, had aged precociously and in its decrepit state seemed in perfect harmony with the other sloping roofs that pressed in on it.

Roccacolomba Alta ended at the bottom of the hill in the maze of modest dwellings that was Roccacolomba Bassa, where the poor people lived. Then there was the river, spanned by the stone bridge with its three arches, which linked the old town to Roccacolomba Nuova, a nondescript abomination built over the last thirty years. After the war Roccacolomba had grown rapidly, thanks in part to the new motorway that, after a long tunnel, linked it with the other towns of the province. Dozens of reinforced-concrete buildings in glaring colours had been built during the anarchic euphoria of the recent construction boom, and Roccacolomba had become a big agricultural town, where the landowners responded to the crisis of Sicily's sharecropping system by investing in machines and technology, thus earning themselves a name for being avant-garde. Where the land did not yield much or was too hard to work, the building industry had done the rest. The prosperity and development of Roccacolomba were assured, but the noble and isolated beauty of the town, founded in the seventeenth century by the princes of Brogli, was under attack and would soon be destroyed. Its social fabric would soon disappear, and everything would change. Pietro Fatta thought that the changes imposed by progress were positive, but he had trouble adapting to them. This incapacity of his saddened him, and he saw it as a portent of his own death.

He looked out beyond the town. The mountains spread out in a wide semicircular curve, in the midst of which lay a jumble of lower hills, on one of which Roccacolomba Alta had been built. Farther away were the hills of the great landed estates, which extended as far as the eye could see. From his "box at the opera" (which was how he liked to think of the terrace) he contemplated this backdrop of hills, whose tops had been levelled by the toil of peasants. Behind him, to the north, the mountains were ranked one behind another, undulating and majestic, clad with dappled woods, interspersed with other peaks that marched on and then plunged to the sea. He looked down. On the slopes of the hills opposite Roccacolomba, on the other side of the river, ploughed fields glittered in the sun. At the base of the valley, the river skirted the hills, disappearing behind one to reappear from behind another, the shining water meandering bright and calm. The panorama was dear to him and he knew it by heart. It always gave him a sense of peace. He would have liked to be a painter, but his destiny was to look after the family lands. He went back into the house and headed for his study.

He didn't feel like working. He sat down beside the fireplace and set to thinking about Mennulara again. Her death was premature. She could have enjoyed a well-deserved and serene old age, after years of toil in the service of Orazio Alfallipe and his family. Indefinable creature, devoted and obedient to her master's wishes, at the same time she was overbearing and imperious in the performance of her unusual managerial role. Orazio used to call her "my household god." Without a doubt, she had halted the family's economic decline by taking control of its administration, yet she had caused an irredeemable breach between the two Alfallipe brothers. Pietro had spent his childhood and adolescence with them, in town and then at boarding school, and the thought of that dispute never failed to sadden him. He picked up a book and tried to find comfort in its pages.

7. *Signora Fatta's granddaughter is fitted for a dress*

Angelina Salviato made the final touches to Rita's party dress, in readiness for the second and last fitting. She laid it out on the table, straightened the pleats of the skirt, laced up the embroidered bodice and puffed up the balloon sleeves; then she took a step back and admired the final effect, satisfied. All smiles and good humour, the housemaids

Lucia and Marianna entered the workroom, followed by Santa's niece, Titina, who had come to borrow the Fattas' vacuum cleaner for the cleaning at Alfallipe House. The girls admired the dress under Angelina's satisfied gaze, every now and then throwing out a comment or two about Mennulara's death, which Lucia had announced in the kitchen at lunchtime.

"What, she's still lying there dead in her flat and they're already busying themselves about cleaning up Alfallipe House? I don't know what they're thinking of. I'd be so sad, I wouldn't be able to think about anything else!" said Marianna. "Look what lovely embroidery on the front . . . You're a marvel with a needle and thread, Angelina."

And Titina: "Signora Lilla's like a sergeant major—do this, do that. Everything has to be done on the double for her. She's become a foreigner, and she talks posh, like they do in the movies. Goodness knows what the silk for this belt cost; it looks like a dress fit for a princess!" She fingered the soft fabric and caressed the ribbon of the belt, for her an impossible luxury. "My aunt Santa has to do all the cleaning at Alfallipe House, with only me and my mother to help her. And what's more, that lot expect us to wait on them hand and foot; they can't even make a cup of coffee for themselves. Born to command, they think they are. Times have changed, and after the funeral my aunt is going to have to talk straight with them."

"If I were your aunt, I wouldn't stay in service there, seeing as she knows what they're like. She's been working for them since before signor Alfallipe died." Marianna was not one to mince her words, which was why signora Fatta had set her to work in the kitchen and why she didn't serve either at table or in the drawing room, a task reserved for the discreet and easygoing Lucia. "Tightfisted—and arrogant too."

Lucia was listening to her, though her eyes were fixed on the dress. She would have liked to learn how to sew like Angelina. She added, "Signor Fatta was saying that Mennulara looked after signora Adriana's dowry—how did she get so clever? Look at the sewing on that hem, tiny stitches like embroidery! You're a really talented dressmaker, Angelina, and you'd make a fortune if you went to work elsewhere."

"Angelina, wasn't Mennulara a relative of your mother's?" asked Marianna with feigned innocence. "Cleverness runs in your family, doesn't it?" She looked at Angelina, on whose pale cheeks red blotches of embarrassment had appeared.

"Well, I didn't even know her. She was related to my mother, but they didn't get on, and as for me, I'm not that good at sewing. I do what I can."

Lucia came to her aid and changed the subject. "Tell us, Titina, did signora Carmela's husband show up at Mennulara's place?"

"He certainly did. My aunt told me that he waited until she died before going there; then they all stuck themselves in signora Adriana's bedroom. You could hear them shouting. They were quarrelling about the property, with that poor dead woman still in the house." Titina was a mine of information, and she continued to churn out more. "They didn't buy so much as a flower, and signor Alfallipe's children, all three of them, each one outdoing the last, don't even want to wear black for the funeral. Signora Lilla said she didn't have any black clothes. Signora Carmela said that out of respect for her husband mourning dress was out of the question. Only Gianni is going to wear a black tie, but without a black armband. He says that's old-fashioned these days. He lives in Catania and knows what he's talking about!"

"And signora Alfallipe?"

"The poor soul is crying her eyes out. They were like sisters. Mennulara was like a mother to her, and to think that she was the younger of the two," said Marianna.

"The masters weren't happy about the fact that those two were fond of each other," said Lucia, rolling her eyes to indicate the Fattas. With a knowing look, she added, "People like us can kill themselves working for the masters. They're rich—they take and they take and they spend and they spend, and then they leave you on your own beam end, as my uncle Paolino always says."

Titina didn't understand. "What are you on about? Get to the point!"

Lucia went on quickly. "Signor Fatta told his wife that she wasn't to go to the funeral, because Mennulara was a servant, but then he said that it was Mennulara who had saved the Alfallipe estate . . . What sense does that make? I'm taking an afternoon off and I'm going to the funeral. The more you work, the less they respect you, so as soon as I've put my trousseau together, I'm getting married, and I don't want to go back into service." Then, turning to Angelina, she asked all in one breath, "If I could learn to sew like you, I'd make frocks for my daughters—look how pretty the buttonholes are, all the same and really tiny—Angelì, will you teach me to sew like you, even just a bit at a time?"

"We'll see, but now I have to straighten up the room." Cautious and silent by nature, Angelina treated the masters with respect. Moreover, she was ashamed of her kinship with Mennulara, a cousin her family had repudiated.

"Mennulara certainly must have had money," Titina went on, "and how she made it, God only knows, or maybe the good Lord doesn't want to know . . . She paid my aunt out of her own pocket and she gave money to the master's children. She must have been a good woman, and she didn't have the chance to enjoy her own money."

Lucia had clear ideas about this. "I say money's for spending. You can't take it to the grave with you."

Titina continued: "It seems the Alfallipes even expected a legacy from Mennulara. When her nephews arrive, who are her real kin, I can just imagine the rows . . . but they're her kin, and they are entitled to her property . . ." She suddenly fell silent, for signora Fatta was coming in with her daughter-in-law and little Rita. The three maids sneaked off towards the kitchen.

Angelina began the delicate task of the final fitting and was complimented again by the ladies. Alone again at last, she carried on with her work, putting her things in order and cleaning the room so that it would be tidy the following day.

A house dressmaker by trade, Angelina worked for only a few families in Roccacolomba, all wealthy and respected. Her teacher in elementary school had encouraged her to sew by having her embroider the handkerchiefs for her daughter's trousseau, instead of teaching her to read and write well. But Angelina and her entire family were grateful to her: from the age of ten, she had never stopped sewing for others.

Angelina earned quite good money, and had taken on the role of the unmarried daughter who supports and looks after her elderly parents. Content with her ordered and serene life, she would spend weeks and sometimes even months in the house of one family or another. In some of these houses, she was even invited to listen to the radio during the long hours of solitary toil, and this had introduced her to music and had improved her Italian. She chatted with the maids during the lunch break, savouring the rich food of the well-to-do. Sweets and biscuits, of which she was very fond, were often set aside for her, and she already had the plump look of a woman who lives a sedentary life, the first step on the road to undisguised and irrevocable spinsterhood.

After the dress fitting, signora Fatta went to the kitchen under the pretext of preparing delicacies for the *consolo*, the traditional basket of food sent to families in mourning, which she wanted Titina to take to her cousin. While she imagined that Adriana's children would not be so distraught as to forget to give Santa orders for dinner, Margherita Fatta wished to observe the salutary mourning traditions and to send something sweet and appetising to poor Adriana, in tacit acknowledgement of her grief at Mennulara's death. Mindful of her husband's request, signora Fatta dallied over the preparation of the basket, chatting with Titina in the hope of picking up information. Titina was very glad to talk and gave full satisfaction, naturally providing the official version of events, toned down and bland, with no criticism of the Alfallipes, as one does when talking to masters. She left Fatta House proudly carrying the large box containing the vacuum cleaner and the basket of sweets and biscuits.

Then Nuruzza Salviato arrived, wearied by the flights of stairs she had to go up and down twice a day to accompany Angelina to and from work. Lucia always offered her something delicious to eat or drink—today a cup of goat's milk with a freshly baked sweet bun. As Nuruzza was sipping the piping hot sugared milk, of which she was extremely fond, Lucia told her the news. "Mennulara died this morning and the Alfallipes are all at her place. Signora Adriana will be devastated. Mennù must have been an angel to look after her that way." Nuruzza nearly choked with rage on hearing the praises of her detested cousin sung in this fashion. She could hardly swallow the delicious mush of bun dipped in sweet milk that she usually guzzled in a flash. Lucia thought that Nuruzza had lost her appetite out of grief for her cousin's death, and she continued to extol Mennù's virtues.

Signora Fatta now returned to the kitchen. She thought it wise to talk to Nuruzza as well; she offered her condolences and asked her, "Tell me, Nuruzza, how was it that Mennù came to work in Alfallipe House? Wasn't her mother in service with the Minacapelli family?"

"My cousin Nuruzza Inzerillo was very ill, and the late signora Lilla Alfallipe took a shine to her younger daughter. That's how she came to enter signor Alfallipe's house, and there she stayed."

Signora Fatta persisted: "They told me that her mother

was a good maid to the Minacapellis . . . You were there at the same time. What was she like?"

"My cousin was a good worker, but she didn't work there for long, since she was in a hurry to get married." Nuruzza could not avoid the lady's questions, but she knew how to reply discreetly, respectfully letting it be understood that she wouldn't learn any more from her.

8. *Nuruzza Salviato tells her daughter the story*

As she walked home with her mother, Angelina asked her questions about her cousin. "You shouldn't talk about these things outdoors," Nuruzza said curtly. "When we get home, I'll explain who Mennulara's mother was, and why the girl ended up in Alfallipe House." In silence, the two women continued down towards Roccacolomba Bassa, their arms closely entwined, the mother small and thin, the daughter plump and ungainly.

That evening, while they were preparing soup for dinner, Nuruzza kept her promise and told Angelina the story of Mennulara's mother.

"We were first cousins on my mother's side, and we were both the second daughters, so we were named after our grandmother Nuruzza, God rest her soul. We were put into service with the Minacapelli family, so we could earn enough to put together our trousseaux, but my cousin Nuruzza also had to earn enough for her sister, Anna, who had a club-foot; no one would have taken her into their home with a foot like that. We two were assigned to kitchen work and general cleaning, the worst job, because we were new and young. But she was a sly one and good-looking, and she managed to get into signorina Lilla's good books; she became her personal maid, leaving me to do all the heavy work on my own."

Nuruzza was absorbed in removing little stones from the lentils, but then she straightened up in front of Angelina, hands on her hips, and added, "She thought she was really something, that cousin of mine, because she was signorina Lilla's pet, and she used to tell us kitchen staff lots of fine things about her. To make us jealous, she would show us the presents she got: hand-me-downs that looked brand-new, ribbons, scarves, cotton underwear as light as a veil, shoes—things that gave her a swollen head." Angelina, who had never received a gift from the ladies, imagined Lilla Minacapelli's marvellous gifts, but she didn't say a word. Her mother went back to cleaning the lentils and carried on with her story. "A good person she was, signorina Lilla. She even tried to teach Nuruzza how to read, but no one knows if she really learned or not. She bragged about it in front of everyone, pretending to read old newspapers that ended up in the kitchen. They were kept there for wrapping the fruit to be stored in the pantry for the winter, for sopping up grease from the fries, for protecting the table when we bottled oil and cleaned vegetables, but certainly not to be read by folk like us."

"Why, where's the harm in reading a newspaper?" asked Angelina, who read all the headlines whenever there was a paper at hand.

"The cook, who could really read and had a little book of recipes written by a real chef, rightly used to say there was a lot of smutty stuff in the papers, and unmarried girls like us weren't supposed to know about such things. But my cousin was just dying to know about them, it seemed," said Nuruzza, thinking that even at forty this daughter of hers, the youngest of the four, was as innocent as a girl.

"And so thanks to signorina Lilla's presents, she finished her trousseau before the rest of us. Rather than give it to Anna, which was her duty, she wanted to marry Luigi Inzerillo, the miner; she made sheep's eyes at him, because miners earn plenty. It wasn't up to her to get married, since it wasn't her turn yet, but she didn't pay attention to that, and she got signorina Lilla involved. In the meantime, signorina Lilla became engaged to counsellor Ciccio Alfallipe and was about to have a big wedding, and she convinced her mother, signora Carmela, to call Nuruzza's father to persuade him to consent to the marriage, promising him that she would take Anna into service, lame as she was, in Nuruzza's place. My aunt was furious about that, but she had to keep the masters happy. She and her husband never forgave Nuruzza, though, and relations between them and the Inzerillos were not good."

"Did you stay friends with your cousin after the marriage?" asked Angelina, fascinated by this love story about her mother's cousin.

"She looked me up when she needed something, but friends, no—you don't forgive certain things. Anna, her poor soul of a sister, had a hard time of it working in a big house like the Minacapelli place, and she stayed in the kitchen as a drudge until she got married," replied her mother, who added, "I'll tell you what she did when her husband up and died on her—that way you'll understand why the Lord punishes those who don't do their duty. She had troubles and illnesses aplenty, did Nuruzza, yet she never swallowed her pride. After her husband's death, his older brother, Giovanni Inzerillo, offered to take in her and her two daughters, as was his bounden duty as a brother-in-law, and certainly not out of choice. His wife wasn't happy about it, because three mouths are a whole lot to feed, and what's more, both Nuruzza and Addoloratina were ill. The three of them stayed for only a few days, but instead of being grateful to him, Nuruzza actually insulted him. There in front of everyone, she gave him lip. Giovanni Inzerillo gave her a thrashing, and that was right, seeing as how Nuruzza didn't have respect for the head of the family. After that, her husband's family didn't have anything to do with her. Nuruzza was uppity, and she never got help from the Inzerillos, nor did she ask for any."

"Why didn't she want to live with her brother-in-law?" Angelina was rapt; Nuruzza Inzerillo's life seemed like a soap opera.

"Because she was snooty. She stayed alone with her daughters and wound up as a laundress with the Alfallipes, but she was still high-and-mighty. She used to say that her daughters would make good marriages and that their children would become office workers or even professionals, like the masters. And look how she ended up," said Nuruzza with satisfaction. "She came to me to ask for help, but only when she was really in dire straits. She sent for me; she was so ill, she couldn't manage to walk, and I went right to her, as we were cousins, after all. She wanted to tell me she was going to die soon, and she suggested that I take in her daughters, because they would give me a fine old age and would make sure I lacked nothing, neither bread nor something to go with it. I already had two good, pretty daughters. What? I said to myself. I've got four children, two boys into the bargain, and this one here's telling me I ought to take in other people's children so I can count on them in my old age! How dare she look down on my children, and say that her daughters would make my fortune? But out of love of the Lord and the Virgin, and because our mothers were sisters, I didn't answer her the way she deserved. All I said was that I would speak to my husband, even though I didn't hold out much hope. The following day, I went back to tell her that we couldn't take her daughters in; I took her some bread, some fruit, and a piece of cheese. She said she didn't need our help: signora Alfallipe was going to have Addoloratina seen by doctors and then placed in an orphanage, while the little one would become the signora's personal maid, and so she felt sure that her daughters would lead a decent life."

"Then what happened?"

"What happened happened! Addoloratina got married and died young. The other one stayed in service with the Alfallipes, and she became worse than her mother, snotty and bossy, and now she's dead, too. The Lord punishes both Turks and Christians for their sins. You know perfectly well what she did to your father . . . Now go outside and pour that dirty water in the chickens' trough, and then put the pot on the stove."

9. *Nuruzza Salviato and her husband curse Mennulara*

After dinner, Nuruzza and Vanni Salviato were left alone while Angelina cleaned up behind the flower-print curtain hanging from a wire. Theirs was a humble home, which Angelina had brightened up with that curtain, which isolated the kitchen from the area where the family lived and slept.

"I didn't tell you before you ate, so you wouldn't choke on your soup," said Nuruzza to her husband. "Mennulara died today."

Vanni Salviato spat on the floor. "I feel the air is fresh and pure, now that it isn't befouled with her breath any more." They remained in silence; then he added, "I lost my health and the will to work, thanks to the way that evil whore treated me. And she was your cousin, too."

"That's no fault of mine. Was I or wasn't I the first one to tell our children that she might as well be dead, that if any of us Salviatos met her on the street, they weren't to say hello but were to look the other way and pretend they hadn't seen her?" Nuruzza didn't take criticism easily, and certainly not from her husband. "Not that we met often in Roccacolomba Bassa. She didn't come here. She felt like she was one of the masters, but she was born a servant and a servant she remained to her dying day. But I walk with my head held high in front of everyone, and I have a respected and honest family. If her mother were alive, she'd tear her hair out over this shameless daughter who betrayed her own people."

"She was shameless right enough. I don't want to know

about the filthy things she was up to at Alfallipe House. I just remember how she treated me," said Vanni.

Nuruzza added, "At Fatta House today, Lucia Indelicato called her an 'angel.' I didn't say anything, because my guts were tied up in knots and I couldn't have controlled my tongue. As soon as we got home, I told Angelina about the mother's wrongdoings, so that this daughter of ours, who really is an angel, will learn what people are like."

At the thought of Angelina, Vanni softened and decided to call her in. Angelina joined them, obedient as ever. Her father beckoned her to sit down beside him.

"Angelina, you mustn't forget what this relative of your mother's did to us all, because when I'm dead you must tell it to all the Salviatos, born and yet to be born, and they must tell it word for word to all those in town who have something good to say about that ill-bred woman.

"I used to enjoy selling fruit and vegetables in the streets. I climbed the steps to Roccacolomba Alta; sometimes I even had to push the donkey, laden with baskets. But people bought from me and respected me. I used to stop beneath Alfallipe House to cry my wares.

"One day, I had some nice apricots, sweet and ripe. She looked out, we agreed on the price, and she lowered the basket from the balcony with the exact coins. I took the money and filled the basket with apricots, she pulled it up, and we said good-bye. I stayed beneath Alfallipe House, selling to people. The apricots were good, and people were snapping them up. That shameless hussy came back to the balcony and started yelling at me, accusing me of having sold her overripe apricots. She said signor Alfallipe didn't want them and that I was a dishonest swindler. Screaming like a lunatic, she threw the apricots in the basket and lowered it back down, demanding that I take them back. She wanted her money back, and she didn't stop shouting until she'd counted the coins—she didn't trust me. People were looking out of the windows, and passersby stopped to listen—she was screaming that loudly. The lies were coming out of her mouth like snakes darting out from those buckteeth of hers; she had become uglier than a maggoty plum. No one had ever treated me like that, and the fact that it was a woman who did it, the daughter of my wife's cousin, was an even greater insult."

Vanni continued talking quietly, his expression grim. "I don't know how I managed to sell that day or the days that followed. The apricots were good; there weren't any rotten ones—and even if there had been, how was I to blame? I had to pay for them all, and I had to sell them all, and better to sell them to rich people, who could throw away half without going hungry. I was over fifty and I was ill, and I needed to work to support the family; otherwise, I'd never have gone back to Roccacolomba Alta. When I went by Alfallipe House, my legs would shake, and not even the donkey wanted to go up the steps to it."

He looked at Angelina and chucked her under the chin tenderly, then said in a loud voice, "You, my sweet daughter, you are good and sensible. Remember this: none of my children and grandchildren must forget that this evil relative of your mother's was signor Alfallipe's servant and whore."

Angelina and her mother opened their eyes wide, amazed and speechless. Vanni, surprised by his own boldness and gratified by their reaction, tried to pull himself up on his own, refusing the cane that Nuruzza held out to him. He rose and headed for the door, walking on his twisted legs without faltering, as if he had finally reacquired his agility of movement together with the dignity that Mennulara had taken from him twenty years before. He stood on the threshold and slowly looked up. Roccacolomba stood out majestically. The lights of the houses on the mountain shone out in the darkness like a nativity scene, at whose foot the hovels of Roccacolomba Bassa lay as if crushed. Vanni turned to his wife, who had followed him, and said, "Nuruzza, up there is the flat of your cousin's daughter the whore. Remember that I, Vanni Salviato, curse her even in death!"

Tuesday 24 September 1963

10. *Signor Bommarito, the surveyor, does not receive his morning coffee*

On Tuesday 24 September 1963, the surveyor, signor Bommarito, was coming up from the square, looking forward to the piping hot coffee that awaited him at home. It was eight o'clock in the morning and he had already finished one of the day's tasks: his customary visit to the barber's after his holiday. The morning air made his freshly shaven cheeks tingle, and signor Bommarito felt pleased with himself. The barber had complimented him, telling him he looked in good form. Don Biagio had entertained him well with the local news, too, the kind that only barbers pick up: about the pretty foreign girl in the whorehouse near the cemetery who was very hungry (for you know what) and how you needed plenty of stamina to satisfy her; about the adventures of Totò Riesi, who was going to break his neck one of these days if he persisted in crossing rooftops by night to visit the pharmacist's wife in her bedroom while her husband earned his living on the night shift.

Signor Bommarito slowed down at the intersection with via Bara, "Coffin Street"—an apt name, he thought, pleased with his own wit—where death notices were affixed to the smooth walls of Palazzo Aruta. He noted two new ones. Let's see who's dead, he said to himself. "Matilde Cacopardo, schoolmistress, at eighty-one years," said the first: he read the usual stock expressions and memorised the hour of the funeral so that he could tell his wife to go. The other announcement concerned a certain Maria Rosalia Inzerillo, aged fifty-five. A stranger, he thought. Poor soul, she was my age. And he went on his way.

He rang his doorbell. But the door wasn't opened for him straight away as he expected. He rang again, but in vain. He took the key from his pocket, slightly affronted by his wife's and the maid's slowness in running to open up for him. Nor did he see them in the hall, and so he proceeded towards the kitchen, still in a good humour and looking forward to his coffee. There they were, looking out of the window. Antonia, the maid, bent over the windowsill so far it seemed she was about to fall, her feet barely touching the floor, her dress hitched up over her backside and revealing her sturdy legs. The buttocks of the foreign girl in the brothel would be a very different sight, he thought to himself, pleased at maintaining the sense of well-being that had been with him all morning.

"I'm back," he said in a loud voice.

The maid paid no heed, so intent was she on listening to what the women on the floor below were shouting about. His wife turned and said, "Ah, Menico, you're back. Did you hear that Mennulara has died?"

Now Bommarito was really annoyed. His wife hadn't even offered him his coffee. "My dear Mimuzza, who was supposed to tell me, the barber?"

"Didn't you read it on the corner of via Bara? The Alfallipes have stuck it up on all the walls," his wife replied excitedly as she gave him his coffee at last.

Savouring the hot drink and no longer annoyed—indeed, lingering on his wife's attractive appearance, for she, too, was just back from the hairdresser and all made up to go to school—signor Bommarito finally began to understand the women's agitation. "It's the first time that an obituary for a servant has been posted by masters, or, as they say these days, by employers. Mennulara has two nephews, her sister's sons, but the death was announced by the entire Alfallipe family, no less. You must see what they wrote—go and read it for me. When you came back, signora Cutrano was repeating it to me. She says they wrote this long screed, and we all know that Mennulara was a battle-axe. I went to school with Carmela, so I know very well," said Mimì Bommarito, and she beat her breast with her right hand, repeating, "I know, and how!" to drive her point home. Her housecoat opened, revealing her voluptuous breasts. Her husband's thoughts returned to the foreign girl, but he reckoned that the whore probably wasn't as curvaceous as his young wife.

And so signor Bommarito did not have the strength to resist his Mimì's sweet entreaties, and he had to hurry back to the corner of the via Bara, where a crowd had gathered to read the Inzerillo woman's obituary, in order to give his wife a minutely detailed account of what was written:

YESTERDAY, MARIA ROSALIA INZERILLO,
A MEMBER OF THE HOUSEHOLD STAFF OF ALFALLIPE HOUSE,
PASSED AWAY AT 55 YEARS OF AGE.

This sad news is given by signora Adriana Mangiaracina, widow of counsellor Orazio Alfallipe; her son,
Gianni, and his wife, Anna Chiovaro; her daughter
Lilla and her husband, Dr. Gian Maria Bolla; and her
daughter Carmela and her husband, Massimo Leone.
From the age of thirteen, she lived in Alfallipe House
and with affection served the family, which, disconsolate, mourns her passing. The funeral will be held
at 3:00 p.m. today in the church of the Addolorata.
The body will be taken to the cemetery of Roccacolomba for burial in the family plot.

The woman living opposite and another two women neighbours were waiting for him when he returned home. They
didn't give him time to repeat the obituary to the end and
kept interrupting him with comments: "Disconsolate, I'll
say . . . Carmela hated her, and it was her fault that Lilla
stopped coming for holidays in Roccacolomba!"

"There's no affection in that house. Not even for a cat."

"Even the family maids are going to the family vault
now? We're all brothers and sisters!"

"If signor Alfallipe were still alive, he wouldn't have allowed a thing like this!"

"And those fine nephews she bragged about so much,
why aren't they mourning their aunt?"

Finally, Bommarito managed with difficulty to disengage
himself from the women and went off to work, leaving them
to gossip. On the way he saw people stopping to read the
death notices and lingering to chat among themselves in
low voices. Mennulara's obituary had been posted in all the

places permitted by the town council: he thought that this Mennulara must have earned a great deal of money for those scrooges, the Alfallipes, given how much they were forking out for her now. He decided that if this shouting from the rooftops for the death of a maid was another innovation of modern so-called democratic times, he would never spend a penny on a maid's obituary; that evening he would remember to talk to his wife about this, before she started making promises and putting silly ideas into their Antonia's head. Then he returned to don Biagio's stories about the foreign girl, someone on whom it was worth spending money, rather than Mennulara, a woman who had never been beautiful and who had never enjoyed the pleasures of the flesh.

As soon as he got to the office, he remembered that he had forgotten to tell his wife about signora Cacopardo's death. Now *she* was important, being the mother-in-law of the headmistress of the junior high school where Mimì, who needed a permanent job, was a substitute teacher. And he cursed Mennulara.

11. *At the haberdashery Maricchia Pitarresi learns of Mennulara's death and curses her*

Early that morning, Maricchia Pitarresi went up to the square to buy embroidery cotton at the Merceria Moderna. She found it full of people: the signorinas Aruta, the owners, were not serving at the counter but stood chatting in Italian with some ladies, leaving the shop assistant to deal with everyone. Maricchia kept to the sidelines, aware of her own social position, while the other women mobbed the counter, dallying over their purchases, apparently intent on making their choice but in reality cocking their ears to listen in on the proprietors' animated conversation. Maricchia, too, was trying to make out the subject under discussion, and she finally succeeded, albeit with difficulty. Mennulara had died. She leaned forwards to listen, but just then the shop assistant asked her what she wanted.

On the way back home, she decided to stop by don Vito Militello's lodge to learn the details of this sudden death. She didn't have a chance to ask questions, for as soon as she came in, donna Enza offered her a seat and gave her a wink with her laughing eyes. "Maricchia, you were the only one missing. Tell us how Mennulara was when you worked together at Alfallipe House; you must know plenty!"

Maricchia didn't like to recall that brief and unhappy period; she accepted that she had to say something in exchange for information, but she wanted to play for time. "Give me a glass of water first. I'm exhausted," she said as she ran her hand over her forehead, leaning back against the wooden chair, listening to the conversation.

Don Paolino Annunziata, his feet resting on the stretcher of his chair, his knees spread wide, laid his hands on the pommel of the walking stick held upright between his legs. He was telling his story with real verve: "I was there the first day Mennulara went into service with signora Lilla. You could see she was used to the country—pretty savage, she was. She came into the kitchen at lunchtime. She didn't want to sit at the table with the other servants; she planted herself in front of the window, looking out at the courtyard like a caged bird."

"A bird? You've become a poet. That one was a she-wolf, I'm telling you," commented don Vito.

"No, she seemed like a bird, small and frightened, a little wild thing in a cage," declared don Paolino. "I can still see her as she was then. She didn't want to sit with us to eat, but she must have been starving, for she was skinny as a shin-bone. Pina Vassallo, the cook, prepared a plate of pasta for her and took it over to her at the window. She ate with her hands, guzzling it down, she was that hungry. She was stained all over with sauce; she didn't know how to eat like a human being. Then Pina gave her a cutlet and she snatched it and devoured it, tearing at it with her teeth, almost not chewing it. She didn't thank Pina, didn't even give her a smile. We were amazed. From then on she ate alone, far away from us, and if she had to sit at the kitchen table, she filled herself up without talking and left right away to get back to work. Uncouth she was and uncouth she remained. If someone asked her a question, she'd flinch, then answer with a grunt. She used to give us looks like a dog with its hackles up. She had black eyes like glowing coals—they looked as if they would scorch whoever spoke to her."

Don Vito added, "And that's the way she stayed. A bad woman. I remember one morning I was going to do the shopping for the baroness and I met her on the steps; she was going back up to Alfallipe House, carrying things she had bought at the market—she used to go bright and early to choose the best stuff. I saw her stumble on the steps. She fell, the shopping bags slipped out of her hands, and lots of lovely fruit and vegetables and even earthenware pots smashed to pieces all over the steps. I ran to help her. She started shouting at me, yelling, as if I was going to assault her: 'Go away, go away, I don't need anyone!' She picked everything up in a flash—fruit, smashed pots, paper—and stuffed it all into the bags, then went on up the steps without so much as a 'Good day.' Those few folk who had come running stood stock-still, watching us. God only knows what they must have thought. I have never felt so embarrassed. I went on saying hello to her after that, because you don't cut anyone dead, but I never really talked to her after that day."

"When's the funeral?" asked Maricchia, who wanted to get away quickly with her information.

"Didn't you see the notice in the street? The Alfallipes had it posted up all over, as they did for their father, God rest his soul," donna Enza said, then added, "Maricchia, don't go. Tell us what Mennulara was like with Orazio Alfallipe, because you must know."

Maricchia had no choice but to speak. "How he was, I don't know, but I know how she was. I entered service at Alfallipe House when she'd already been there for five years. She had become signora Lilla's personal maid. But when the mistress's son Orazio came from Catania on holiday, she was all ready to serve him. She had her eye on him, the whore, though he didn't even look at her." Maricchia paused to gauge the reaction to her words and to get her breath. Don Paolino turned to the door that gave on to the porter's lodge and frowned sceptically. Maricchia picked up her story again: "A woman like her should have walked with eyes lowered, after the things she did when she picked almonds, but the

Inzerillos were a shameless bunch. Signora Lilla was fond of her, and she believed the spiteful tales Mennù told her. A good thing I left to get married." Maricchia had said enough, and, before she had to answer any more questions, she got up to return home.

On the way, those inauspicious times at Alfallipe House unfolded before her eyes. She had been engaged to a cousin, with whom she was in love and whom she wanted to marry soon. She had decided to go into service so that she could make up her trousseau quickly. Orazio, still a student, noticed her and was attracted to her. Maricchia knew she was good-looking, with her glossy, wavy hair and shapely body, but she was an honest girl and wanted to keep her virginity for her cousin. Orazio was relentless: he would summon her to bring him a glass of water, asking her to serve him in his room, and she had to obey, even though she understood that he was mentally stripping her. She would tremble when she was alone with him, but she made it clear that there was nothing in it for him.

Mennulara noticed Orazio's attentions. She gave Maricchia the most unpleasant and heavy tasks in the kitchen and storehouse, which kept her far from the eyes and the intentions of the young master—not to protect her but because she was jealous. Although they were almost the same age, she never showed Maricchia either friendship or courtesy. One day signora Alfallipe sent for her and told her that some embroidered handkerchiefs, which Maricchia had put in the clothes drawers, were missing. "I haven't stolen anything. If you can't find them, then it's obvious that someone else took them," Marrichia replied, offended by the insinuation. From then on she felt that Mennulara and the mistress were watching her.

A few days later signora Alfallipe asked her if she knew the whereabouts of some fine woollen blankets, which she had recently washed. Maricchia took the hint, and she begged her mother to take her away. And that's what happened. Just as she was leaving Alfallipe House, Mennulara, who used to speak to her only to give orders, came up to her and gave her an envelope. "Signora Lilla told me to tell you that she doesn't want you to speak of this to anyone or even to thank her. It's a gift for your trousseau." There was cash equal to two months' wages, an enormous sum, which she could use, and Maricchia didn't have the courage to refuse.

"It's horrible being poor," said Maricchia out loud, sure that Mennulara had given her the money in order to be forgiven for her perfidy. That Mennulara never enjoyed Orazio's attentions—in fact, had to serve the whole family and even had to take his widow into her own home—was proof that the good Lord punishes the wicked. And her only reward is that now the Alfallipes are paying for her funeral, thought Maricchia, laughing to herself.

Maricchia Pitarresi and her family did not go to Mennulara's funeral.

12. Don Giovannino Pinzimonio recalls the past in the Conversation Club

Zu' Peppino Coniglio had wasted time at the baker's. Panting his way up the steep steps that led to the square, he was late for the Conversation Club and feared that some other member might have already taken the copy of *La Sicilia*, depriving him of the pleasure of being the first to read it.

He was so surprised to find his old friends in animated conversation rather than fighting over the paper, which lay still untouched on a chair, that it didn't even cross his mind to grab it. Instead he stood there listening, oblivious to the rheumatism in his legs, his hands clasping his shopping bag, which gave off the fragrant aroma of freshly baked bread.

Don Giovannino Pinzimonio, aged eighty-three, was holding court that morning. The others were seated around him, sniggering like schoolboys, interrupting from time to time to add details to the story he was telling with such gusto. At first, zu' Peppino didn't understand who it was they were talking about.

"She'd climb the trees like a monkey, one foot here, one hand there, straddling the branches and leaping from one to another. And she'd hang from those laden with olives and shake them, jumping up and down on the branch below, as if she were dancing." Don Giovannino got up and began to mime the movements, his legs wide apart, flexing his knees. "She'd climb up barefoot; the bark didn't scratch her, she was so agile and light she barely touched the trunk. In sixty years of work, I never saw anyone like that girl. The olives rained down like hail and the children on the ground gaped at her and tried to get closer under the tree, but the old overseer kept them at a distance."

"They wanted to look up her legs, never mind the olives!" exclaimed Mario Lo Garbo, his eyes shining at the memory of pleasures almost forgotten. The others laughed. Each one of them had his own.

"What legs!"

"A good-looking girl!"

"Small, but with a woman's body!"

"What do you know about it? Did you ever touch her?"

Zu' Peppino asked, "Who?" but the members ignored him, blissfully engrossed in their spicy recollections and amused by the witty cracks they thought they no longer had in them.

Don Giovannino finally spoke to him. "Do you remember Mennulara when she was a little girl working on Baron Putresca's land?"

"Yes," said zu' Peppino, disappointed because he had thought he had come in on fresh gossip about a more interesting person than the Alfallipes' maid. "But why are you talking about her?"

Mario Lo Garbo, tears of laughter still in his eyes, said, "Didn't you read the notice on the street? She died yesterday."

"A fine thing to talk about the dead, with them still warm, and to laugh about it. I hope you won't do the same for me when I go to my reward," said zu' Peppino. He was cross about missing their fun and was determined to spoil it, old grouch that he was.

"With you it's all doom and gloom!" retorted Mario Lo

Garbo, and the others laughed, thinking zu' Peppino deserved the put-down.

Don Giovannino felt justly reproved, but he was still taken by his reminiscences, and wanted to go on. "Peppino, it's true, Mennulara did die yesterday, may she rest in peace, but we weren't saying bad things about her; actually, we were praising her beauty."

Gaspare Ponte added, "I say that if the dear departed knew that we still admired her, she'd be glad about it. When she was young she knew she was pretty—and how! She liked to be looked at!"

The members started talking about Mennulara again, in a more reserved tone than before, but not for long. Chuckling, Gaspare Ponte said, "She'd whack anyone who reached out a hand to help her, and hard!"

"Why, did you make a pass at her, too?" asked don Giovannino.

"No. Who'd have had the nerve to do that? The swear words that used to come out of that mouth, when she was riled . . . and what a lot of them she knew!"

"And could she shout!"

"She had the loudest voice of all of them. When someone far off had to be called, the overseer would ask her—she was like a singer."

"If only she had been a singer! I really loved it when the women and boys used to sing the old folk songs; her voice would soar up, full of melody, and she'd bump and grind, wiggling all over!" added Mario Lo Garbo, getting up and imitating her, putting his hands on his hips and clumsily rotating his pelvis above his thin and twisted shanks.

They roared with laughter again. Zu' Peppino gave up

and laughed with them, for he wanted to contribute to their recollections. "When they weighed the sacks with the day's crop, she'd toss them onto the scales as if they had feathers in them—made of iron, she was."

"She was made of iron and fire," said don Giovannino very seriously. He hadn't forgiven zu' Peppino for the earlier reproof, even though it had been justified. "And then that fire went out, poor soul," he added, determined to make him feel guilty for having joined in the fun.

The members gradually calmed down, but they didn't fall silent. Blood rejuvenated by their reminiscences of Mennulara continued to flow fast in the tired veins of the old men. Seized by memories, they carried on nostalgically about country life. For once the members of the Conversation Club lived up to its name, and the newspaper languished untouched on the chair.

Towards midday, the members prepared to return home for lunch. The younger ones would meet again in the afternoon. Don Giovannino suggested, "With all the laughs she has given us, I think it's our duty to go to her funeral. What do you say?"

Thus, forgoing their siesta, as a token of their gratitude for the laughs they'd had and slightly ashamed about the lack of respect they'd shown the deceased, a numerous delegation from the Conversation Club attended Mennulara's funeral, to the amazement of the others present.

13. Gaspare Risico, a postal clerk and leader of the Roccacolomba branch of the Italian Communist Party, and his wife, Elvira

The bookshop closed half an hour early on that morning of 24 September in order to allow the proprietor, Rosalia Mangiaracina Pecorilla, to prepare lunch and go to Mennulara's funeral. Elvira Risico, the shop assistant, took the chance to buy some fresh sardines for her husband from the fish merchant. Her husband loved fish, and not just on Fridays.

Elvira was in the kitchen, busy frying the sardines—cleaned and filleted, with a good coating of flour—when her husband sneaked in and tenderly put his hands around her hips. They had been married for eight months, and people rightly said they were mad about each other. As he kissed her neck, clammy from the heat of the sizzling oil, Gaspare asked her why she had come home so early.

"Don't distract me, Gasparu'. Can't you see I'm frying? They'll go soft if I don't fry them right away," said Elvira, losing conviction as her husband's caresses intensified. He was feeling her breasts, her thighs, and down there, and she felt damp and sweetly juicy all over. "The maid who worked for the Alfallipe family died, a relative of signora Pecorilla's, and so she closed the bookshop early to go to the funeral."

The embrace slackened for a moment, then resumed. Her husband, clasping her hips and pressing against her, said, "It must be the Inzerillo woman. I spotted her in the post office last week, and she looked tired." After a pause, he added, "She was a nasty piece of work—one of those people you have to watch out for."

With every day that passed, Elvira had more reasons to admire this intellectual husband of hers, a man who knew about everything and everybody; he reflected before making a judgement and had deep, wise thoughts. She said, "And to think that signora Pecorilla told me that she was a good woman, and that she loved the Alfallipe family as if they were her own and served them all her life . . . " She paused, regretting that she had used the bourgeois word *served*, ashamed of her ignorance. Gaspare carried on nibbling at her earlobe.

At table, they chatted contentedly, devouring the hot, crunchy sardines. "But why have the Alfallipes posted the notice on the streets, and why are they organising the funeral? Isn't that the responsibility of the dead woman's family?" asked Elvira, who came from near Siracusa and wanted to fit in in her husband's town, where she would live all her life, unless Gaspare's political career took them to some big city.

"That scum have to learn to treat workers and employees with respect when they're alive, not when they're dead. The Inzerillo woman is a perverse example of a proletarian who let herself be dominated by the capitalists, and who treated others terribly. I know, because I had to put her in her place lots of times in the post office. She gave herself airs, like a baroness, the baroness of sweet fuck all, she was!" He said no more, for he didn't feel like admitting that in reality it was Mennulara who had scolded him, and more than once, for not being in the complaints department during working hours: he'd sneaked off to Party offices to read *l'Unità*, as he did every day, a habit that was tolerated by the manager, his aunt's brother-in-law, thanks to whom he had got the job in the first place. Mennulara had lectured him as if he were a schoolboy. This woman who was barely able to write had told him that she knew about his regular absences from work and that he ought to set a good example if he wanted the workers' respect.

The effect of Gaspare's diatribe, very short indeed compared to the sermons he usually gave his wife to raise her political consciousness, was surprising. All amorous smiles, Elvira laid a hand on his shoulder and, fondling his neck, said, "Today I have a surprise for you," while with her other hand she slowly unbuttoned her housecoat, releasing her full breasts. She was completely naked.

They didn't finish eating the four remaining sardines, and Elvira had cause to bless her husband's political commitment, which forbade the employment of a maid, or even daily help, for that Tuesday 24 September, Gaspare Risico made love to his wife right there on the lunch table, with all the crockery wobbling merrily at the thrusting of his hips. Apart from Marxist philosophy, he had taught his wife some marvellous little tricks. After the first session of lovemaking, Gaspare drew himself up and moved away from the table, where Elvira was lying sated and wonderfully beautiful, the better to look at her; he sipped from a glass of wine. Then he decided to pour the rest into the small and perfect hollow of Elvira's navel, and from there the wine started trickling down her soft, pulsing belly until it penetrated her intimate parts and dripped over her open thighs. And so Elvira knew the joys of cunnilingus.

That afternoon, Gaspare Risico forgot to warn his comrades not to go to the funeral of that "traitor to the working class," the Inzerillo woman. There was no need, because none of the members of the Roccacolomba branch of the Communist Party so much as entertained the idea of going to a funeral at three o'clock in the afternoon; this did not prevent Risico from boasting in the days that followed that, thanks to his sagacious timing, he had prevented the Party's being discredited in the eyes of the citizens.

14. *The funeral*

Dr. Mendicò, arm in arm with his sister, signora Concetta Di Prima, was heading for the church of the Addolorata to attend Mennulara's funeral. He was silent, absorbed in his thoughts. Then, as was his wont in his old age, he suddenly spoke. "There's something I don't get about this death. She should have made it at least until Christmas! She was in a hurry to leave, and she got her way this time too."

"What are you talking about, Mimmo? Calm down," signora Di Prima said, trying to pacify him. At that point, some acquaintances came up, also heading for the funeral, and they entered the church together.

Dr. Mendicò and his sister sat in one of the front rows. The doctor liked to contemplate the Baroque altar with its coloured marbles; the statue of the Blessed Addolorata with its melodramatic gaze, in the Mannerist style of the provinces; and the decorative work with cherubs, wreaths of flowers and fruit that covered the apse, a munificent gift of the prince of Brogli, perhaps to ease his guilty conscience: for dynastic reasons he had forced his eldest daughter to become a nun, and she had become the abbess of the convent. The doctor's glance fell on the coffin and he thought that Mennulara had unwittingly chosen the appropriate church for her funeral: both women had been sacrificed by their families, one for prestige and the other for survival. "The nobility and the poor have a lot in common, but they don't know it," he whispered to his sister. Signora Di Prima nodded in vague agreement, thinking that, with old age, her brother's reflections were becoming more and more extravagant.

Assisted by the young parish priest, Father Arena was dressing in the sacristy prior to the funeral service. This was the church where he himself had once served as priest. Since his retirement he had almost forgotten he was a priest, and he lived quietly in his godson's cottage in the country, looking after his vegetable patch and cultivating the garden in front of the house. He lived like a peasant—he of all people, son of one of the prince of Brogli's sharecroppers, chosen and destined by his family, with the prince's help, for a different and better life.

The previous May, Mennulara had got back in touch with him and they had met several times, rekindling their warm friendship. Betraying no emotion, she had told him that she would die before the winter, asked him to help her write a few letters, as in the old days, and then she asked if he would officiate at her funeral. You couldn't say no to Mennulara.

Father Arena donned the purple-and-gold vestments for the funeral Mass. The lace trim of the new priest's white linen surplice barely covered his knees. Goodness knows what he had done with those fine long surplices that the nuns in the convent had sewn especially for him because he was tall—unusual among the countrymen and poor folk from whom the clergy sprang. Father Arena was, in fact, very tall, slim and frail, and he had often wondered whether the benevolence of the prince of Brogli towards him hadn't had something to do with his mother, who was said to have been extremely attractive as a young woman. He was unlike his short and stocky brothers, and had been sent off to the seminary when very young, not because he had manifested a precocious vocation, which, in fact, he had never felt, but in order to avoid any embarrassment that his appearance might have caused. Like Mennulara, he contented himself with what was offered him, and he could say that he had lived a simple life and, on the whole, a satisfying one.

Celebrating Mass had always terrified him, because of his stammer, which he managed to control thanks to the stratagem to which he owed his popularity: he had learned to recite the prayers and even to preach at lightning speed, so his Masses were over in a quarter of an hour, a real record. The wealthy families of the town, partly because he was the prince's protégé and partly because of his speed and good nature, vied for him for weddings, baptisms, first communions and funerals, as well as at family Masses held at home or in the country chapels. As a result he often sat at their well-provided tables; he appreciated good cooking and was very fond of food, but all without guilt, because he had access to these good things thanks to his work as a priest.

Father Arena had thought at length about his funeral sermon for Mennulara. He had even written a page of notes, which he had already lost. "That does it. Here goes nothing," he said, straightening his vestments, and he entered the church at three o'clock sharp, followed by the parish priest.

He was surprised to see so many people. In the first row, there were the Alfallipes. Only signora Adriana was wearing mourning dress. Santa and the other maids were packed into the pew behind, dressed in black, their heads covered. There were also some of signora Alfallipe's friends, which heartened him; they would support and comfort her in the following days. And then there were the former servants of the Alfallipe household, several townspeople, poor folk, greengrocers, the porters of the great houses of Roccacolomba Alta, tradesmen, and acquaintances of Mennulara. Father Arena looked at the rest of the congregation; he hadn't expected all those people. There were various worthies of the town—Vazzano, the notary; Dr. Mendicò and his sister; the agronomist Masculo and his wife; the mother superior of the convent, schoolteachers—and even a clutch of old men from the Conversation Club. And that was not all: there were also some field hands from estates that had once belonged to the Alfallipes—lots of them, occupying four or five rows at the back. They sat in a tight group, cloth caps in hand and the contrite look of schoolchildren on their faces, and yet more middle-aged men nearby who looked like out-of-towners, perhaps pruners or field hands. Perplexed and confused, Father Arena turned to the coffin. Poor Mennulara. Who would have ever imagined that he, so much older than she, would be officiating at her funeral, and before so many people . . . Heaven knows where they had all sprung from!

He began the Mass at top speed, as usual. When the time came for the sermon, he went up to the pulpit and spoke forcefully, with no stammers: "It is always hard to talk of the dead. Sometimes I try to say words that the dear departed would have appreciated, sometimes words that the family would like to hear . . . Only rarely have I decided to say what I want to say. For Maria Rosalia Inzerillo, I will say what I feel like saying, because I knew her from the time she was twelve years old and I loved her like a daughter. As she grew, she became a true friend, and I knew her well—Mennulara, as she was called by the townsfolk by way of nickname, and Mennù in the Alfallipe household. She worked like a dog all her life. She didn't know the meaning of repose. A restless creature in body and soul, she always sought to do more and better. Difficult and wary of strangers by nature, she rarely laughed, but she had a sense of humour all her own. She devoted her life to the Alfallipe family and did for them what she believed was right. She had few friends, even though now I see many people here, so perhaps she had more than I thought. But she had enemies, too: she did not forgive easily and there was no one as stubborn as she. God will forgive her these failings because she suffered terribly from childhood, when she gathered almonds on the estates . . ."

At that point Father Arena felt himself pierced by two penetrating and terrible rays that guided him inexorably towards an unmistakable figure in the back of the church, standing in front of a column in the portal, arms folded and legs apart: don Vincenzo Ancona. The overcoat hanging from the heavy, solid shoulders looked like a mantle of power that seemed to create an aura around his body.

Father Arena fell silent and remained motionless as a statue. With an immense effort, he pulled himself together. Skipping all the other things he would have liked to say, he finished quickly: "And she also suffered in dying when still young. I tell you, she was an admirable woman and one whom with time people will learn to love, for she always kept her word and was a loyal servant and friend. I offer my condolences to her nephews and her brother-in-law, who are unfortunately not present, and to the Alfallipe family."

Only then did Father Arena manage to wrench his gaze from that of don Vincenzo and turn it to signora Alfallipe. He felt faint, and he hung on to the pulpit. Like a suckling lamb in need of maternal approval, he sought don Vincenzo's gaze again. But don Vincenzo Ancona was no longer there. He had vanished like an apparition—no sound of a step, no creaking of door hinges: he and his men had disappeared.

15. Don Paolino Annunziata wets himself for the second time in his life, and again it is Mennulara's fault

Don Paolino was not religious. He went to church only for funerals, christenings, and weddings, and donna Mimma was most displeased by this, even though her husband had a good excuse for his scanty observance: he suffered from arthritis and had trouble getting in and out of the wooden pews, what with the infernal footrest contraptions that trapped his feet, the folding kneelers on which he banged his knees, the little bookshelves for the missals that jutted out and hampered his movements. Once, at a grand-daughter's wedding, it had taken three men to extricate him from the pew after he fell and got stuck inside.

In the church of the Addolorata, he preferred to let his wife and his niece Luisa take a conspicuous place in one of the front rows, in the central nave, while he luckily found a chair near the church entrance, where he ensconced himself so that he could be among the first to leave after the service. He was fondly observing Father Arena, whom he had driven many times to the Alfallipes' country house in signora Lilla's day, when they still used to have Mass said in the chapel. A good man, this Father Arena. After all, he wasn't too "priestly"; he had got his housekeeper, donna Maricchia, pregnant, and she a widow who was older than he, and they produced a fine boy who was the spitting image of his father. Father Arena did not conceal the matter, as many priests do, and during their car trips the two men had often talked of their respective children.

To listen to Mass said by Father Arena was a relief, thanks to its predictable brevity. Don Paolino compared it to a car journey. Father Arena would start off puffing and stut-tering, then would pick up speed by swallowing his words and skipping phrases, to arrive in a flash at the "*ite, missa est.*" Certain that the sermon, too, would be brief, don Paolino was listening attentively to the priest's words. Well done, Father Arena, he said to himself, noting that the priest was speaking clearly and without stammering. He must be getting better with old age, he thought, looking on him with a benevolent eye.

But suddenly, after the first few sentences, Father Arena broke off. It seemed to don Paolino as if the priest was staring at him, but that wasn't it, for the priest's gaze slid beyond him. I shouldn't have assumed he'd got rid of his stutter, because here he goes again, he doesn't want to start stammering and he doesn't know how to go on, thought don Paolino, calmly confident that Father Arena would soon begin speaking again. But the priest remained silent and seemed petrified by an incomprehensible terror, his gaze fixed above don Paolino's right shoulder, like a hare dazzled by the lights of hunters in the night, a powerless victim. Don Paolino felt a strange disquiet, as if he had something to do with the situation, as if from behind his back there came a hostile shaft of withering light that immobilised Father Arena.

Forcing himself into a painful contortion, don Paolino, still curious, managed to turn round and look behind him: leaning against the door of the church was don Vincenzo Ancona, his ruddy old face with its taut, glossy, and almost completely unwrinkled skin exuding energy and power, his gaze fixed on Father Arena. Around him stood four men in dark clothes, their eyes darting from one corner of the church to another. Don Paolino was instantly noticed. A warning glance fell upon him from one of the men, a look that transmitted the message: mind your own business and remember that you saw nothing. With miraculous speed and without the slightest twinge in his bones, don Paolino turned back to his former position and lowered his head as if in prayer. His sight was blurred and he was shaking with fear. He sensed a slow feeling of warmth inside, which descended from between his thighs, spread out over his legs, and seeped up his buttocks: don Paolino Annunziata was pissing himself.

The Mass was over and people were slowly preparing to leave the church. Don Paolino remained glued to his chair, embarrassed at the thought that the others might notice that his trousers were wet. He told his wife that he wanted to say hello to Father Arena and would wait for him in the church. His sight was clearing again and he began to feel better, but he was sticky, and, as the urine cooled, he began to feel extremely uncomfortable. He got up cautiously and headed for the sacristy, taking care to hug the wall as he walked in the shadows.

Father Arena was alone. He had taken off his vestments and was standing before the portrait of the first abbess of the convent, the blessed Carmela di Brogli, with her dark, hard eyes, as if beseeching her to intercede with the Lord. Don Paolino went up to him. He understood that the priest was asking courage of the nun, perhaps an ancestor of his, and he waited for a few moments. Then he lightly touched the priest's cassock to attract his attention. Father Arena started. "Oh, it's you, Paolino. You gave me a fright."

"I saw him, too, Father, and I pissed myself."

With a half smile Father Arena said to him, "You mustn't worry, either for me or for you. Here, use this." He handed Paolino a linen cloth and clumsily helped the man dry himself.

Shortly afterwards the two old men, one tall and straight,

imposing in his fluttering black cassock, the other small and with shakier legs than usual, bent over his stick, appeared together in the courtyard, where people were lingering to chat, waiting for Father Arena. "Stay in touch," said the priest to don Paolino, and he joined the funeral cortege. He took up his position at the front, together with Gianni Alfallipe, and the hearse moved off.

Don Paolino lingered in front of the church, hoping the breeze would dry him off. To affect some sort of composure he cast a respectful gaze at the cortege which, like a slow worm with an elongated head, was snaking its way along the winding road that led down towards the cemetery. When the undulating, voluble tail disappeared from sight, he returned home crestfallen. He told donna Mimma that the stuffed sardines he had eaten for lunch had given him heartburn, and he slipped into bed, hoping his trousers would dry without leaving any trace of his shame.

That afternoon, he slept soundly. It was already evening when he awoke; the air carried the sweet smell of frying onions and other preparations for dinner, and he felt protected. Mennulara shouldn't have done this to me, he said, laughing at himself. Twice is too much. It must have been fifteen years since the other piss, and she was involved that time, too.

It was a dark December evening, when night falls at four in the afternoon, and the pair of them were coming back from the country in the car. Mennulara was sitting beside him, as she used to do when they travelled alone; she didn't play the boss with him. She had taken over the reins of management of the Alfallipe lands, and it was a period of strife between her and the sharecroppers, who were reluctant to accept her authority. It was also in the days of the bandit Giuliano, when the field hands were demonstrating, and when the old order was struggling against a mafia undergoing a profound transformation, a mafia that was more and more aggressive and aware of the part it was about to play in the political and class conflicts of Christian Democratic Italy. Every visit to the countryside provided an adventure and a new clash. For don Paolino, a lover of the quiet life, the best moment was the one when they would leave the farm, laden with victuals and produce from the vegetable garden, and return to Rocca-colomba.

That day the car was fragrant with the freshly picked greens and the scent of the first oranges of the season. Don Paolino was driving carefully, looking forward to the steamed vegetables that he would eat for dinner with a drop of new oil and a dash of lemon. He was proceeding slowly and attentively along the track, which was pitted with potholes and strewn with treacherous rocks. Cautiously, he negotiated the sweeping bend that followed the side of the mountain, overlooking a steep gorge full of briers and rocks. Just then, after the bend, they were stopped. Three men were blocking the road; they had been waiting for them. One was in the middle of the track, the others at the sides, their sawn-off shotguns pointed towards the car; you could see only their eyes, narrow slits between the flat caps and the scarves covering their faces.

Mennulara's reaction was instantaneous: she laid her hand on his thigh without embarrassment and said, "When I tell you to go, put her in first gear and put your foot down, understood? Now stop and do as they say."

The man in the middle of the road shouted, "Switch off the lights!" In his confusion don Paolino switched on the low-beam headlights and stopped. "I told you to switch off the lights, you moron!" the man shouted again. Don Paolino obeyed, and they were left in the dark. In the meantime Mennulara had wound down the window and without waiting for the man on her side to approach, she stuck her head out and said in a loud, confident voice, "What do you want?" The man moved slowly, his shotgun still pointed at them, and, still looking her right in the face, he asked, "Is this signor Alfallipe's car?" His companion was checking the rear windows to make sure there were no passengers in the back.

Mennulara replied, "You know very well that this car belongs to signor Alfallipe and that I am Mennulara, Maria Rosalia Inzerillo, and that the man at the wheel is don Paolino Annunziata, the signor's chauffeur. I have to go back to town to carry out my duties at Alfallipe House, so hurry up and tell me what you have to say." She withdrew her head and sat with her back straight against the seat, her neck and head swivelled to one side, her eyes fixed on those of the man standing menacingly nearby. He let his shotgun slip down and slowly rested his left arm on the lowered window; taking all the time in the world, he spoke. "Signorina, this is a warning for you. Going into the estates is not good for you. The air in town is much healthier and you'd do better to remain a maid at Alfallipe House and not bother your head about things that don't concern you."

The tension was palpable. Don Paolino looked straight

ahead. Aimed at him was the mouth of the shotgun held by the ugly thug who was standing right in the middle of the road like a stone giant, his legs apart. There was a hesitant tremor in Mennulara's hand, which still lay heavily on his thigh; he felt the pressure of her nails through the cloth of his trousers. She was afraid, too, and he thought he was doomed.

Her thunderous voice made him jump. She was shouting loudly, yet her words were clear and simple: "No one speaks like that to me, but I realise it's not your fault nor that of the gentlemen with you today. Things haven't been explained to you very well, and it's not up to me to explain them now. Be so kind as to tell don Vincenzo Ancona that Mennulara sends him her greetings and that she'll call him soon, that he is not to go to the inconvenience of contacting me. I'll send him word when I'm ready to talk to him. And he's not to worry—I'm a woman who knows how to keep her mouth shut, and I'm going to stay that way. Give him this message without delay. Also tell him that I've taken no offence at this encounter with you. Anyway, there will be no more encounters, and you've made me a little late in returning to town. I have to go now, because as don Vincenzo is well aware, I am a servant with the Alfallipe family. He knows this because that's the way it is, he knows everything—and he also knows I have to look after the counsellor's property. I must come to the countryside, and the country air does me a world of good. When I need help, I won't be ashamed to call him; he knows that I respect him. In the meantime, Merry Christmas to all of you, and now get out of the way, because I'm late."

She was gesturing as she spoke, and she had withdrawn her hand from don Paolino's thigh, but at that point she let it fall again heavily. Her voice now strong and confident, Mennulara gave the order: "Let's go, don Paolino," and she turned back to look at the road ahead without deigning to give a further glance at the individual who had addressed her. She had dismissed them all. Don Paolino started the car and it slowly moved forwards. The man in front of the car remained motionless, the shotgun still pointed at him. Mennulara's hand obliged him to proceed. Don Paolino thought that maybe his time had come—either from being shot to death or crushed to pieces in the gorge; only that hand, pressing on his thigh as heavy as a rock, gave him the strength to drive on, like an automaton. Slowly, the man began to move towards the mountainside, his arrogant posture unchanging, and gave way to the car; his shotgun was still pointed at don Paolino. The car moved forwards quietly.

Mennulara leaned out of the window and called out a farewell in Sicilian: "*Salutàmu*, go and tell don Vincenzo Ancona what I said to you. I wouldn't like you to get into trouble, as you don't deserve it for so little." She gave don Paolino's thigh a vice-like squeeze. He switched on the headlights, put his foot down, and the car took off in a cloud of dust. It was then that he realised that he was sitting in a pool of cool liquid; he had pissed himself.

They made the return journey in silence. At Alfallipe House, Mennulara said to him, "Go up to the kitchen. I'll give you a pair of the counsellor's trousers and I'll wash yours. Tell your wife that you got oil on them. And remember, not a word to anyone." Don Paolino did not speak of the event, and after that things in the country went smoothly for Mennulara.

16. *After the funeral, Dr. Mendicò offers the necessary condolences to Santa and converses with Angelo Vazzano, the notary*

After the funeral, Dr. Mendicò once more offered his sympathies to the Alfallipes. He thought it his duty to offer them to Santa, too. He tried to spot her in the crowd and found her outside the church, surrounded by a group of women noisily commiserating and trying to outdo one another in effusive expressions of grief. The doctor waited patiently for a lull to get in among them and catch Santa's attention; in the meantime he listened in on their conversation.

Santa was enjoying her moment of glory; she was extolling Mennulara's culinary and domestic skills, without forgetting to emphasise her own virtues and the high esteem in which Mennulara had always held her. The women were hanging on her every word.

"Mennù taught me lots of things in the kitchen, even though I could cook, and well, too: sweets, biscuits, meat pies, rice croquettes, meringues, profiteroles . . . She would leave the kitchen spotless; she never wanted me to wash pots and pans for her. And she never left me to eat on my own. She laid the table for signora Adriana and served her in person, and to think that it was her own flat, her own property, yet she treated her as if she were the mistress in every sense."

The noisy interruptions of the other women's admiration and surprise drowned out Santa's words, until she began to sing the praises of the heroine's last deeds. "The week before she died, she wanted to make almond biscuits and marzipan. She had some almond flour but didn't like it; she said it needed bitter almonds as well—she knew all the tricks, she did. She asked signora Carmela to buy her some, and then she went off to the kitchen to prepare the sweets. She got out of bed to do this, though you could see she was ill and in pain." Santa began weeping again, submerged by a chorus of sorrow from the women: "She was a good woman." "What an angel she was." "What will you do without her? . . . " Encouraged, Santa continued her tale. "Just to show you how much respect she had for me, I'll tell you this. She put two lots of biscuits in the oven; one batch came out burned, the other nice and crunchy. She said to me, 'You'll be in for it if you eat the burned ones, they've gone bitter. You and signora Adriana must take the nice golden ones, which are sweet.' She took the burned biscuits to her room and ate them alone, because she wouldn't hear of waste."

A gap opened up in the circle and Santa saw the doctor. She threw her arms around his neck and held on to him for a good while, proud to show the other women that Mennulara's doctor considered her a family retainer, worthy of receiving his condolences in public, setting the final seal on the importance she had assumed that day. Finally, the doctor found a way of extricating himself from her embrace and went on his way.

On the street, Vazzano, the notary, approached Dr. Mendicò, and they walked together for a while. "She was a unique character, with an enviable nose for business . . . Just think, she managed to minimise for the Alfallipes the damage caused by the government's breakup of the big estates, and well in time she sold off to poor folk the land that was all rocks and brushwood. She knew the Alfallipes' land better than a field overseer. I was dealing with a professional, mark my words. For all her bad temper, she was a good woman and devoted to the Alfallipe household," the notary concluded. The doctor concurred.

"There's something I'm curious about, Mimmo. You who were her doctor . . . Is there a will?"

"I don't know."

"I'm asking because some time ago she had me draw up a deed of gift, by which she left her flat to signora Alfallipe, and I thought she'd make a will, too, but she didn't, and I was amazed at that. I thought she trusted me. She couldn't have made a holograph will—she could hardly write, as we all know—yet she must have had property. She had no declared income—no one wants to pay taxes—but when cash was needed, Mennulara found it. I always wondered where she got it from."

Dr. Mendicò had never liked Angelo Vazzano, and the question irritated him. "You ought to know better than I, I'm only a doctor. As for cash, I never let her pay me."

"Maybe she didn't have time to do it. After all, she seemed well only a few weeks ago. And I think she also went on holiday in August. She didn't expect to die so soon . . . What do you say?" the notary added, hoping for a more exhaustive response.

He got little more than a monosyllable. "She did; I didn't." The notary understood that Mimmo Mendicò would say no more, and he took his leave.

Left alone, Dr. Mendicò meditated on Santa's words and the notary's comments. Mennulara had certainly died before her time. He had diagnosed her tumour in May, advising her to have tests done and to seek the advice of a specialist, but she had said no. He warned her that this foolish refusal would probably shorten her life, and Mennulara's only reply was to ask him if she would manage to live until the autumn. He told her it was possible, and Mennulara replied, "It's fine by me if I die at the end of September."

Yet the unexpected worsening of the previous week had taken him by surprise; despite fierce stomach pains, Mennulara again refused to be admitted to hospital for tests; and at the end of September, she was dead, as she had decided. Dr. Mendicò shook his head and said to himself, with infinite sadness, It's time I gave up medicine. I'm no good at it any more, I have to admit.

17. Don Giovannino Pinzimonio observes the passìo and reminisces about Mennulara

After the funeral, don Giovannino Pinzimonio felt worn out. He stopped at the Conversation Club for a breather before tackling the climb towards home. The chairs were standing out on the pavement, lined up against the outer wall. Don Giovannino slumped into the first chair handy, without trying to find his favourite. The straw-bottomed chairs of the Conversation Club all seemed the same, but each member had chosen one, and heaven help anyone who took it from him. There had been big rows about this in the past.

The sun was still beating down on the cobbled street. The light was dazzling, and don Giovannino struggled to keep his eyes open. He dozed off, then was awakened by the chatter of people passing by in the square: the *passìo* had begun. Instead of going home, as was his custom by now, he ordered a coffee from the waiter to keep himself awake, and then set to watching.

The Conversation Club quarters were found in a run-down eighteenth-century building; they consisted of a large room on the ground floor, furnished with chairs and tables, and four rooms on the first floor, now abandoned and full of piles of useless old furniture. In times long gone by, these rooms were said to have been used for surreptitious encounters with women. An elderly waiter saw to all the club's needs: he acted as cleaner, intermediary, sometimes even secretary and administrator. The rich bourgeoisie of the town had frequented the place until 1860, when they transferred to the new United Italy Club. After that, the Conversation Club went into decline. Many of its lower-middle-class members were retired, and the building became more and more decrepit. Despite this, don Giovannino and the other members were proud of it and boasted they had the best premises in the province, thanks to its position. The building stood at a widening of the square—that's to say, on the main street of Roccacolomba, close to the *chiesa madre* and the most elegant shops, opposite the most fashionable café. It was undoubtedly the best place for observing the *passìo*.

In the cooler part of the day, people would pour into the square for the *passìo*, every afternoon and on holidays. This was an agreeable social activity, good for one's physical and mental health, which don Giovannino, too, had engaged in as a young man—to look for a wife, to find clients, to attend to social relations, then to show off his fine, pretty daughters of marriageable age, and to pass the time. Despite the changes of recent years and the advent of television, lots of local people still strolled through the square, rich and poor but all well groomed. On Sundays, the maids of the rich families also promenaded, but Mennulara had never been seen among them. Today there were lots of girls—the majority of the strollers, in fact. He spotted three or four young ones arm in arm, passing in front of him again and again, all chattering at once, giggling and looking around. In front of the café, male territory, they slowed down.

Respectable men, who didn't promenade very often, would generally go only in the company of their wives, well dressed and rested after their siesta. They preferred to meet in the café, their turf, to watch the women strolling by, and only womanisers would join the *passìo* to walk behind women. Orazio Alfallipe had been one of these; he would walk by himself, following the women's swaying hips.

The same little group of young girls passed by don Giovannino again. One of them, petite and rather plain, shot an ardent glance at a young man leaning languidly against the counter of the café. Their eyes met fleetingly every time the girls passed by; then the girl would turn her head the other way and continue her stroll, accentuating the movement of her hips.

All the chairs lined up against the wall were now occupied by silent club members, watching to spot the jounce of a breast, the movement of a fine backside, mentally stripping the few curvaceous women who dared to wear tight-fitting dresses as they strolled by on the arms of husbands, fathers, brothers. Don Giovannino's thoughts turned to Mennulara's youthful body, still not fully formed. He struggled to keep his eyes open, but his creased and wrinkled lids fell over his pupils and his sight dimmed. Images of the past flitted before him, as if he were at the cinema.

18. *Don Giovannino remembers*

Don Giovannino was an honest and respected surveyor of agricultural produce. His work involved going around the fields on horseback, and he could boast a good knowledge of all the estates in the province.

He would leave Roccacolomba at sunrise and return at sunset. Before his eyes he could see the little girl, four or five years old, walking alongside her father on the road in the pale light of dawn, upright and proud. Luigi Inzerillo was a poor devil; having lost his job in the mine through illness, he had been obliged to work in the fields in order to provide for his family, even though he knew his lungs were rotten. He took his younger daughter along because his wife was ill, too.

While her father toiled, the little girl would gather snails, capers, wild fruit, wood, all she could find to eat and to make kindling. On his return to town, Luigi would shuffle along, dead tired, while the little girl would walk at his side with her chest out, despite being weighed down with the bag containing her harvest. Sometimes she even carried her father's hoe. Don Giovannino refrained from inviting her to climb up onto his mare because he feared that Luigi would collapse on the road without her beside him.

At six years of age the little one started to work in the teams of almond pickers. She was one of the youngest, but none of the women was as good as she; she bustled about with dogged concentration, willing to help the others and to learn. Her tiny fingers never missed an almond, an olive, a pistachio; it was as if her fingertips had eyes. She unearthed them among the sods of hard earth, among the stones, in the bramble bushes. Where those minute little fingers passed, no berry or fruit was left to be picked, either from the ground or in the branches. Fearlessly, she climbed the big trees to get the almonds that didn't fall under the blows of the canes.

After her father's death, she was the one who, at the age of eight, supported her mother and sister. There was no task that she would not accept, anywhere and for any pay, so long as it allowed her to go back to town in the evening. When she gathered almonds her quick, bony fingers looked like a spider's legs weaving a web. That was when they started calling her "Mennulara," the almond picker, a nickname she never lost.

She worked almost joyfully. Don Giovannino recalled her kneeling, absorbed, but alert to everything. She would hear his mare coming at a distance and would be the first to greet him with a shrill but respectful greeting: "*S'abbena-dica*, don Giovannino." He watched her become a well-proportioned girl, her body thin from hunger but harmonious, her oval face, her bright eyes with their long lashes, her beautiful smile that revealed irregular, protruding teeth. She had a seductive singing voice; when the girls joined with the young men in the *stornelli*, the call-and-response folk songs, she put all the passion and sentiment of youth into her singing. She would play with the boys, and she was not intimidated by men. She learned their strong, vulgar language, which she used like a beast if one of her peers did her wrong or if she thought she was the victim of an injustice. And she knew how to behave with her superiors: when the supervisor or woman overseer was unfair to her, she would fall silent, a sullen look on her face.

From early childhood Mennulara had a strong sense of her own dignity, and this seemed incompatible with her social and economic position. She looked people straight in the eye, she asked questions without being artful or disrespectful, and she expected a reply, which she would usually receive. She didn't go to school—she knew her duty, which was to support her family. During lunch breaks, she would keep to herself with her ration of bread and something to go with it, putting a good part to one side to take home. In her pocket she kept crusts of hard bread, dried fruit, and pieces of cheese that she picked up here and there, and she would eat them when she was hungry, saving the best food for the sick ones waiting for her at home. When the working day was over, if there was still enough time, she would return alone to the fields to gather fruit, vegetables, and greens left after the crops had been picked, which she'd shove in her bag and take with her back to Roccacolomba. She had no fear of dangers on the road or of the long walk.

When she was thirteen Mennulara no longer showed up in the fields. Rumour had it that she had had a relationship with a fellow that had ended badly. There was no talk about the affair, because the boy belonged to a powerful family. Don Giovannino, whose work led him to see a great many things and to say little, asked no questions. The less you knew the better, he felt. Some time after, they told him that she had gone into service at Alfallipe House.

He saw her again about twenty years later. He had heard it said that, after the death of signor Alfalippe's mother, she was the one who gave the orders on the estates. She called him in to make an estimate of the almond crop.

They met at the farmhouse, where she behaved like a boss. No longer attractive, she seemed diffident and distant. Don Giovannino rode into the almond grove. Absorbed as he always was when working, he didn't notice that she was following him on foot; once she caught up with him, she never left him for a second. She stopped when he stopped to observe the blossom on a tree or a pruned branch; she never said a word, but her eyes never left his face. Don Giovannino felt uncomfortable.

On their return to the farmhouse, Mennulara withdrew to the offices and made him wait for a long time. Then she came out holding a notebook and stood in front of him. Employing the usual roundabout expressions of the trade, don Giovannino began to talk of ordinary things, the rainfall that year, the hoeing that had been done and was still to be done, before coming to the eagerly awaited moment of the estimate. Mennulara listened in silence. Don Giovannino was embarrassed by her silence; he was in a cold sweat, unable to understand the behaviour of this servant who was now in charge. Maybe she meant to strike an attitude, or make him realise that the boot was now on the other foot; goodness knows what devilment was going through her head. But he was sure of one thing: he couldn't wait to take his leave and return to town. He tried to finish quickly.

He was about to pronounce the verdict and give the estimated figure, when she stopped him. Holding out her right arm, palm up, she said, "Before you say anything, don Giovannino, read the estimate I have written here and see if you think it's correct," and she proffered her notebook.

As he recalled that moment, don Giovannino shivered again. Written there was the exact figure that he had calculated. Amazed, he wanted to know how she had managed this. Had she perhaps read his mind? In a simple, unassuming way, she explained the observations that had led her to the same conclusions he had reached.

"How did you manage to learn so much?" he asked her admiringly.

"I used to like working in the fields, remember?" was her laconic reply. Don Giovannino could have sworn he glimpsed Mennulara's dark eyes become moist. From then on, his services were no longer required, and surveyors were no longer seen on the Alfallipe estates.

She was so different from the others. Where did she get that brain and that presence? Certainly not from her father, don Giovannino said to himself, for Luigi Inzerillo wasn't very intelligent, nor did he have any special fondness for work . . . So from whom? All of a sudden, he recalled that in church he had glimpsed a man who reminded him of don Vincenzo Ancona. He was startled by the thought that crossed his mind. Perturbed, he told himself that there are some things you shouldn't even think about.

He opened his eyes now, settled himself better on his chair, and went back to observing the strollers.

19. *In town on the evening of the funeral*

Before the funeral, there was much gossip in Rocca-colomba about the Alfallipes' decision to organise such a thing for their maid. People also talked of the deceased, as was proper, though they had little to say apart from what was public knowledge. Comments on her private life were very limited, for, having always worked in service with the same family, she had not given any grounds for salacious gossip; true, in the families that knew the Alfallipes well, there was no lack of allusions to Orazio's love affairs, and people whispered with a snigger, and not without a certain incredulity, that the list of his conquests might also include his maid. This possibility was soon discarded, however, because Orazio was known to have preferred women who were married, buxom, and more cultured.

Those few well-to-do townsfolk who took the trouble to go to Mennulara's funeral at three o'clock in the afternoon on Tuesday, 24 September—not out of grief and even less so out of respect for the Alfallipes, but spurred by curiosity about this unusual event—were not disappointed. They saw with their own eyes the scant sorrow of the Alfallipe son and daughters at the death of the maid who had raised them, as amply demonstrated by the skimpy floral wreath and modest funeral, without any music; they tried to estimate the cost of the imposing wreath sent by Mennulara's nephews, and they marvelled again that they were not present at the funeral of their only maternal aunt—unless the Alfallipes had expressly excluded them.

The mourners thus had the opportunity to observe the others attending the funeral and to repeat—at home, at the club, and in the salons—their versions of the event, which they embroidered upon with great authority. What a congregation there had been at the Addolorata! Apart from the Communists, absent to a man, all the town's classes and factions were represented; they said that even don Vincenzo Ancona had deigned to honour the funeral with his presence. Unfortunately, they hadn't seen him face-to-face. Only a few had noticed him, but the rumour flew around town. The children who had been playing football in the churchyard at the time said that they had seen a shiny black car arrive in the square when the funeral Mass had already begun. It drew up right next to the main door, and four men got out along with a big, beefy old man; they had slipped into the church, only to come out soon after, while the service was still going on. They got back into the car, took off again at high speed, and vanished.

After Tuesday afternoon people talked about Mennulara with caution and a certain respect, although her life was scrutinised down to the smallest detail, given that there wasn't much to say about her. The fear that the name Ancona inspired in Roccacolomba was such that it was never pronounced in public; even when people met in shops or in the square, they spoke in whispers, for walls of houses and cobbles in the street have eyes and ears and report to those who should know. It was wise to ensure that this did not happen.

People marvelled yet again at Mennulara's extraordinary career—to have started as a maid and gone on to become a businesswoman managing the Alfallipe assets, saving them from bankruptcy and allowing them to carry on living like gentlefolk while she was content to continue working as a maid and a manager at the same time. Of course, they had to accept that she played the boss and interfered in their business, and probably that she put money aside, but after all, she'd been devoted to the family and had taken the counsellor's widow into her own home, relieving the children of this worry too.

The general opinion was that she was ignorant but intelligent and able, an unpleasant and imperious woman whose life had been devoted to serving the Alfallipes. The rich disapproved of them for allowing a maid to interfere with family decisions, which was indecorous and intolerable for any sensible person, but the Alfallipes differed from others in this as well: as long as they could suit themselves they would have sold their souls to the devil. The poor criticised Mennulara because she had sided with the masters to the detriment of her own folk, her nephews included, while all she received in return was a modest funeral. The mark of respect shown by don Vincenzo Ancona remained inexplicable, but the common people and the bourgeoisie wisely preferred to gloss over that topic.

Only in Baroness Ceffalia's salon, in the presence of a few intimates, was this subject discussed freely, as a way of showing the contempt the upper classes had for the mafia. Among the visitors from Catania, guests invited to the forthcoming Vazzano wedding, the talk was once more of Orazio's adulterous affairs, Massimo Leone's vulgarity, Lilla's arrogance, and Gianni's spinelessness. They talked about the financial situation of the Alfallipes, who had allowed this maid to become their manager, the very family that had become rich in the previous century by managing the lands of the princes of Brogli. They were lucky, because Mennulara had not emulated their greediness: all she had bought with their money was a modest flat. There were many cases of estate administrators who made fortunes at the expense of noble and incompetent masters, and so in a certain sense it was just, and certainly not unusual, that such families met with a similar fate in turn as they went into decline. But this had never happened with a woman, and a servant at that.

The dependence between masters and servants in the Alfallipe household was, by itself, extraordinary, but it was made yet more so by the younger generation, who, seeming at first to have rebelled against it, had in fact perpetuated it and gone farther. They considered Mennulara part of the family and had made this public by posting the death notices and arranging her funeral as if she had been a close relative.

On the other hand, there was something that didn't make sense: the presence at the funeral of don Vincenzo Ancona, the acknowledged mafia boss of the province and the father of an important person who lived on the mainland, a modern man of honour who was known to be a supporter of the government. This was an astonishing, worrisome occurrence, worthy of discussion. After heated debate, two theories held up, both of them bold and rather implausible: that Mennulara's real father was Vincenzo Ancona, whose cunning she had inherited; or that he had been her secret lover in her youth. Thus it happened that don Vincenzo Ancona, a mafioso who had killed ruthlessly and unhesitatingly for the honoured society, who had sentenced a brother-in-law to death for "talking too much," a father of four and a practising Catholic, came to be seen as a sexually indiscreet person and a romantic, too, a victim of his passions.

In the porter's lodge of Palazzo Ceffalia, the talk was obviously only about the funeral. Unlike the masters, no one was foolish or impolite enough to dare to think that Nuruzza Inzerillo or her daughter might have been don Vincenzo Ancona's lover. With the wisdom of the common people, they considered two concrete hypotheses: that Mennulara had been a member of the mafia, which would have been extraordinary, given that she had been both poor and a woman; or that she had done Vincenzo Ancona some favour big enough to deserve her posthumous honour. In any case, respect for Mennulara grew, although don Vito Militello continued to point out that she had been an unpleasant woman nonetheless, God rest her soul, who had kept to herself and had had no friends, and that she had gone over to the masters and ridden roughshod over her own people.

Wednesday 25 September 1963

✖✖

20. *Contrary to expectations, Mennulara is still the subject of conversation, and Gaspare Risico avenges himself for her insolence by mistreating Carmela Leone*

On the morning of Wednesday 25 September, the gossip about Mennulara's funeral was repeated to those few who still hadn't heard it, enlarged upon and embellished after a good night's sleep, but still with a good deal of circumspection. Then finally in the mansion houses and in the porters' lodges, the people of Roccacolomba began to agree there was nothing more to discuss, criticise, sift through, or recollect about Mennulara and the Alfallipes and that everyone was tired of talking about them. The topic was mined out and would be a dead letter by tomorrow. The forthcoming wedding of the daughter of Vazzano, the rich notary, would take its place in the town gossip. But things didn't turn out quite as predicted.

With a terrible sinking feeling, Carmela Leone accepted her family's decision that she was to go to the post office to pick up any correspondence addressed to Mennulara, as she was the only Alfallipe child still living in Roccacolomba and well known and respected there.

She had discussed this mission with her husband, down to the tiniest detail, until the small hours: What should I wear? What if they catch me at it? It's illegal to pick up post addressed to someone else, and worse if the person's dead. What should I do? Should I take a friend along? It was decided she would go to the post office in the late morning, elegantly dressed. She would explain that it had just occurred to her to pick up letters for her mother, signora Alfallipe, who had found it more convenient to have them addressed to her trusted maid.

On the way, Carmela felt very anxious and as if she were being watched. Her legs were shaking, but not because she was wearing high heels, and she made her way unsteadily along the cobbled street, sweating and a bit desperate. She managed to control herself only by affecting the air of superiority typical of her family, and it was in this state that she arrived at the post office.

They had all taken it for granted that the clerk at the counter would have known about Mennulara's death. But there was a new clerk, a woman, and Carmela forgot the little speech she had learned by heart and thus did everything wrong. She asked in a murmur if there was any post for signorina Maria Rosalia Inzerillo. An elegant lady like herself, wearing jewellery and obviously married, could never be a "signorina" Inzerillo. The clerk realised this and asked if she was picking up post for a third party. The question wasn't a refusal, for it was acceptable for relatives to get letters addressed to their spouses, parents, uncles and aunts, or children, just on their word, without any formal proxy.

Carmela got flustered and couldn't manage an answer to this simple question. Instinctively, she fell back on ancestral hauteur and made a scene that looked set to degenerate into a row, so loud were the words and threats she levelled at the poor clerk, who naturally felt responsible for this customer's reaction. Carmela accused her of impertinence, of not knowing who she was—she, the daughter of counsellor Orazio Alfallipe—and ordered the clerk to hand over all the letters for signorina Inzerillo without delay. She had better things to do than stand at a counter waiting, and besides, the queue of people behind her was growing longer.

When the clerk asked whether she was related to signorina Inzerillo, Carmela said that the latter was in service with the Alfallipe family, and she had the right to ask if there was any post for her, which she could also pick up, since all of signorina Inzerillo's correspondence belonged to the Alfallipes and the clerk should have known that. If she wouldn't hand it over, then she, Carmela Leone, née Alfallipe, would complain to the manager, whom she knew personally.

When the clerk flatly refused, Carmela decided to tell the truth. She had come at the request of her family. Her mother, signora Adriana Alfallipe, lived with signorina Inzerillo, her maid, in the home of the aforesaid signorina Inzerillo, who had died of cancer two days before. Signora Alfallipe was grief-stricken and certainly could not come in person to pick up the post, which arrived addressed to signorina Inzerillo but in reality belonged to the Alfallipes. It was not hard to understand, she said, and she had to take the post to her mother that morning.

Carmela did not achieve the desired effect. Her story, basically true but incomplete, seemed implausible to the clerk, who by then had become suspicious and stuck to her original position; she also refused to give Carmela information about the late signorina Inzerillo's postal business. Carmela insisted, continuing to repeat her points, raising her voice more and more, and ending up hysterical, asking the clerk at least to tell her if there was any post for signorina Inzerillo in general delivery and declaring she wouldn't budge from the counter until she obtained this information.

The clerk asked her to go away, saying there was a crowd waiting to be served. Then Carmela began to threaten her, asserting that it didn't matter whether signorina Inzerillo was well or ill, alive or dead, for there were family matters that needed resolving immediately, and the clerk had to tell her if there was any post, or else there would be all hell to pay. The clerk, who was new to the job, didn't know what to do. She called a colleague for help. Carmela turned purple in the face and became almost apoplectic; having no intention of leaving, she stood her ground, hanging on to the counter. Workers and customers watched the row unfold, irked by the delay but amused, too. Those among them who knew Carmela Alfallipe quite simply enjoyed the whole scene and listened eagerly.

The post office staff agreed that the only solution was to take the customer to signor Risico, a colleague who out of the goodness of his heart had chosen to deal with complaints from the public, and so they did. It took two clerks to persuade Carmela to move away from the counter; each of them holding her by an arm, they escorted her, ranting and raving, into his office.

With an exquisitely polite "What can I do for you, madam?" Gaspare Risico invited Carmela Leone to take a seat in front of his desk. His two colleagues went off, their eyes twinkling, snickering together. They appreciated the way Risico did things and found him an able and understanding colleague, as well as a good-looking man. Risico armed himself with paper and pencil and carefully wrote down the date. Carmela sat in front of him, her back not in contact with the chair, her legs nervously folded, ready to leap to her feet. Silent at last. In purring tones, Risico asked signora Leone to give him the particulars as he set out to make a written record of the conversation. This behaviour alarmed Carmela, who haughtily ordered him to write down nothing whatsoever, to listen to her, and to stay calm and civil, as she, signor Alfallipe's daughter, was. All she wanted to do was to pick up her maid's post, she said, adding that she was a personal friend of the manager and expected the matter to be resolved speedily, for everyone's sake, including signor Risico's.

On hearing the name Alfallipe, Gaspare Risico couldn't believe his luck. Only a moment before, he had been reading *La Sicilia* and had not welcomed his colleagues dragging this madwoman into his office, but now he was pleased to have the chance to teach an Alfallipe a lesson, given that she was in his clutches.

Risico was blessed with the ability to put people at their ease and to get them to talk freely, only to pounce the moment they felt safest, when he would lead them to the point where they were defeated but grateful for his courtesy. There were few complaints he couldn't resolve, and even then the complainants were left with the impression that somebody had taken them seriously and appreciated their contribution to the smooth running of the postal service. The fact that he was an attractive man didn't hurt, either.

He decided to pretend that he knew nothing about the Alfallipes' affairs. He had Carmela tell him what had happened at the counter, and he agreed with her that the users of a state service deserved to be treated with respect. By asking her easy and encouraging questions, using the dialectics of body language—his hands motionless on the table, palms turned up towards her, his lips barely parted in a half smile— Gaspare Risico managed to lead Carmela Leone to the desired point. The poor soul, little by little and confusedly, revealed the real purpose of her request. Risico looked at her straight in the eye, only to lower regretful lids at the accusations levelled at his colleague and, nodding his head in agreement, respectfully encouraged her to continue. In the end the hapless Carmela admitted that she was expecting important letters addressed to Mennulara, letters that probably contained money, and she would have forged signorina Inzerillo's signature and taken them away in order to have them immediately. Carmela added that if Risico helped her, she would bear this in mind and, in addition, would put in a good word for him with the manager.

Gaspare Risico's inviting silence might have encouraged her to say more, but she had said enough. He silently exulted. Gotcha! he thought, and straightened in his seat. Brandishing his pencil as if it were a spear aimed at Carmela, he berated her harshly, accusing her of intended theft, impersonation, forgery, and fraud, of making false statements and false representations to a public official regarding her own and other people's identity and personal attributes, and of threatening and attempting to corrupt a public official in the course of his official duties. What's more, she had dared to lodge a complaint about the counter clerk, who had suspected nothing of her plot to perpetrate a fraud to the detriment of the legitimate heirs of the late signorina Inzerillo.

He rose to his feet with icy dignity and solemnly announced that he would write the report and consign it to the manager, stating he had two reasons for doing so, which he would explain in detail. At that point he paused to observe Carmela's reaction. She was dumbfounded. Fat tears streaked down her puffy face. Gaspare Risico sat down again to rattle off these reasons under her nose. Wagging his index finger at her, he said, "The first is that I am paid by the state to serve the public. Dissatisfied with our service, you came to me to lodge a complaint, if it may be defined as such, and it is your right to expect it to receive serious consideration. The second is that you told me you are on friendly terms with our manager. You must have had a reason to say so. It certainly cannot be that you wanted to accuse the manager of corruption or incompetence, because he is an honest and respected person. So perhaps it was to threaten me, and in that case it is my duty to tell the manager so that he may make a final decision about whether you are right, whether we refused to provide you with information and to entrust you with post that you have the right to collect, or whether you are a thief or an impostor who was trying to get what belonged to the late Maria Rosalia Inzerillo. As far as I am concerned, you have absolutely no right to collect another citizen's post without a proxy or a letter from a lawyer, as prescribed by postal rules and regulations, let alone to get information regarding the affairs of a deceased citizen."

Carmela's face had undergone a grotesque metamorphosis: her fringe had deflated, the hair clung to her sweat-soaked forehead in graceless clumps, her eye shadow was running down her cheeks, and the red of her lips, which she had been biting to keep from bursting into tears, had made a smudged halo around her mouth. In this moment of supreme peril, Carmela Alfallipe clung to her pride and vanity: she held back her tears and pleaded with Risico to let her go. She must have failed to make herself clear, she told him. Things weren't the way he thought. She had talked too much because she was grieving over Mennulara's death. With a "Let's pretend that we never met, although I find you extremely courteous and it would be nice if we could meet under different circumstances," she tried to give him an alluring smile with her swollen and discoloured lips.

Gaspare Risico replied severely, as he would repeat complacently to his wife that evening: "Madam, you represent the Italian people, who are exposed to abuses of power on the part of state bodies that exist solely for the purpose of serving the citizenry. You exercised your prerogative as a citizen to lodge a complaint. Justice will be done, and I intend to do my duty."

That said, he gathered up his notes, and, with a wonderfully courteous "Excuse me," he walked out, leaving Carmela dazed and silent. But not for long.

21. *Massimo Leone punishes his wife for her foolishness*

It soon became public knowledge that at the Rocca-colomba post office that Wednesday, the assistant with a certificate in first aid had to be called in to deal with Carmela Leone, who was having a full-blown fit of hysterics, but even she hadn't been able to calm her down.

The deputy manager of the post office had been obliged to call the husband, Massimo Leone, to get rid of the woman, who was refusing to budge. It was as if signor Leone had been expecting the call; he rushed over in his car, parked in front of the main door, and charged into the offices, led by the postal workers who had been waiting for him impatiently. As soon as he saw Carmela, he grabbed her and clamped her arms behind her back in a vice-like grip, then forced her to get up from the chair. Shoving her along, Massimo frog-marched his wife along the corridor with her arms locked behind her back, holding her so hard that her skin visibly reddened. She was trembling and sobbing as he pushed her along from behind with his knees, until they came to the entrance and went out the door. The only words that Massimo said to Carmela, according to the crowd of office workers and passersby that formed around them, were "Come on!" and "Get moving!" as if she were a donkey. And then, in front of everyone, he flung her into his stylish motor car. As soon as she was seated, Carmela bent forwards and a river of yellow vomit gushed from her mouth.

Massimo had barely opened the door of their flat when the phone started ringing. He was holding Carmela with one hand under her armpit; he tightened his grasp and picked up the receiver with the other. It was Lilla, anxious for a report on the morning's activities. Massimo told her that there was no post, that Carmela had a migraine headache and was about to go to bed. He gestured at Mimma, the maid, who had come running to answer the phone, to go away; then he shoved Carmela into the bedroom and pushed the door to. In silence, he gave her a sound beating, kicking and punching her on the thighs, hips, belly, groin, breast, and back. No one would see the bruises, for he knew how such things were done. There was no need to close the bedroom door, as Mimma would hear no shouting or weeping, only Massimo's panting and the rhythmic blows raining down on Carmela, who was lying in a faint on the carpet.

Massimo washed his hands and combed his hair, then sat down at the table for lunch, served by Mimma, who wouldn't talk. After lunch he went out, without returning to the bedroom. He didn't want to take the car—he needed to let off steam by walking. His wife's behaviour had filled him with disgust—not only had she soiled the interior of his new car but she had made a scene that would cause a scandal in town and God knows what other problems. He desperately regretted having married her; he had done so out of pleasure in defeating the opposition fomented by Mennulara within her family, and not out of the hope of a handsome dowry, as they said in town. Now he was stuck with this good-for-nothing wife. Massimo stomped along Roccacolomba's empty streets until he came to the open countryside. He wanted to be alone. Keeping up a brisk pace, he sweated in the autumn sunshine, which was still dazzlingly bright.

Without realising it, he found himself on the road to the

cemetery, the same one he had slowly walked along the day before, behind Mennulara's coffin. He was seized by an irresistible desire to go and smash up the family vault, which that woman had had built right in front of the Alfallipes' private chapel. The cemetery gate was closed. He stood there under the fierce sun, his hands clutching the wrought-iron bars. His rage was mingled with thirst, he felt unwell, and he decided to return to town.

On the way back, he noticed that the shutters of the brothel were open. He went in and stayed until late afternoon. He left exhausted, but without the usual sense of wellbeing. The madam enquired if the foreign girl had been to his liking; on receiving the money, she offered halfhearted condolences for Mennulara's death. Massimo cursed and added, "She even screwed mafiosi, and now that she's dead her dirty little secret is out."

22. Father Arena pays a duty call to offer signora Alfallipe his condolences and reproves Lilla Alfallipe for making unseemly proposals

Father Arena was fond of signora Alfallipe. She had borne with silent dignity the unfaithfulness of signor Orazio Alfallipe, who had inherited his father's carnal instincts but, rather than amusing himself with whores, had preferred to lead respectable women in both the town and province into temptation and mortal sin. She had been a faithful and resigned wife to him, unlike her mother-in-law, who had openly despised her husband, and she had channelled her scant energies into the amusements permitted to a woman of her social position—afternoon visits with lady friends and card games—glad to leave the running of the house to Mennulara, who served her with the same devotion she had shown for her mother-in-law. She did no one any harm, nor did she do anyone any good.

The only criticism made of her was that she spent too much money on clothes. Father Arena thought that this was a minor fault, and anyway as a young woman her good looks had given pleasure to lots of men, him included, without leading them to sin. The fact was that she was a good woman, like many others, who had shown herself to be surprisingly unconventional only once and then sensationally—when on her husband's death she left the family mansion to move into Mennulara's flat.

Early in the morning, as befits a priest on a mourning visit, he rang the bell at the main door of Alfallipe House. Until quite recently, with Orazio's death, there had always been someone in the porter's lodge. Father Arena had dark forebodings about signora Adriana's future in this kind of second widowhood; he hoped that it would not be too painful for her, that she would manage to adapt to living alone in the big gloomy house, and that her children would look after her and not abandon her.

Lilla came down to the door, apologising for having made him wait, and accompanied him up the stairs to the main floor. The red stone stairway led to a landing with a large stained-glass window that gave onto the inner courtyard, then a second flight of stairs to the main floor and two doors of solid walnut: one the main entrance to the family home, the other leading to the counsellor's office, three large and imposing rooms, luxuriously furnished, as befitted the manager of the estates of the princes of Brogli.

Lilla led the way up the stairs and stopped in front of the window to wait for the priest. The sunlight filtering through the glass fell on her fair hair. She looked very much like her mother had as a young woman, and Father Arena brightened at the memory of the kind and graceful Adriana he remembered as a young bride.

"Father, I'd like to talk to you alone for a moment," said Lilla. "I know that you saw Mennulara often these last months. My father gave her a free hand, as you know, and she wound up administering our property. Not everything was distributed to us children at his death, and out of respect for our mother, who has always had a soft spot for Mennulara, we tolerated this." Father Arena continued to look at her, and her hard, determined tone made him realise that she was like her mother only in appearance. He tried to work out what she could want from him, a mere priest.

"I shall have to return to Rome soon, so we need to find out quickly what she did with the inheritance we were entitled to and where she may have hidden it. I think that you have information," said Lilla, finally revealing her intentions. "In the past, you wrote letters for her, and of course you were her spiritual father," she added.

Father Arena stood looking at her, incensed at her request. Sensing his unease, Lilla realised that she had made a mistake and changed tack. "It goes without saying that if you help us, we would all be grateful and would bear this in mind once the situation has been resolved. You have my personal word on this." Then, puzzled by the priest's prolonged silence, she added, "There is a lot of money involved, which could come in handy for you, now that you're retired."

Father Arena replied heatedly, stammering in refined Italian, "You have been living on the Continent for many years and maybe you have forgotten many things, but surely you haven't reached the point of forgetting that a priest does not betray the secrets of the confessional. This is so throughout the Catholic world. Mennulara honoured me with her friendship, and it's common knowledge that I used to write her letters for her. I wrote the draft of the one she left you and I informed her nephews of her death. If you wish, I can give you their address. I have nothing else to say to you. As for the offer of money, if I have understood you correctly, thank you, but I'm not so poor as to sell my integrity. And as for you, signora Lilla, you should be ashamed of such behaviour, which is unworthy of an Alfallipe." He looked away and continued on his way up the stairs. "Let's go up now. I have come to pay a call on your mother."

Signora Alfallipe received Father Arena with her customary warmth and thanked him for having been close to Mennulara in her last days. The pair slipped into reminiscences of the past. "She was stubborn, Father. Remember how many times you encouraged her to learn to write . . . but she never wanted to try. Yet my mother-in-law often used to say that it was you who taught her to read," she said. And, turning to Lilla, she added, "You didn't know, perhaps, but grandmother wanted this. She told me that Mennù suffered terribly when her own mother died and almost stopped speaking altogether. Hoping that she might find solace in reading prayers, she asked Father Arena to teach her to read and write."

"I was a young priest," said Father Arena, warming to the memory, "and signora Lilla had a liking for me. I used to come to hold Mass on Fridays and to confess the household staff. I would stay for lunch and in the afternoon give Mennulara lessons. She learned quickly and she read well, but she didn't know Italian. I gave her an Italian-Sicilian dictionary, which opened the world of reading to her. I don't think she ever read prayer books, but she read a great many others. Signor Orazio allowed her to use his library, and with his permission she would sometimes lend me books of modern literature. And so I was amply rewarded for those few lessons of many years before."

At that point, in a fit of generosity, Adriana Alfallipe made him an offer that was well received. "Father, allow me to give you some books as a present. There are lots of them, and no one reads them. You go and choose. I wanted to do this after Orazio's death, but I was afraid it might upset Mennù. She used to close herself up in that library for hours every day, and she was terribly jealous of all the bits and pieces that Orazio used to collect, as you know."

"Father," said Lilla on noting the priest's embarrassment, "if you trust me with the choice, I'll go right now to get some that might interest you."

"Thank you, signora Lilla," he said. "They are all in alphabetical order. Mennù sorted them all out after your father died."

Lilla went off, leaving the two old people to their agreeable conversation. She returned shortly afterwards with a full bag. Father Arena refrained from opening it, but deep down he was thrilled. He devoured so many books that he was reduced to buying secondhand ones. With the promise of another visit, he left signora Alfallipe comforted and smiling.

"Father Arena is a good man," commented her mother when Lilla came back to the living room, having shown the priest to the door.

"I don't see how you can say that," said Lilla resentfully. "You know perfectly well that it was he who helped her write the letter and who told her nephews about her death."

"Where's the harm? Should he not have done so?" replied her mother. "What books did you give him?"

"The first ones I saw, all D'Annunzio, which Mennù had put under the letter A, by the way. That's how well Father Arena taught her the alphabet!" was Lilla's acid reply.

Signora Alfallipe's reaction was surprising. "You've made a big mistake! Your father wanted those books to go to Pietro Fatta! I was going to give them to him this very day. It was his specific wish—he repeated it many times before he died—but Mennù was against it and told me she would deliver them afterwards. She must have forgotten, and only last week she asked me to give them to Pietro. What were you thinking of, giving D'Annunzio to a priest? I don't understand you. Those books are on the Index." Signora Alfallipe, snuffling like a little girl as she wrung her hands, kept repeating, "Now what'll we do? What a mess!"

Lilla could no longer contain herself. She turned on her mother, yelling that she had had enough of everything and everyone and was dying to get back to Rome. Signora Alfallipe dissolved into desperate sobs. But it was time to receive guests, and the mother and daughter had to recover their composure and welcome them.

And so the Lodato Ceffalia family, on a mourning visit, noticed that Adriana Alfallipe was in a lake of tears right from the start. Not even her husband's death had left her so distraught. After the visit, Baroness Ceffalia and her two daughters busily discussed the Alfallipes: grief-stricken Adriana was on the verge of a nervous breakdown; Lilla was no comfort to her and avoided looking at her, as if she was angry at her for some reason; she couldn't conceal her impatience to leave for Rome and talked of the dead woman with no affection. It was clear that she wanted it known around town that she was looking for information about Mennulara's financial situation and was staying on only for that reason.

23. An afternoon of disagreeable encounters for Pietro Fatta

Pietro Fatta's siesta had been disturbed by visits from Girolamo Meli and Lilla Alfallipe.

The manager of the post office, who hailed from Ragusa, had telephoned him before lunch to request an urgent meeting. They didn't know each other very well, and Pietro was rather surprised; he decided to receive the manager formally in his study. Meli was as white as a sheet and talked fast, jumping up from his armchair to pace around the room, although avoiding going near the open balcony, as if he feared he was being stalked. He told Fatta about the report drawn up by his clerk, Risico, an able young man but unfortunately a Communist, one of those idealistic, honest ones. Risico had suggested involving the police because he suspected that there was something shady about Carmela Leone's actions, grounds to suspect an offence. As Meli had to make the final decision, he had made discreet enquiries regarding signorina Inzerillo's correspondence. She had received parcels and registered letters, as well as copious other correspondence, apparently books and magazines from Italy and abroad. It was thought that these last were addressed to her for Orazio Alfallipe's convenience. Some of them were still arriving, perhaps subscriptions still in effect or promotional offers. After the counsellor's death, she had been receiving post for the last few years from a bank in Lombardy, a branch or an associate of some Zurich banks, the kind that have a certain type of clientele. The manager was sure this post contained cash. These letters arrived punctually on the twenty-fifth of every month, except today, as if the woman had had a presentiment of her death and had informed the senders.

But there was more. The manager could have sworn that no one had noticed his enquiries, but he soon realised he was mistaken. A clerk put in the office by the mafia, an untouchable, had presented himself in Meli's office to advise him not to concern himself with signorina Inzerillo's post, which would not be arriving any more. It was the first mafia warning the manager had received since he had begun working in Roccacolomba, and he was afraid.

He also wanted to discuss another delicate problem. He had been reliably informed that Massimo Leone was heavily in debt and had dealings with small-time criminals. In addition, he was violent and had been involved in brawls. The female workers were worried about Carmela Leone's safety and feared that her husband, in a fit of rage that he had managed to control but not hide that morning, would beat her badly. Meli felt it his duty to inform Pietro Fatta of this and to ask his advice, since he was a friend and relative of the Alfallipes and an upright man, one whose wisdom was respected throughout Roccacolomba.

Chairman Fatta did not disappoint him. He suggested that he do nothing and wait. He confirmed his full support of Meli and his actions, and thanked him warmly for having turned to him. With the promise to keep each other informed about further developments (unless this poor soul asks for a transfer—he's obviously crapping himself with fear, thought Fatta), they parted.

Pietro Fatta hoped that now he might finally be able to rest, but then his wife came in, looking troubled, to tell him that Lilla Alfallipe was in the parlour and had something urgent to say to him. He hadn't seen Lilla in about a year; she was the best of the three children, intelligent, determined, and elegant. She gave him a cursory account of Mennulara's orders regarding her funeral, but it was clear that this was not the purpose of her visit. Pietro Fatta asked her to get to the point. Composed as ever, Lilla explained, omitting details she thought embarrassing. "After Papa's death, Mennù wanted to carry on managing the estate. We refused. I think that was when she decided—to spite us—to resign her position and oblige Mama to agree to that unseemly cohabitation with her in her flat. Clearly, she kept control of other assets, ones that were not part of the inheritance, perhaps to avoid paying tax. I believe they were cash investments or stocks. She did not want to give us details of the bank accounts or the people who controlled the investments. She paid us the accrued interest in cash, on the twenty-fifth of every month, punctually. It arrived in the post.

"We expected to receive information through Vazzano, as had happened with our father's inheritance, or through some other professional, or through someone Mennulara trusted, in order to come into possession of the funds, but no one knows anything. Carmela tried to find out something, so she went to the post office, but it seems that the staff refused to hand over the post addressed to Mennù. I know that after Papa's death she came to you for advice. Do you know anything that might be useful to us? I also know that Father Arena helped her to write some letters, but he told me very little. Perhaps he would talk more freely to you. What do you think?"

Pietro Fatta was relieved. He had feared that Lilla might tell him about Massimo Leone's violence towards Carmela. That spineless Meli had exaggerated. He advised her to speak to some other professionals in the province, people whom he respected and with whom Mennulara had had business relations, then added, "You surprise me with this story about Alfallipe money under Mennulara's control. As far as I know, she always kept you informed about everything. She was very meticulous and honest. If I were you, I'd follow her instructions to the letter."

With a deep sigh, her clear eyes darkening, Lilla said, "So we're going to have to obey her orders again?" And she got up to go home.

"One moment. Where's Carmela?"

At that question, Lilla stopped and gave the reply she had prepared beforehand: "Massimo told me she had a migraine and was staying at home."

"Then allow me to give you another piece of advice. Go and see how she is and ask her exactly what they told her in the post office," said Pietro Fatta authoritatively.

Lilla realised he already knew what had happened, and she sat down again. She told him about Massimo's violence and about the couple's economic problems. Since January, Mennulara had been paying Carmela's bills directly, so obviously she too had known about the Leones' financial situation. Lilla didn't know how to protect her sister. "Gianni wouldn't have the courage to talk to a fly. Who's going to talk to Massimo?"

Pietro Fatta dispensed the same suggestion he had given to the post office manager: wait and keep your eyes open.

24. Chairman Fatta meditates

The Fattas spent what remained of the afternoon together in Margherita's parlour, which surprised Lucia when she went in.

Margherita was shocked by Lilla's revelations and feared for Carmela's safety. She sighed and continued with her embroidery. Pietro, in the armchair beside her, was thinking. Every so often, they exchanged words dense with meanings, the kind known only to those who have spent a lifetime together. "Well . . . Yes indeed . . . What a life . . . ," "True, what a life . . . Different world . . . It's crazy."

Theirs was a quiet and affectionate marriage, yet Pietro had never been in love with his good wife. He had remained faithful to her for fear of losing his reputation for probity and the cloistered harmony of his home, both of which he held dear. They respected each other and together they had raised a fine family, for which he was immensely grateful. Margherita was weeping in silence. Pietro tried to cheer her up, saying that everything would work out fine, that Orazio's children were histrionic. His wife pulled herself together and caressed his cheek before leaving him to pay a call on Adriana. Pietro took her hand and planted a long kiss on it. At his death things would go differently—he had no doubt about that.

Alone at last, he recovered his composure, drank a coffee, the last one of the day, and took refuge in his study. There he kept a secret collection of books—some antiquarian, some new—erotica and pornography that were hidden behind the false shelves he had designed with Orazio Alfallipe. These books were his solitary and silent solace. As a young man, he had had few real amours, and none after his marriage.

His bosom friend Orazio, almost a brother, had had no such problems. Although his parents had made him go into law, he practised it sporadically and with such a lack of interest that when he decided to retire few people noticed. He agreed to marry Adriana Mangiaracina to keep his parents happy, just as Pietro had done when he married her cousin, but Orazio did not give up or lessen his active interest in women—what he called "the chase." With his special sense of humour, he maintained that his energies were concentrated on the demographic increase of cuckolds and on the genetic renewal of the people of Roccacolomba, among whom marriages between blood kindred were predominant. Orazio knew how to behave; not only was he a discreet and considerate lover but he also managed, once an affair was over, to maintain affectionate and collusive friendships with most of the women he had seduced.

Between the two of them there had been no secrets. Orazio would talk to Pietro about his women and together they would plot his conquests, from courtship to seduction. Pietro contributed his refined and vast erudition; it was as if he too lived Orazio's affairs, thanks to the empathy that bound them and the wealth of details and sensations that his friend lavished upon him.

Orazio was a cultured man with a variety of interests. Indulged by his mother, he was accustomed to satisfying all his whims and to being the centre of attention. Thanks to their connection to the princes of Brogli, in summer the Alfallipes were able to keep company with the aristocrats who spent their holidays in the mountains. Orazio was sought after and appreciated for his brilliant conversation and wide knowledge. He loved music, especially opera, and was a born collector. For brief but intense periods, he would devote himself to collecting everything that kindled his current enthusiasm, only to abandon this in favour of a new object of interest, just as he did with women, squandering his fortune. He didn't care about his assets or even about his family. Had it not been for his mother's and then Mennulara's shrewd management, they would have been reduced to poverty, like many others.

With Mennulara's death, it seemed that the family was disintegrating as the foolishness of its members became clear. Pietro Fatta selected a book and soon forgot Roccacolomba and the whole world.

25. Massimo Leone makes peace with his wife and receives a warning, while the Alfallipe family makes some important decisions

In the early afternoon Carmela Leone was lying in bed, aching but comforted by her sister's unexpected visit. Dying with curiosity to hear the account of the sortie to the post office, Lilla had rushed, right after lunch and while her mother was resting, to the Leones' house, where she found Carmela still lying semiconscious on the floor. She had immediately called Dr. Mendicò, who diagnosed some probable fractured ribs and various bruises. He prescribed rest for at least a week. Left alone, the sisters wept together and talked for a long time. Distressing as it was, the conversation seemed to bring them together. After Lilla's marriage, relations between them had become infrequent and formal, for the respective husbands were totally different from each other, and Lilla was ashamed of the provincial traits that Carmela had picked up or perhaps just maintained. But now, for the first time, Carmela talked openly with Lilla of Massimo's disastrous financial situation and his violence, though she added that she loved and needed him despite everything. She wanted to stay at home, and no one, not even Gianni, was to know what had happened. Then she fell asleep, exhausted.

Her husband woke her up. The maid had told him about the afternoon visitors, and he went in hesitantly. Carmela nodded at him to sit down on the edge of the bed, then apologised for not having been able to conceal the incident from Lilla. "She came with no warning," she murmured, weeping. Massimo bowed his head and covered it with his arms, his elbows over his head, his chin sunk to his chest, his hands clasped behind the back of his head, and he too wept.

"What's going to happen?" he asked, breaking the silence.

Carmela had devised a plan as she lay dozing. If her mother asked any questions, she would say that they had had a row but everything had been worked out. It wasn't worth worrying about. Her shattered looks were to be put down to her grief at Mennulara's death. She and her husband didn't speak of the events at the post office and decided to dine at Alfallipe House in order to avoid arousing suspicion. Lovingly, Massimo helped Carmela wash and dress herself.

When they were ready, Massimo went to get the car, which was parked in the usual place. From a distance, he thought it was sitting lower than usual. Thinking that he too was tired and that his sight was beginning to deteriorate, he drew closer. That afternoon he had parked it alongside the wall in the lane behind the house, after taking it to the car wash. It had been in perfect condition. But now the wheels were flat, the tyres covered with long, deep gashes. Fearfully, he walked around the car in silence. The old man who lived in the basement across the lane observed Massimo from a seat outside his front door, his wizened face expressionless and immobile. No point in asking him anything, thought Massimo, opening the car door and taking out a sheet of paper that was lying on the seat. "Keep your mouth shut and mind your own business," was written on it in block capitals.

Carmela, surprisingly, was not disconcerted by this news. Without emotion, she said, "We're being watched," and they went straight to her mother's in her small car.

They all dined together in the main dining room. Massimo had seldom eaten at his mother-in-law's house because of Mennulara. The massive, lugubrious dressers along the walls looked like gigantic menacing figures that were leaning forwards to listen, the sets of plates and glasses piled behind the glass doors tinkled when anyone passed by, and the faint light of the low-wattage lamps created a seedy atmosphere of blurred shadows. The rancid stink of uninhabited rooms permeated everything, as if the soul of the house were offended and it too wanted to punish and warn them. They ate little and without enthusiasm.

During dinner they reviewed the situation. Gianni was distraught and didn't have a clue what to do. Their mother was wholly taken up with her aches and pains; that afternoon's visits had wearied her, and she didn't even notice that Carmela was walking with difficulty. Lilla felt discouraged, but they had to come to some decision. Everyone agreed that the warning given to Massimo sprang from Carmela's visit to the post office, which by common consent they glossed over. Mennulara clearly had been in contact with mafiosi, and it was probable that she had left orders to have the family humiliated even further. It was her revenge for their refusal to let her manage their properties after their father's death. The three children were convinced of this, but such was their arrogance that none of them dared suggest the obvious move: to obey her orders and rewrite the obituary.

Massimo spoke up. "I don't care if people make fun of us, but I don't want our cars' tyres slashed or worse. There's nothing else for it: we have to correct the death notices and put in the text she wanted, the way she wrote it, and right now." They all agreed.

26. The Risicos analyse the situation

After dinner, Elvira Risico took her husband's empty coffee cup from his hand. "What could there be that was so important in a domestic servant's post?" she wanted to know.

"Massimo Leone is a nasty piece of work, a layabout and a womaniser," began Gaspare, who then went on to say that there were even rumours of an indecent assault he'd made on a laundress in his youth. The only son of a small lumber dealer, he had led the family firm to the verge of bankruptcy in just a few years. The business was taken over by his brother-in-law, who gave him a phony job. The marriage with Carmela Alfallipe was a big stroke of luck; in town, they said that the Inzerillo woman considered him unworthy of Carmela and never wanted to meet him. They had married in summer, while she was away visiting her nephews. Massimo regularly cheated on Carmela and beat her, too.

"You don't beat up women," he said, troubled, correcting the didactic tone he normally used when talking to Elvira.

"They say his father used to thrash him, but why do the same to his wife? . . ." And there he stopped, disturbed, as if he couldn't believe it himself.

Elvira, for her part, had some sensational news: that afternoon, signorina Aruta had gone into the bookshop to whisper to signora Pecorilla that a customer had said that someone had slashed the tyres of Leone's new car. What's more, that morning signora Pecorilla had spoken very circumspectly with Father Arena about an important personage who had turned up at the funeral. She hadn't dared mention the name, but the priest had lowered his gaze in assent. Elvira hazarded a suggestion. "What if the mafia is involved?"

Gaspare wanted to hear no talk of priests or the mafia. "Let's analyse the situation logically," he said, lapsing back into his usual tone. "From what I have explained to you, right up to Inzerillo's death there was nothing suspicious about the behaviour of the Alfallipes or of Leone, despite the oddity of the situation. There's something shady about today's events, which I don't understand. Inzerillo received packages, magazines, and letters. This could be explained by her duties and by the idleness of the Alfallipes, who didn't even take the trouble to pick up their post. But the post continued to arrive after the death of Orazio Alfallipe, and I don't know what to make of that. It was very expensive material, pornography, art, archaeology—goodness knows who read it. We can rule out Inzerillo, semiliterate; it's most unlikely that it was signora Alfallipe, a fatuous bourgeois of limited intelligence, according to those who know her, and certainly a woman with no interest in antiquities. So who read it? Did the subscriptions continue out of inertia, and did the post remain unopened? I doubt it, given how tight-fisted the Alfallipes are."

"What if the two women read the books together, out loud, the way we do? After all, they did live in the same flat, and the winter nights are long," suggested Elvira, snuggling up under her husband's arm.

"A lesbian relationship . . ." murmured Gaspare, fondling her hair.

"What are you talking about, Gaspare, those two old women!" she protested.

Gaspare curled a lock of her hair around his finger. "The story takes a new twist with Carmela Leone's visit to the post office. Inzerillo received registered post on the twenty-fifth of every month. I remember that once she complained about a delay of barely a day; I made a note of the sender, a bank, and I'm waiting for a colleague to check this out. But today the letter didn't arrive. Someone is expecting it and needs it. That's why Carmela Leone made her threats, and that's why she was so afraid. What's behind these letters? Who is it she's afraid of? And why?"

Elvira straightened up, freeing her head from her husband's hand, and shrugged. She had no answer.

"And the mafia element? Where does that come into it? I just don't get it. Elvira, let's go to bed. We'll see what happens tomorrow," said Gaspare.

"Maybe the letter will arrive late," she murmured as she switched off the light.

27. Chairman Fatta and his wife have a talk

In the Fatta home, it was well known that the chairman didn't like to be disturbed when he retreated to his study. It was a sort of unwritten rule, which was frequently broken by his granddaughter, Rita, to whom he could deny nothing. Margherita Fatta complied scrupulously with her husband's strict habits, but that evening, on returning from her mourning visit to Adriana Alfallipe, she walked straight to the study, knocked without hesitating and went to sit in an armchair opposite the one where he read by the fireplace, listening to classical music.

"What's up, Margherita?" asked Pietro, looking up from his book and closing it slowly. It was an erotic novel, the last one brought to him by Mennulara, the innocent recipient of a particular publishing house's materials, which she would deliver to him at his home, dutiful and faithful to Orazio's orders even after his death.

"I'd like to tell you about my visit to Alfallipe House and a request Adriana made, as you asked me to," said his wife timidly. "There were lots of people, many of whom were there to pry and gossip, but Adriana needs company—she's so lonely . . . Carmela wasn't there, and Lilla is hard on her mother. Adriana isn't happy there; she misses Mennulara's flat, which she had got used to and where she had all her comforts. At one point, she took me into her bedroom to tell me something in private. You won't believe this, but what she had to tell me was that Father Arena had paid a mourning call this morning, and Lilla had given him some books that belonged to Orazio."

Pietro raised his eyebrows as he did when he was curious, especially when the talk was of books. His wife continued: "Adriana told me that Lilla went into Orazio's study, took all the books by D'Annunzio, put them in a bag, and gave them to the priest as a gift. Poor Adriana was in tears—she struck me as being really not quite all there. Anyway, it seems that Orazio had instructed her to give those particular books to you after his death, and Mennù had refused to let Adriana do this, as she wanted to keep the library intact. As usual, Adriana had obeyed her. It seems that it was Orazio's last wish. Did you know that?"

"No," replied Pietro, puzzled. "I wasn't expecting any gift from him. He was already pretty generous with me in life."

"Adriana made me promise to tell you that she wants you to ask Father Arena to give them to you, and she will let him take some others, ones to his liking, but those books are meant for you."

"I must remember to speak to Father Arena about this when I see him," said her husband.

"No. Adriana was most insistent that you talk to him as soon as possible. Father Arena lives in the country and seldom comes to town . . . Please do as she asks. The poor soul has so many other worries."

Pietro Fatta wanted to change the subject, for his wife was annoying him, so he asked, "What else did she say?"

"It seems that don Vincenzo Ancona went to the funeral. Not many people saw him, but the rumour is going round."

The news that a powerful and aged mafia boss had attended the funeral of a maid was gossip that didn't interest

Pietro Fatta in the slightest. "Perhaps Mennulara had dealings with him, but I don't understand why he took the trouble to go to her funeral. It must have been a token of respect for the Alfallipes," he said.

"But he didn't go to Orazio's funeral," Margherita pointed out. Her husband did not reply, irritated even more by her insistence. She carried on conscientiously with her account of what she had learned around town. "At the Merceria Moderna, the signorinas Aruta were talking about Carmela and Massimo. Everyone knows what happened; people are talking and talking. They also say that somebody slashed the tyres of Massimo's car. That boy definitely keeps bad company. Maria José Sillitto, who, like a true daughter of Baroness Ceffalia, never stops gossiping, told me that after beating poor Carmela, Massimo went off . . . well, to a house of ill repute." Pietro smiled at his wife, who was all red with embarrassment. She couldn't bring herself to utter a word like *brothel*. "And he told everyone that Mennulara was one of them." Pietro smiled again. Maybe Margherita didn't even know the word *whore*, she was so innocent. "And that she associated with mafiosi, too. I didn't ask anything else—it didn't seem right—but tell me, Pietro, who could have given Maria José such information?"

"I don't know," he replied, patient and resigned to his wife's naïveté, which verged on stupidity. The habits of Salvatore Sillitto, an unfaithful and rather indiscreet husband, were common knowledge. "Thanks, really. I know you would have preferred to stay home and play with the children instead of going out to listen to this gossip, but it was necessary. Now I have to finish reading. I'll see you at dinner."

Pietro Fatta lowered his eyes to the book resting on his knees, and Margherita got up from the armchair. He had finally managed to get rid of her.

28. *Rita Parrino Scotti thinks about the past*

Rita Parrino Scotti, the notary Parrino's only daughter, had returned to live with her parents in Roccacolomba as the still-young widow of the illustrious Professor Scotti, who had held the chair in Italian literature at the University of Palermo. A curvaceous, attractive woman, she had decided of her own free will not to remarry, and had devoted herself to the arts, especially music. She had had various affairs, conducted with discretion, all with married men, including Orazio Alfallipe. She wasn't a home-wrecker and was convinced that she made a happy contribution to the conjugal lives of her lovers. This belief of hers was apparently confirmed by the continuing friendship shown her by the betrayed and almost grateful wives, who assiduously frequented her musical afternoons.

Rita looked down on Adriana Alfallipe and Mennulara, whom she considered responsible for the premature end to her affair with Orazio, which without a doubt had been the most intense and satisfying of her mature years.

It had been easy for them to enjoy each other's company without having to fall back on the usual subterfuges, provided that there was no scandal. They would meet frequently in Rita's villa in the country, under the pretext that Orazio was very interested in botany and eager to visit the Parrinos' beautiful garden. An imaginative and generous lover, Orazio spoke little to her about his family. Besides, Adriana seemed to accept her husband's frequent infidelities almost with relief.

Rita was curious about Mennulara, the servant-administrator. At first, she had thought that she was secretly in love with Orazio and that this was the reason for her devotion. Under Orazio's guidance, Mennulara identified fragments of shattered antique pottery, reconstructed the pieces, and helped him to catalogue them. Orazio laughed at the idea that Mennulara was in love with him: he explained to her that he had known Mennulara ever since her arrival at Alfallipe House at the age of thirteen and that she had never been jealous, nor had she aspired to what she knew to be unattainable. She was a servant in the Alfallipe household and as such was rightly devoted to him and the entire family. She did her duty, and that was that.

This was confirmed when Rita found out that Mennulara took on other responsibilities that should have fallen to Orazio in order to give him more time to spend with her, Rita, even to the point of inventing plausible reasons for Orazio's business trips to the mainland, which in reality were their delightful holidays. And it was Mennulara who left his messages and gifts in Rita's porter's lodge in order to avoid arousing suspicion. To Rita, Mennulara was a woman with a craving for power, overwhelming and oppressive in her devotion to the Alfallipes. She had persuaded Orazio and Adriana to join her in opposition to Carmela's marriage to Massimo Leone, a person of little worth and hence perhaps not a suitable match for their daughter. Nothing was decided in that family without Mennulara's approval.

On their return from a particularly happy trip, made under the pretext of attending a conference on music, Orazio decided to invite Rita and her parents to his home for dinner, so that he could show them an Ionian vase purloined from the dig at Bosco Littorio, near Gela. It was an unusual event at Alfallipe House: Mennulara did not allow them to entertain guests in the evenings, claiming that she was too tired to prepare dinners, despite the fact that she bent over backwards to organise summertime lunches in the country and the usual afternoon entertainments for Adriana's lady friends.

Orazio had never shown Rita his study, which he had refurbished at considerable expense, nor his collections, of which he was very proud. The invitation therefore represented a solemn occasion. The conversation at table flowed pleasantly, the food was excellent, and Mennulara served in silence, as was correct. When they finished eating, Orazio offered to take Rita to his study while Adriana accompanied the elder Parrinos to the drawing room.

At that very moment, Mennulara returned to the dining room with the silver coffee tray. She slammed it down so hard on the table next to Adriana that all the cups rattled on their porcelain saucers. "I'm not going to serve that whore," she said, and went off, closing the door behind her.

Adriana showed an unexpected presence of mind. "Forgive me, I don't know what's got into her. She has never been disrespectful to me, and I don't understand why she should insult me, especially in front of guests." Orazio said nothing. They all tried to pretend that nothing had happened, but shortly afterwards the Parrinos took their leave, and the visit to Orazio's study did not take place.

Rita was certain that Mennulara's words were aimed at her. She had proof of this the next day. Orazio sent her a letter of farewell: "Beloved Rita, I realise that my domestic happiness, a source of support and delight for me, has been jeopardised by our precious love, and I am obliged to make a painful decision. Adieu, my muse. With eternal gratitude, your Orazio."

She saw him again a few days later at a concert in the provincial capital, together with his wife. Adriana came up to her to apologise again for the maid's behaviour: "She's so very good and faithful, but sometimes she goes too far . . . She's had her problems and she took it out on me. I'm truly mortified. Please forgive me." Orazio remained at his wife's side, impassive. Rita hated Adriana: she wasn't the insignificant wife that Orazio, that blockhead, had described her as being, but a hypocritical and frigid harpy who enjoyed an undeserved reputation for sanctity. As for Mennulara, Rita had been wrong about her, too: she was a woman who defended her territory, who wouldn't give up her power without a fight. Probably she feared that the Alfallipes might end up by separating, thus destroying her own position at Alfallipe House, which could remain impregnable only so long as the family remained united. She had sided with the wife and they both had browbeaten that weakling Orazio.

After that, Orazio underwent a radical change: he showed up at musical events but not at social receptions. He associated with a few male friends and lived at home like a recluse, devoted to his collections. In town, they said that this behaviour was caused by the illness that led to his premature death a few years later.

When Adriana was widowed and decided to go to live in Mennulara's flat, Rita finally understood their game. Adriana didn't like men; probably the maid was like her, or she had wanted to pander to her mistress's tendencies for her own convenience or vice. Rita was now sure that a preexisting lesbian relationship between the two women was the key to the mystery. To the townspeople they appeared like Orazio's victims, one because of marital unfaithfulness and the other because of her burden of responsibility, but in reality they had cut him out of family life and lived in perverse and satisfied symbiosis. The two wretched women had feared that Orazio and Rita might destroy the ambiguous ménage established in Alfallipe House. How stupid and perverse. If only they had known that she, although she loved Orazio, would never have sacrificed her freedom for a man . . .

Rita had concealed from others both this theory and her immense contempt for the two women of the Alfallipe household. Now, with Mennulara dead, she was disgusted when she heard people speak of this servant with respect and admiration. She would dig through the pasts of both these unworthy women and get at the truth. At Adriana's death, she would do it again.

29. *At the musical afternoon in the Parrino home, no one listens to the music, while the talk is of the Alfallipe family and Mennulara*

The Parrinos' home was crowded not only with ladies but also, unusually, with their husbands. As a rule, the men brought their wives and then returned to pick them up after the musical afternoon, an innovation in the social life of Roccacolomba introduced by Rita Parrino, as she was still known then. The ladies tried to comply with the tried-and-true formula of these get-togethers, but today they failed: the husbands showed no signs of leaving, and none of the guests seemed to have any intention of listening to music. They mingled in large and small groups, depending on the importance of the news and the gossip about the extraordinary events that had recently occurred in Alfallipe House. They separated and reformed like amoebae at the first hint of spicier or more improbable tittle-tattle from neighbouring conversations. And even though there was nothing amusing about the events under discussion, the atmosphere seemed light-hearted, given the dislike of—not to say rancour towards—the Alfallipes, who, once they had ensured their position as managers of the Brogli estates, got rich by buying Brogli land at rock-bottom prices and put on Brogli airs at the same time.

The atavistic pleasure of backbiting overwhelmed the sounds of Wagner, which soon became mere background music. Carmela Leone had been spotted getting out of her car in front of her house late that morning, bent double and shaking all over, walking with difficulty and spattered with vomit. Massimo had held her up as far as the door, his face twisted with rage. What had happened to her? Baroness Ceffalia, who rarely deigned to visit the salons in town and who had at first feigned a reluctance to divulge such bad news, was now regaling a closely packed crowd with a flood of details obtained from a reliable source, according to whom Massimo had beaten Carmela. Dr. Mendicò had found she had several fractured ribs. The baroness omitted to mention that the "reliable source" was her porter's wife, Enza Militello, who had the information from the husband of the woman who ironed for the Mendicòs, who had gleaned the news by eavesdropping on a conversation between Dr. Mendicò and his sister, signora Di Prima, news she had rushed to tell her husband when he came to take her home.

Unwittingly diverting the attention of the other guests from the baroness, signora Mimì Bommarito exclaimed, "She was a real Cassandra, that Mennulara! She foresaw everything. My maid told me that she opposed Carmela's marriage because she knew that Massimo Leone was violent—he had even slapped his mother—and she was right not to want him in the house! All Mennulara wanted was the good of the Alfallipe family. If only they'd listened to her . . ."

The guests, fascinated by the news, neglected to ask the baroness any more questions. And she, outraged, refused to appreciate the contribution made by the schoolteacher, Bommarito, a woman of humble origins, who naïvely thought she might acquire some culture by frequenting these afternoons in the Parrino home, which—as everyone knew—were organised to show off the notary's silverware and not for love of music. She therefore determined to nip this fleeting celebrity in the bud, saying indignantly, "One mustn't believe what the common people and servants decide to tell one; they are not people worthy of trust. What's sure is that Massimo Leone broke three of poor Carmela's ribs, and it wasn't up to a maid to abuse the misplaced trust the Alfallipes had in her by interfering with the marriage of their daughter. That was the sole province of Orazio, the head of the family, but everyone knows he was a spineless character, under the influence of certain women, and she, that maid, always had the upper hand."

Happy at having struck two targets with one well-turned observation, the baroness shot a fleeting glance at Mimì Bommarito, who flushed with embarrassment, accepting this lesson in sagacity and style; then she looked Rita Parrino squarely in the eye, for the latter, who had recently become the lover of her son-in-law Salvatore Sillitto, had sown discord and distress in the home of her daughter Maria José.

The guests continued to run down the Alfallipes, their arrogance, and the weakness of their men, starting with Orazio's father and his voracious sexual appetites.

Before leaving, the baroness took a final dig at Rita: "It's easy to see, in a family in which the men aren't worth much, how a maid like Mennulara could rule the roost. I'll tell you, Orazio lived under the influence first of his mother and then of Mennulara, who at least saved his wealth and was faithful and loyal to him. And she didn't eat him out of house and home the way I'm told that certain lady friends did with holidays and gifts, no matter what other people may say!" Yet again the baroness hit the bull's-eye. Rita blanched visibly and shot her a furious look. The baroness gave her a faint smile, enjoying her embarrassment, and moved off to another group of guests.

As they took their leave, the guests complimented one another and their hosts on the success of the musical afternoon. As soon as Rita was alone with her parents, she complained of a bad headache and retired to her room. Her mother went into the kitchen to check that the maids had washed and dried all the silverware, then counted the cutlery herself and locked it away in the cupboard, together with the trays. Signor Parrino was left alone and pensive. He had noticed the humiliation inflicted on his daughter by the baroness's words, and he mulled over thoughts of revenge as he paced up and down the corridor with long and heavy strides, his head lowered and his fingers nervously intertwined behind his back, oblivious to the looks of amused amazement on the faces of the domestics. Then, to take his mind off things, he went to his club.

30. *The menfolk talk business at the United Italy Club*

Pietro Sannasarda, a land agent who had recently bought a building business, had won at poker, and he offered a drink to the losers. They were surrounded by other members, and the talk was of the Alfallipes' troubles.

The old lawyer Ettore Manzello theatrically declared that he was sure that Risico, a nasty breed of Communist, would lodge a complaint against Carmela, and that the grounds for prosecution were plain as day: it would spell the complete ruin of the family's reputation. "The Alfallipes are off their heads. What do they think they're ever going to find in that servant's post? We all know, those of us who were of an age with poor Orazio, that he used to receive certain risqué magazines from Paris, with five-year subscriptions paid in advance, and he had Mennulara pick them up at the post office and take them to the Fattas' place, he was so afraid that his late lamented mother would find out about them. Carmela can easily pick them up, if the subscriptions are still valid, but I'd like to be a fly on the wall to see the Alfallipes' faces when they open the envelopes! The truth is, the children were unhappy about poor Orazio's inheritance and didn't trust Mennulara's administration, although as far as I know she was honest." He drained his little glass of liqueur and with an "If you'll excuse me, I'll see you later," he got up from the table and went off towards the other room in the club.

Pietro Sannasarda was a friend of the Leone family, and so he defended the behaviour of the Alfallipes: "Mennulara was still managing Adriana Alfallipe's dotal property, and the children were right to want to find out whether the family property was coming to them and not to Mennulara's nephews. If Carmela Leone went over the top at the post office, then her conduct was perfectly understandable. With all those worries on her mind, she probably overdid it. Women are like that, weak-minded; it happens to lots of them." Then he added, "But Massimo Leone's wife was right to go to the post office and to investigate around town. That servant, may God rest her soul, was holding Alfallipe property, and the Alfallipes couldn't have got it all. Otherwise, explain to me how this Mennulara could have permitted herself to own a flat and have her mistress stay there for free. She was the daughter of poor people, she lived on a maid's wages, and we all know that the Alfallipes were never generous with their employees," he said, looking around. Then he shrugged and threw his hands up in the air. "Gentlemen, the figures just don't add up!"

"Pietro, you're forgetting that business of the sale of the land at Puleri," said the notary Vazzano. "Mennulara had five percent on that, an agent's entitlement, and she deserved it for her business sense. She advised the Alfallipe brothers not to sell the land and suggested they wait a year. Orazio and Vincenzo made a lot of money by following her advice. Within a year, several acres of woodland at Puleri were fenced off for building. After that success, Orazio put the administration of all his properties in her hands. But Vincenzo, who was too big for his boots, didn't like that, and he argued with his brother. If it hadn't been for Mennulara, the Alfallipe brothers would have sold that property at a loss, and it went on to become a gold mine for the family. I handled all the conveyancing for the lots, and I know."

Sannasarda was unconvinced. "She was a maid, and she couldn't know about certain things. She got lucky. Who can be sure that they intended to sell Puleri, and that they didn't want to wait? . . . You can never trust the Alfallipes."

Vazzano didn't back down. "I'm telling you, they had stacks of debts, and Vincenzo Alfallipe wanted cash right away. Orazio, as we all know, was good only for spending. The two brothers instructed me to draw up the agreement to sell for twenty million lire, which was a big sum in the 1950s.

One day, Orazio summoned me to his house. I remember it well because Mennulara was in the study, busy dusting some vases that he had bought, old pottery that he threw his money away on, and she stayed in the room as we talked, which struck me as very odd. I swear I never heard Orazio speak so firmly. He told me that the sale was not to go through and that I had to explain this to the buyers. He wouldn't hear of counter-offers, not even at twice the price. And she kept an eye on him from a distance, throughout."

Sannasarda was still not convinced. "But if Puleri and the other land around was designated for building, where does she come into it? You don't mean to tell me that it was thanks to her, or that she had friends in the town hall and maybe in the provincial administration, too? How could she have known this? I don't believe she had informers—who could they have been? Just as our wives pick up information from the maids' gossip, the maids pick it up from them, but you don't get to know about such things from our wives, and not even from other members of the household staff. She got lucky, really lucky, and what's more, she took a fine commission from the Alfallipes for that sale, without deserving it."

The notary Parrino was listening with interest. At that point, he said, "Remember that the new town was supposed to be built on the other side of the mountain, at Baiamonte. No one could ever have imagined that it would be built at Puleri, absolutely no one. I was surprised myself, and I lost money on it: I had bought some land at Baiamonte, which remained agricultural."

"Shit!" exclaimed Ettore Manzello, commiserating with

Parrino about his bad investment. But the notary took no notice and carried on. "That woman had someone who protected her and kept her well informed, and it wouldn't have been another maid."

Pomice, an engineer who was a provincial councillor and an up-and-coming member of the political Right, a man of few words and an attentive listener, said, "You're wasting time making these inferences. She was probably lucky—it happens sometimes."

Manzello the lawyer came back from the games room and rejoined the conversation, laughing. "Lucky Mennulara and very lucky Orazio. After this first-class deal, he trusted her totally, and he was never to regret it, which wasn't the case for Vincenzo, who sold off his inheritance for a pittance. In December 1950, before the restrictions on land ownership came into force, she made me work like a mule to prevent the breakup of the Alfallipe properties, settling disputes old and new, sorting out inheritances held in common with other Alfallipes, and making fake sales to nominees. She always managed to keep the best lands for the Alfallipes. She knew their estate inch by inch, like a surveyor. And when she made genuine sales, she sold stony ground to those poor peasants who bought a few acres thinking they'd become landowners and could forget forever the sweat of labour and hunger."

Sannasarda said, "I don't believe it. You must be mistaking her for someone else."

"What are you talking about? Old, yes, I'm old, but I'm not stupid yet. Let's ask Angelo Vazzano . . . You drew up a bunch of deeds for the Alfallipes at that time. Is what I'm saying true or not?"

Vazzano lowered his eyes and nodded twice, his face inscrutable, and they all understood.

Fortified by this corroboration, Ettore Manzello went on in a loud voice: "Orazio lived the life of a carefree bachelor—he was always telling me so, and he joked about it. He said that Mennulara was a devil of a businesswoman and that she did everything, at home, on the estates, and with the investments. He found it hard only when he had to save face and behave as if it was he who was making the decisions—sometimes you need a man, since a woman, a servant, and an illiterate one at that, can't handle certain people. All Orazio was interested in was having money for his amusements and for buying useless things. And when it came to spending, he spent a lot, on both himself and his women. Those so-called respectable ladies cost him millions, far more than women of easy virtue!" Manzello broke off—he had just noticed the presence of Giovanni Parrino. The notary, discreet man that he was, stood impassively by the table, then moved off towards another card table.

When they felt sure that Parrino was no longer in earshot, the members carried on chuckling about the same topic. Even Vazzano took the floor: "Orazio maintained that life wasn't worth living without women and that you didn't regret the money spent on them. It's ironic that he could allow himself to satisfy his love of women through the work of a spinster maid."

The conversation began to take on a racier tone as the old men talked about certain "special services" rendered the masters by young servants. "Right," said Manzello, "you might say that Mennulara provided Orazio and the entire Alfallipe family with a unique kind of special service: she was a donkey that shit money! Really enviable. If she had been as exceptional in bed as she was at housework and in business, then Orazio would have been the luckiest man in the world. But you can't have everything, and Orazio got a whole lot from life."

"I envied him Mennulara. She was a great worker . . . Honest women and loyal employees like her are just not to be found," said Vazzano.

Parrino came back into the room. Although apparently following the game at the next table, he had been listening in on their conversation, thinking of his adored daughter and the suffering she had endured on Mennulara's account. He joined the little group and said, "A worker, yes, but an honest woman, I don't know. Prominent persons certainly don't trouble to attend the funeral of any old servant . . . but they just might attend that of a lover." Having said this, he bid good-bye with a "Good night, everyone," turned on his heel and left the club, politely greeting members he met on his way but without lingering over the usual pleasantries.

The members were taken aback at this forthright comment from a man known for his tolerance and discretion, but then they went back to chatting pleasantly, now ready to let rip in their gossip about Rita Parrino's love affairs, absorbed in long salacious disquisitions on the "comforts" allowed widows within the limits of morality and good taste. Soon they moved on to the Parrinos, and to the almost indecent way they indulged their widowed daughter.

Late that evening, signor Vazzano left the club in the

company of signor Pomice. They walked along the road in silence. When they parted company at the crossroads, Pomice said, "If I were a friend of the Alfallipes, I'd tell them to mind their own business and to forget about the property; they could have other problems. If I were a friend of Parrino, I'd advise him to talk less. He said too much this evening, and he should watch his step. Seeing that I'm your friend, my dear Angelino, I'll say this to you: it would be better all round to speak neither good nor ill of certain dead people." Vazzano gave him a long and grateful handshake and went off home, comforted by the trust shown in him by Pomice, a man who was going places in regional politics and therefore an "important" friend and one to keep sweet.

During the night between Wednesday 25 and Thursday 26 September "persons unknown" seriously damaged the garden of the Parrinos' country villa.

As chance would have it, it was signora Rita who noticed this first, on Thursday morning, when she went out into the garden with some bulbs to be planted for the following spring. She found that disaster had struck. Trees and bushes had been uprooted, and the flower beds were in a shocking state: their beautiful plants had been dug up and destroyed, then the soil had been scattered with stones and lime; elegant terra-cotta pots had been smashed to pieces, the flowers they had once held cut and trampled on; the older trees had been mutilated and the trunks gashed with an axe; the sculptures and stone seats had been overturned, every statue decapitated. The lily pond, with its crystal clear water, Rita's pride and joy, was full of soft, stinking mud, and small coloured fish floated in the slime, dead. The larger ones, their bellies slashed and their guts hanging out, were carefully laid out in rows on the lava stones that served as benches around the pool.

The caretaker of the villa, a countryman, swore on the souls of his children and on his father's grave that he knew nothing about it. The previous evening, he had watered the garden and had left it scented and luxuriant. He had heard no noises during the night, a fact confirmed by his wife and children. That morning, he had gone to dig some land a good distance away, and his wife, who normally stayed at home, had gone into town to visit her mother, who was on her deathbed. It was sheer bad luck that barefaced scoundrels had made this awful mess while he and his family were absent. They were probably delinquents who, now that you could easily reach Roccacolomba from the motorway, were roaming around the countryside causing trouble. Wringing his hands in desperation, he added that it was even more tragic that signora Rita had discovered the damage before he had, so that he hadn't had a chance to clean up the garden, remove the rubble and branches, throw away the uprooted plants and stinking fish, and thus spare the signora, whom he loved like a daughter, the displeasure of finding her beloved garden in such a state.

Thursday 26 September 1963

✕✕

31. Father Arena meets Chairman Fatta in the square and they have a granita

Father Arena left the Pecorilla bookshop and went back up the street, sweating and laden with books. The autumnal breeze, still warm, ruffled his hair but did not refresh him. He was glad he had finished his business in town in time to get back to the country that same morning; he felt a burning desire to get out of Roccacolomba and was eagerly looking forward to reading the books he had exchanged at the bookshop for the ones Adriana Alfallipe had given him. He could already see himself sitting in his little garden, where the Michaelmas daisies in full bloom would make the perfect backdrop on which to rest his tired eyes.

"Good morning, Father Arena." Pietro Fatta's voice made him jump.

"My respects, chairman," replied the priest.

"May I offer you something?" added Fatta in the polite but authoritative tones of someone who is rarely refused.

And so Father Arena set aside his hopes of catching the morning bus and found himself sitting at a table in the Bar Italia in the company of Pietro Fatta, whom he had known for years but never well.

As soon as the waiter went off with their order, Pietro Fatta explained the reason for his invitation. "Forgive me the indiscretion, Father, but I know that you have some books by D'Annunzio, chosen for you by Lilla Alfallipe from Orazio's library. Adriana told my wife that Orazio wanted to give them to me. Frankly, I don't know why. I read them once, and he's an old-fashioned writer whom I have no desire to read again. But Adriana was most insistent, and I want to keep her happy. Would you mind exchanging them for other books?"

Father Arena was unnerved by this request. He stammered confused words; his granita went down the wrong way, and he only just stopped it from dribbling onto his chin. He had to take a sip of water; he couldn't think of a way of avoiding the embarrassment of revealing that he had already sold signora Alfallipe's gift in exchange for the very books that now filled the bag lying at his feet, half-hidden beneath his cassock. Father Arena would have liked to stick himself in that bag, too, flattening himself out to become a book page like any other, to pass unobserved, and to get out of the chairman's mellifluous clutches.

Pietro Fatta guessed that the priest didn't want to part with the books. As a young man, Father Arena had transgressed; perhaps he had long wanted to read D'Annunzio, and this request would rob him of his one chance to possess the books innocently. Compressing his lips to restrain an ironic little smile, he said, "Don't worry, Father, keep them; they belong to you. But would you let me take a peep at them? Sometimes Orazio would comment on passages . . . I promise to give you them back by tomorrow."

With a look like a hunted dog, Father Arena explained with dignity and a certain reserve, stammering, that he didn't like D'Annunzio either, and that Orazio's books were on sale in the secondhand book section of the Pecorilla bookshop. Reading was his great love, but he couldn't afford to buy new books, and signora Pecorilla had let him exchange those he had already read for works of modern literature that were more congenial to him. With great embarrassment, he added that he meant no offence to signora Alfallipe and counted on Pietro Fatta's discretion. They smiled at each other, relieved and by now partners in crime.

Manzello the lawyer came into the bar with his wife. Spotting them at that precise moment and assuming they were talking about Mennulara, he came up to them and exclaimed jovially, "I bet you're talking about the second obituary for Mennulara. What a farce!" Father Arena and Pietro Fatta responded simultaneously and identically with a characteristic Sicilian expression: brows knitted and lips pursed in a slight pout. Manzello put them in the picture: new, elaborate eulogies about Mennulara had been pasted onto the funeral notice, and a new obituary had appeared in the *Giornale di Sicilia*. He leaned on the table, waiting for an invitation to join them, but at that moment his wife called and he had to join her, to the relief of both Father Arena and Pietro Fatta.

Left alone, they drained their glasses of water with long, slow draughts, in silence. "There's something wrong at Alfallipe House, Father, and that worries me," said Pietro Fatta. "I, too, was fond of Mennulara. I'd like to talk this over with you at my place—there are too many people around here. May I invite you to lunch?" Father Arena had to get away from town for the rest of the morning, so he pretended he had a prior engagement but agreed to call on Fatta at four in the afternoon on the following Monday. The two men separated and Father Arena went on his way with a heavy heart. He deliberately did not buy the paper or join the crowd of inquisitive people who were reading and commenting on the corrections pasted onto the death notice on the wall.

Pietro Fatta went straight to the Pecorilla bookshop, hoping that at that hour he would not find his wife's cousin there. But there she was, loudmouthed and indiscreet, as usual. They were both aware of their mutual dislike, but, while Pietro took care to avoid Rosalia Pecorilla, she would perversely take every chance she had to have disagreeable conversations with him, full of innuendo.

She promised to let him have the books he had asked for just as soon as the shop assistant had put them in order; they were in a pile of secondhand books in the back of the shop. "I can wait, there's no hurry, thanks a lot. Good day," said Pietro, and made to leave.

Signora Pecorilla stopped him. "Wait, Pietro, what's going on at Adriana's place? I hear worrying things . . . It all sounds very comic, but I wouldn't want it to turn into tragedy."

This relative of his wife's insisted on speaking to him with a familiarity that their distant kinship did not justify. Irritated, Pietro said brusquely, "You read too much. There's no big drama. It is just the death of a middle-aged woman."

"Oh, that's what you say . . . But it's also about what happened to Carmela, the warning given to Massimo, the mafiosi who went to the funeral. There's even talk of doubts about the cause of Mennulara's death. And you think I'm exaggerating!" Signora Pecorilla was indignant, and the pitch of her voice began to rise. Pietro Fatta shot her an icy look, doffed his hat, and went out repeating, "Good day again, and thanks." He walked back home, taking the steps that few people used, hoping to avoid further encounters.

Signora Pecorilla turned to Elvira Risico, who had been listening to them, and said, "Don't worry about finding those books. Look for them on Monday. My cousin's swollen-headed husband can wait. If it weren't for that saint of a wife of his, no one in Roccacolomba would have anything to do with him. He gives himself such airs."

32. Roccacolomba is puzzled by the additions to Mennulara's death notices

The people of Roccacolomba were surprised, but not for long, when they noticed that Maria Rosalia Inzerillo's death notice had been corrected. Stuck below the personal details of the deceased, there was a strip of paper of the same colour, bearing the words: "Administrator and member of the household staff of Alfallipe House. With deep sorrow, the Alfallipe family announces its inconsolable and eternal loss." Another little strip farther down added: "Almighty Lord, forgiveness and limitless love, in praise eternal." The *Giornale di Sicilia* also published a complete version of the obituary, including the date of the funeral, by now of only historical value.

Those few who did not know the Alfallipes and Mennulara might have deduced that she had been a beloved servant, and that in the confusion following her death, the Alfallipes had not agreed about the text of the obituary among themselves and had wanted to rectify this formally, strange as it might seem.

People who knew a bit more and those who had direct contact with the Alfallipes were even more surprised: judging by the behaviour of the children at the funeral and during the mourning visits, they would have expected that any changes to the death notice would have toned down the eulogies to the deceased rather than making them more elaborate.

"Why all these obituaries?" was the first question that everyone asked. The explanation had to be simple: the Alfallipes had lost their heads.

"Why have they lost their heads?" was the second. They couldn't find a rational answer to this one.

The immediate reaction of the Alfallipes' friends and acquaintances was to rush to their house, taking advantage of the fact that only mourning visits could be made without an invitation or sometimes even without prior warning. Adriana Alfallipe accepted their condolences all over again with gratitude and her usual courtesy. She seemed worn out and a little vacant; she dissolved into tears easily and often. The visitors were so many that no one had the chance to ask her about the reasons for the most recent notices.

Adriana Alfallipe wasn't, in fact, the person for whom people troubled to make these calls. They came to see her children, to try to establish from their behaviour, or from the answers to the oblique questions that one makes in such situations, the reason behind the new notices. The Alfallipes must have anticipated this, because Gianni slipped off to Catania and Carmela stayed with her mother only for a short while before going home, saying that she had a migraine—though everyone knew she was still getting over the beating her husband had given her. Lilla kept busy welcoming and showing to the door the many visitors who came to Alfallipe House, and she managed to avoid direct questions about the death notices until the Aruta cousins showed up unexpectedly at lunchtime.

Mariella and Tanina Aruta were old maids and were distantly related to the Alfallipes. They weren't rich: their grandfather had married a servant, and for this transgression he had been disinherited. They eked out a living from the Merceria Moderna, and they were well liked in Roccacolomba for their good manners and kindness: they never spoke ill of people and they were always prepared to help others. And they had another, much-appreciated good point: although they never gossiped deliberately, they were incapable of keeping a secret. They would repeat everything that was told them and recount everything they saw, not only without exaggerations or embellishments but also without negative judgements; they were Roccacolomba's bush telegraph.

Mariella Aruta asked Adriana to show her some embroidery and the two ladies went off to the parlour. Lilla remained alone with Tanina Aruta, who said with her usual frankness, "You must tell me why you changed the obituary, Lilla. Lots of people have asked me in the shop, and I'd like to give a truthful answer. Otherwise they'll think the worst."

Lilla, who had previously agreed with Gianni on an explanation to give to people, took the opportunity to give it to her in Carmela's absence: "What you are reading now is not a changed obituary, but the one that should have been printed in the first place. I'm sorry to have to say this, but it's all Massimo's fault. He volunteered to see to the publication of the obituaries we wrote together. You know that Mama and Mennù were very close, and on Mama's insistence we arranged to have the notice put up on the walls and printed in the newspaper, written as Mennù wanted. I don't know how or why, but the death notices that appeared on Tuesday were incomplete. Massimo must have forgotten something, or he didn't read the drafts carefully—I don't know which. The fact remains that Mama was very upset, and we said to ourselves that for us it was more important to please her than to be criticised in town. Finally, people can read the right version."

Massimo and Carmela, in their turn, gave a slightly different version: it wasn't clear how, but both the printer and the assistant sub editor at the *Giornale di Sicilia* had omitted a few words of the original text. Massimo had complained bitterly about this, explaining the distress that the omission had caused his mother-in-law, and those responsible had corrected the error at their own expense.

The signorinas Aruta did their best to spread the version of events supplied by Lilla, but they found few people prepared to believe it. As for the Leones' version, the printer denied it.

33. *Lilla tries to make sense of the whole business, recalls events of the past, and ends up agreeing with Mennulara*

On the morning of Thursday 26 September Lilla had a long telephone conversation with her husband, who was furious about the second obituary in the *Giornale di Sicilia*. Gian Maria demanded a rational explanation, which was impossible, because there wasn't one. Bursting into tears, Lilla told him about the presence of the mafia boss at Mennulara's funeral, about the damage done to Massimo's car, and about the obviously mafia-style message—which she attributed to their having failed to publish the obituary as requested by Mennulara. She confessed that she was afraid of her; it seemed as if she had been transformed into an evil spirit that hovered over the family and would not be appeased until they obeyed her orders. Lilla was convinced they were being spied on and feared for her own safety and that of their daughter. Her husband told her to come home the next day.

Anticipation of her imminent return to Rome had a calming effect on Lilla, who pulled herself together and stoically put up with the procession of visitors. That evening, finally alone in her room, she began to pack her suitcase and to think things over. There had been no other warnings, and she was beginning to feel ashamed of her hysterical behaviour that morning, which she put down to her aversion to Roccacolomba and her own family.

When her father was still alive, Lilla had gladly come back home for brief visits. But her mother's decision to move in with her maid had made these visits intolerable for her, and this too had been the fault of Mennù. Lilla's relationship with her had become extremely difficult after her father's death.

It had started when he fell ill. Her parents and Mennù had insisted that there was no need to call in a nurse, that Mennù would see to things. Dr. Mendicò had approved that decision, and Mennù, who had looked after her own mother and after Grandmother Lilla, had proved to be an excellent nurse. But when Lilla returned to Roccacolomba a few days before her father's death, she discovered Mennulara behaving very differently. While she did not neglect her own duties, she was often absent from her father's room during the day, when the family was at his side, although she continued to attend him during the nights. Mennulara would say that she had to see to the estates and other business matters, and so it happened that, at the moment of her father's death, Mennù was away, precisely when she was most needed at home. On her return, she expressed her grief in a contained manner before plunging into her domestic chores and the preparations for mourning.

One evening a few days after her father's death, the family was together for dinner—with the exception of Massimo, who was out of town. Since Mennù had not accepted Carmela's marriage, she would withdraw whenever Massimo called on his in-laws; on the rare occasions when he lunched at the house, she would refuse to serve at table, leaving this duty to another maid, Santa. Although Lilla was not in favour of her sister's marriage, she found Mennù's arrogance insufferable, as she did the submissiveness of her parents, who allowed her to behave in this way. But that evening

Mennù served dinner, as in the old days. At the end of the meal she placed the fruit bowl at the centre of the table, then took a chair that was standing against the wall and sat down together with them. This had become established practice ever since she had become their administrator, whenever she wanted to discuss important matters with the family. "I am a servant of the Alfallipe household, and when I came in to your house I promised the late signora Lilla that I'd serve her son Orazio for all my life. I've kept my word and I've done my duty. Now I'm tired, my bones hurt, and it's time I took a rest. I tell you that I don't want to go on working." She lifted her hands from the table and laid them in her white apron—small tanned hands, gently tapered and uncallused, unusual for a maid. Her dark eyes briefly lingered on each of them in turn. She betrayed no emotion and sat impassively, waiting for a response. None came, and Mennù continued: "I've bought myself a flat near here. It has two bedrooms, it's completely furnished, and it has central heating and air conditioning. I shall continue to serve you for one more month, to help you with the division of your father's inheritance, and I am also prepared to administer it, unpaid, if you wish. Then I will leave Alfallipe House and go off to my own place."

"What are you saying, Mennù? Are you leaving now, of all times, now that Orazio is no longer with us?" Adriana's voice was feeble. Big tears fell on the fruit peelings on her plate.

In a pathetic attempt to confirm his recent position as head of the family, Gianni said in an authoritative voice, "I don't think this is the time to talk of such unexpected and radical changes."

"But I do," replied Mennù. "Once the two-week mourning period has passed, each of you will get ready to return to his own home and go about his own business, and all will be as before, but you must understand that things have changed for your mother. This house is very big, and it has no central heating; you'd need to spend money to make it comfortable. Your mother and I are getting older every day, and the time will come when I won't be able to serve her the way she is accustomed to, and she doesn't deserve that. It's the right time to make decisions—for you, too." The others were silent. Mennù's answer brooked no argument.

Then the mother looked up with a piteous expression and asked, "Mennù, who will come to live with you?"

"I have no family in Roccacolomba," she replied, lowering her voice.

"Would you take me to your flat? I wouldn't be a nuisance, I can't live alone, as you well know." Her children turned to stare at her. Tears were now falling copiously.

Mennù remained impassive, but she did not hesitate to reply. "If you are all agreeable, it's fine by me, but the terms must be clear: I will serve signora Adriana as I have always done, in my home, but she must hold her card games and receive her visitors at Alfallipe House. I'll keep the rooms and the bedrooms clean for all of you when you come to Roccacolomba, but she will eat and sleep at my place, as my honoured guest."

Carmela was the first to speak: "I really don't understand what's happened to you, Mennù. Is this the time to bring this up? . . . Papa is not long dead. Can't you wait a few days more? I haven't talked about this with Massimo. I know you don't want to see him, but he's my husband, and I don't want to make decisions without him. Mama could move in with us, perhaps. Another solution might be found." And she burst into loud sobs, hiding her face in her Flemish linen napkin. Lilla and Gianni were speechless. The silence in the room was broken only by their mother's soft weeping and Carmela's muffled sobs.

"You're stupid!" Mennulara's voice was full of disdain, and she addressed Carmela as if she were a little girl. "You're stupid now and you were stupid then to take that dowry hunter for a husband. Don't you understand that this solution will save his face before the entire town, because your mother can receive him as and when you wish in Alfallipe House? He can even sleep here."

Lilla had to step in. "Couldn't we postpone this conversation at least until tomorrow evening? I'd like to think that Papa would have appreciated it if we didn't argue, and Mama is crying."

"You're right. Tomorrow it is, then, but let it be clear that I shall work only one month more, and I expect an answer quickly." With that Mennù got up and began to clear the table in silence.

That evening, the children had their first major row with their mother. Carmela offered to put her up in her home; the other two suggested instead that she remain in Alfallipe House and they would find another maid. They agreed that the time had come to get rid of Mennù, who would turn into a real tyrant now that their father was no longer there to restrain her. Lilla assured her mother that her husband, who detested Mennulara's interference, her coarse dialect, and her familiar attitude towards their daughter, would never tolerate the little girl's learning that her grandmother lived in her maid's flat. He would not allow Lilla to bring their daughter to Roccacolomba. Adriana Alfallipe, for her part, did not consider the arrangement inappropriate and seemed content to live in Mennù's home wherever and however it was.

The arguments between mother and children continued during the next days without any agreement being reached. Mennù carried on working in silence and did not bring up the subject again. In the meantime the three children informed her that they would manage the family property without her help. She replied that they were making a mistake but that she would help them anyway if they needed it.

Thus it happened that, at the end of the month, Adriana Alfallipe moved into Mennù's modest flat, to the disapproval of Gianni and Lilla, who visited her less frequently. Lilla did not return to Roccacolomba any more, and the grandmother could see her granddaughter only when she went to Rome in the summer. But Carmela dropped her opposition to this cohabitation because it was convenient for Massimo, who feared he might otherwise have to shoulder the burden of his mother-in-law.

The three children, unversed in the management of their assets, encountered some difficulties. Reluctantly, they had to seek Mennulara's help. Once she had solved the problems, she repeated her offer to resume the management of the estate, and when they refused she said that she would no longer help them, which offended them deeply. They asked their mother to divest Mennulara of the administration of her personal assets, but she wouldn't agree. Relations between them all cooled even further.

After the Mass held in Roccacolomba on the first anniversary of their father's death, Mennù asked for a meeting alone with the three Alfallipe children. She made a surprising proposal to them. "The late signora Lilla, God rest her soul, and your father would be unhappy if they knew that you seldom visit your mother and that you telephone her just as seldom. You owe her this respect. It pains me to see you estranged from her, and I understand that this is because you are angry with me, that there is war between us. I don't want to ask you to make peace, because I believe I acted justly, and you know that. Too much has been said. But signora Adriana is unhappy because she doesn't see her children often, and I don't like that. It's my wish that Lilla and Gianni telephone her every week, and come to Roccacolomba to see her every month, while Carmela will visit her four times a month.

"My cash is invested well and I have a good income. I'll make you an offer: at the end of every month I'll give you half a million lire each, but you must come to my place to pick it up. It will be at your disposal on the twenty-fifth of every month. If for any reason you don't call on your mother, as agreed, you lose the payment."

The three children accepted; after that, Adriana Alfallipe lived happily in Mennù's flat, and the townspeople praised Lilla, a really affectionate daughter, who never missed her visit at the end of the month.

Thinking of all this now, Lilla had to agree that, despite the burning humiliations Mennù had inflicted on them, on the whole she had been right about their inexperience in managing their father's estate and about Carmela's marriage. Now that Mennù was no longer alive, Lilla would miss the considerable sum that she had received every month. She felt alone. Her brother and sister, so different from her, had chosen to live in worlds far distant from hers. Her mother, physically present during her childhood and adolescence, had always been emotionally distant, a sublime egoist. As a child Lilla had suffered because of her mother's marked preference for Gianni, but now she realised that this was another burden for her brother, the victim of an obtuse and oppressive maternal love.

Her father had inculcated a love of art in her, but he had never been around when she needed him, and he had also badly neglected Gianni and Carmela. Her parents lived under the same roof, but in fact they led separate lives; each partner's requirements always had absolute priority over the other's and the children's. Yet despite her father's chronic infidelity, you could say that theirs had been a successful marriage: Lilla had no recollection of affection expressed between them or towards their children, but she also had no memory of rows or disagreements. Mennù had worked hard to maintain the family equilibrium and financial stability. Perhaps they should have been grateful to her for that.

Thinking of her return to Rome, Lilla fell asleep almost at peace.

Friday 27 September 1963

✕✕

34. The post brings the Alfallipes some hopeful news

It was about eight o'clock in the morning. Signora Alfallipe and Lilla were having coffee in her mother's bedroom before Lilla prepared to return to Rome. Taking leave of parents always involves difficulties, but in this case it seemed easy and devoid of emotion except for a certain relief. Mother and daughter had been humbled, so to speak, by the events of the week.

Santa came into the room, agitated. The postman was in the porter's lodge, waiting for someone to sign for a registered letter. Lilla went down and then returned with an envelope; the address was typewritten. It had been posted in the provincial capital. Lilla opened it impatiently. Dated the previous day, 26 September, it was written in Mennù's large block letters and wasn't signed. Lilla read it out loud.

You didn't do as I told you, but now that you have placed the announcement in the Giornale di Sicilia *as I wanted, I forgive you, provided you do as I tell you.*

Go into your father's study. Behind the Enciclopedia Treccani *there is a false shelf. Take out the volumes of the encyclopedia. You will see a large hatch. Open it. Behind it are three shelves. There you will find eight crates wrapped up. Don't open them. They contain antique vases that—today or tomorrow—I want you to take to the regional museum of archaeology by car. Take care not to knock them about. Drive slowly. It would be a disaster if they got broken. At the museum, ask for Dr. Palmeri. He is expecting you. Tell him only that you have come on behalf of Mennulara, and give him your name; explain that you need a certificate of authenticity and that the vases belong to you three. Don't touch anything else in the house, and don't look for anything else.*

After you receive the certificate, wait for another letter. Remember to do as I say.

Lilla put the letter on the table and said, "Let's go to the study." The two women got up. They set off—passing through the salons, the billiard room, down the corridors, through the antechambers, before reaching the study by the internal door. Wrapped in their pale dressing gowns, they slipped along over dusty majolica floors. Slim and light-footed, they opened the doors of the empty dark rooms with their bolted windows and then carefully closed them behind them, switching the lights of every room on and off as they went with the synchronised rhythm of a dance with no music. They finally reached the study, and there they stopped.

"What now?" asked signora Alfallipe, ready for action. Lilla glared at her reproachfully. Her mother complained of fatigue and pain whenever her strictly idle routine changed, but now she seemed ready and willing.

"I don't want to open the shutters; people might see us . . . Let's take down the books and see if things are as she says," Lilla replied.

When Lilla had gone to get books to give to Father Arena, she had hurriedly tossed others on the floor. Apart from this pile, the imposing study was dusty but in order. It had that particular and invasive odour, a blend of stratified dust, damp, and the sweet rottenness of worm-eaten paper, which lingers in uninhabited rooms as if they wanted to punish and reprove the masters for having loved them and left them.

They set to work with a will, keeping up their synchrony of movement in an almost religious silence. Lilla scaled the elegant rolling library steps, took out the heavy leather-bound volumes, and handed them to her mother, who laid them one by one on the floor, one on top of the other, forming little pillars of equal height. When she had taken out the last volume, Lilla climbed back down and, dusting off her hands on her hips, stood in front of the shelves. Her mother came to stand next to her: their dressing gowns, slightly dishevelled by the unaccustomed movements, hung down over their elegant bodies in graceful folds as they silently gazed at the bookshelves. "Let's open it," said Lilla, and she turned the handle of the false door, which opened with a creak.

There they were: eight identical crates, lined up in their hiding place, wrapped in heavy paper, bound well with several loops of strong cord, ready to be transported to the museum. A comforting sense of well-being descended upon the two women, who looked at them in silence. Signora Alfallipe said, "Everything will go just fine, you'll see." "Let's hope so," replied her daughter, adding, "We'll have to call Gianni. I could take them to the museum myself today, but one of the men must go with me—they're fragile. We'll leave things as they are for the time being, and we'll lock the door."

They retraced their steps through the house, their hearts light. As they neared the bedrooms, they heard Santa yelling coarsely. The maid had gone to get the coffee tray and, not finding the two women, had looked for them all over the place in vain, never imagining that they might have gone as far as the study. Fearing that signora Adriana might have collapsed or succumbed to some other disaster, Santa had repeatedly gone through the rooms the family used; she had even gone down to the porter's lodge, into the inner courtyard and into the storehouses, calling for them at the top of her voice.

So they had to put up with a scene from the serving woman, who had ended up slumped in the mistress's armchair all hot and bothered and asking for water. After she refreshed herself, she took them to task for having given her such a fright. Lilla had to restrain herself from scolding Santa and reminding her that this was no way to treat her masters. She would see to her at the right time. They were going to have to fire her, for she seemed to think she had the right to behave like Mennù. But now she allowed the woman to let off steam and explained that they had gone into a room in the back of the house to pick up some things for Lilla to take back to Rome.

As soon as they were alone, Lilla called her husband and her brother and sister. With the same diligence and economy of words, they organised the transport of the vases to the museum that morning. They were relieved and optimistic, although puzzled by Mennulara's continuous, inexplicable vigilance and presence in their lives. Signora Alfallipe felt calm all day. When it was time to take leave of Lilla and the vases, she said, "Mennù is protecting us from heaven. We must do as she says . . . Remember that, all of you: she is in heaven, thinking about our good."

In the general confusion, none of the Alfallipes thought of opening at least one crate to check its contents, nor did anyone wonder about the provenance of these finds. Their basic problem—to discover the origin of the monthly payments—was far from solved; on the contrary, this was a further and suspicious complication. But none of the Alfallipes gave this so much as a passing thought. It was enough that Mennù had got in touch, no matter how or why. They were in no doubt that the cash source would flow for them once again.

After the corrections to the death notices, the mourning visits had multiplied. The townspeople found the Alfallipe family well disposed, the children full of praise for their late servant: an exceptional human being who had devoted herself to them totally and had loved them like a second mother. She had even supervised and encouraged them in their studies; she had been really eager to learn and had acquired a certain culture—no more, of course, than that small amount a maid could learn—by indulging their father in his craze for collecting. The visitors were amazed by this abrupt change, and they hastened to tell others that madness was now rife in the Alfallipe household, where Mennulara, no longer deprecated, was being hailed as their guardian angel and even a woman of learning.

Dr. Palmeri, the archaeologist at the regional museum, received Lilla and Gianni with courtesy. He promised to examine the contents of the crates without delay, adding, "Please pay my respects to signor Mennulara. He is a remarkable self-taught expert in the Attic pottery of Magna Graecia." By now, nothing could surprise the Alfallipes, not even the fact that Dr. Palmeri thought their maid was a man and an art expert. Lilla and Gianni, duty-bound by Mennù's orders, didn't bat an eyelid. They smiled and took their leave.

35. *Lilla Alfallipe has some pleasant memories of Mennulara*

Lilla was on the plane, bound for Rome. She didn't like to recall episodes from her life as a young girl in Rocca-colomba, but some images of her childhood she thought she had forgotten or perhaps removed were beginning to return.

It was the time of the Allied landings in 1943. The family had been evacuated to one of their most remote properties, in a high inland valley. Leaning against her father's legs, Lilla was looking at the illustrations in an art book, which they were reading together, sitting on a blanket beneath the broad crown of a mulberry tree, and she was happy to have her father's attention all to herself. After a few moments she began to feel she was being watched, and she looked up. Mennù was also sitting under the tree, with her sewing; she was looking over at them with tender pleasure; her hands rested in her lap, having relinquished the wooden darning egg inside the sock she was mending. Lilla smiled at her, and

Mennù's full and protuberant lips opened in a complicit smile.

That period had been especially pleasant for Lilla, despite the nature of the events that were its cause. They were living in a peasant's cottage concealed by trees, near a stream. The family had taken refuge there with their grandmother, and, fearing the worst, they had brought along only don Paolino, the chauffeur, and Mennù to serve them. The children didn't know about the invasion of Sicily, although they knew the war was still going on, and they were enjoying this country holiday, which seemed as if it would go on forever. Mennù had suggested to their father that he might make up for their lack of schooling by teaching the children what could be learned about the countryside, and every afternoon, while his mother and wife were resting, Orazio would take them out together with Mennulara. Lilla had never been so close to her father as she was then.

Another sweet memory surfaced. They were beneath an enormous carob tree; her father was pulling down the lower branches and giving botany lessons, explaining the long journey that sap makes in trees, telling them of the miracle of pollination, and identifying the parasites on the foliage. Mennù was listening, rapt. During the lessons she would often go off to pick up stones, berries, and little creatures, which she would bring to Orazio, as if she, too, were a pupil. He would take them one by one, holding them delicately between his slender fingers, which Lilla loved so much, and observe them closely before telling their fascinating story. Mennù would listen and then make her contribution, derived from her own experience in the fields, and sometimes she would even correct him. She had a good knowledge of the medicinal virtues of plants, antidotes for the bites and stings of animals, and their habits during the different seasons.

Suddenly Lilla remembered a specific moment in her memory of that day: her father and Mennù examining the long carob pods and laughing together, looking at each other. Lilla had felt a high excitement, as if she was part of something powerful and intimate, which she did not yet understand.

But this idyll was short-lived. Mennù soon became their sole teacher. Their father, taken by a love affair with a lady who had also been evacuated and was residing nearby, had lost interest. Mennulara would take them around the fields and then suddenly stop, gesturing at them to keep quiet, when she saw an unusual bird in the trees, a frightened rabbit, a rock with a curious shape, or an abandoned object. She spotted everything before they did. She explained the life of the animals as she understood it, the effects of pruning on trees, the wonders of grafts that transformed pear trees into peach trees, the way a caterpillar turns into a butterfly. Lilla enjoyed it all. It seemed to her that the whole world was in continuous wonderful transformation, and she felt truly free.

Mennù used to prepare delicious snacks with what little food could be found during those difficult days—sandwiches filled with omelet, onions, and olives, anchovies marinated in oil and lemon juice—which they would eat under the trees. When it got hot, if they were alone, she would take off the thick stockings she wore throughout summer and winter and go barefoot. She would lie down on the ground and stare at the sky. She seemed completely happy. When the wind blew hard, it would muss the chignon at the nape of her neck. Then she would let it down—"The wind always gets the upper hand anyway," she would say—and her hair would puff out, as if it had been imprisoned before, forming a mane of big thick curls that hung down over her shoulders. She was almost beautiful then.

When the period of evacuation was over, they went back to Roccacolomba. Grandmother Lilla was in poor health and there were financial problems. Lilla went back to the monotonous and oppressive life that characterised her childhood. They saw little of their father, who was engrossed in his various interests outside the family. Their mother spent the afternoons playing cards. They were hard times, and changes were always for the worse. There was often talk, at home, of selling property in order to live off the capital.

It was decided that Mennù would also look after the kitchen, and the domestic staff was reduced. Nevertheless, Lilla's parents decided to engage a young woman who had some years of schooling to look after the children. Their familiarity with Mennù, who spoke only Sicilian, would have kept them from learning Italian properly, and Lilla would be of marriageable age in a few years' time. Both her grandmother and her parents feared that she and her sister might become "common" as a consequence of continuous contact with the servant, who saw to their studies in her own way and generally supervised them closely in all things. Mennù was kept ignorant of their worries and was very upset about the arrival of the newcomer, which she considered an unjustified intrusion in her sphere of competence, and she said as much. But the Alfallipes did not yield to her remonstrations. Lilla recalled that this young lady, whom she and her siblings disliked, was dismissed not long after when more cuts had to be made. This left only two servants: don Paolino and Mennù, occasionally assisted by women who worked parttime.

Mennù was therefore once again responsible for the children. But she had changed. She still attended to her duties punctiliously, but Lilla felt that she was distant and almost hostile. And then, some time after their grandmother's death, Mennù took over the management of the estates. Swamped with work and worries, she became bad-tempered, imposing her will on the house and the family, giving priority to their mother's requirements and to their father's wishes and whims, while the children became of secondary importance, as they were for the parents.

Even then there was something enigmatic and elusive about Mennù. Gradually, she rose to the role of servantmistress, the person to whom parents and children alike turned with requests for money; yet she continued to be proud of her work as a domestic, and she went on serving them as before. She didn't want Lilla to learn to cook or to do those little tasks that girls enjoy, such as embroidery. She did everything. She took no days off except for the two weeks in the summer that she spent with her nephews, with whom she kept up a close correspondence, dictating the letters to Lilla. Her time off during the day was in the afternoon—between 2:30 and 4:00 p.m.—when she would retire to her room or to the study next to that of Lilla's father to see to the accounts. No one dared disturb her. Even her father had to ask permission to go into the study during those hours, and she didn't always give it.

Lilla had no other pleasant memories. She was painfully aware of her father's extramarital affairs, which hadn't seemed to bother her mother. Life in Roccacolomba was claustrophobic; many well-to-do families there had sold their houses and moved to the city. Lilla had enthusiastically returned the love of a surgeon from Lombardy and married very young, glad to leave a family without a soul and a town without a future. Mennù had approved of this decision, on condition that Lilla continue her university studies, and she urged the Alfallipes to give their daughter a grand wedding reception.

That evening, home at last in Rome, Lilla told her husband of the week's extraordinary events. The episode of the vases was relevant because it proved that there was a complex system of checks and controls on the Alfallipes' conduct, planned by Mennù with the help of persons unknown and implemented by a variety of people. The notice in the paper was probably a coded message. The reasons for and the purpose of this complex arrangement were not clear. Lilla and her husband wanted to know more about Mennulara, and so they decided to telephone her nephews.

Sunday 29 September 1963

✗✗

36. Lilla Alfallipe and her husband meet Gerlando Mancuso, Mennulara's nephew

"He could pass as one of us," remarked Lilla to her husband as they headed towards the group of armchairs in the hotel lobby where signor Mancuso was sitting. Of medium height and dark, he was well dressed in a wool blazer, nice casual shoes, and with a small, elegant watch on his wrist. He was reading the newspaper while he waited. After the initial pleasantries, Lilla offered him her condolences, as was proper. She felt liberated, pleased to be able to pass them on to someone else and not to have to receive any more of them herself.

"It is I who should be offering condolences to you, signora Bolla. Aunt Rosalia, in our view, loved you like her own children and us like nephews, and I am sure the feeling was mutual. After all, she always lived in your home, and she only spent two weeks of holiday with us every year," he replied. Lilla was not expecting things to start this way, and Mancuso, noticing this and thinking he had spoken out of turn, looked embarrassed.

"Thank you, but now I'd like you to tell me about your aunt . . . She was an extraordinarily reserved person, especially regarding her private life. I'd like to understand her better." Lilla was unable to say more.

"You're right: it's not easy to explain her. There's no doubt that she was remarkably intelligent and she had even acquired a degree of learning: a complex woman. At home we used to laugh at her secrecy. My father, who was in the carabinieri, would say that if she had been born a man she would have become a mafia boss; he said she was a *fimmina di panza*, a woman who could keep her mouth shut."

Gerlando Mancuso spoke the gentle Italian of the mainland, with a French *r*, but he pronounced the Sicilian expression perfectly. Gian Maria pointed this out tactfully. "Unfortunately, we were born and brought up in the north. I have never been in Sicily, but we kept up the dialect to communicate with Aunt Rosalia, who stubbornly refused to speak Italian. I think she was ashamed of her lack of education and her limited knowledge of etiquette." Again Mancuso feared he had spoken out of turn, giving the impression that a Sicilian accent was unusual, and turning to Lilla he added, "If I may say so, signora Bolla, your Sicilian accent shows through delightfully in your perfect Italian."

Lilla didn't like people to notice her southern origins, and so she smiled and went straight to the topic that concerned her most. "As you will certainly know, signor Mancuso, your aunt managed our family assets until our father's death, after which she continued to manage our mother's estate. Her sudden death has left us rather confused about various aspects of her administration. She died prematurely and didn't have the time to set her own and our affairs in order . . . Perhaps she entrusted you with some settlement, a memorandum, or a will?"

"Aunt Rosalia discussed business with me, since I was her

eldest nephew, but she gave me nothing for you, nor did she intend to make a will, as far as I know. I wouldn't have expected her to, because she made us gifts in the past and was most generous with us. We are expecting no inheritance. What she possessed will all go to the Alfallipe family, I'm sure of that. We discussed this in August, during her last visit. She was pleased because she had put everything in order with the bank. 'I shall die easy because I have done my duty towards the living and the dead'—those were her very words. She was farsighted, and she would have organised things to avoid death duties. And so, signora Bolla, as far as I know, her estate is destined to go to you Alfallipes."

Lilla was speechless, and her husband intervened. "The Alfallipe heirs know nothing of this. They received sums of money from your aunt every month, sums that were actually sent to her directly through the post, running the risk of money being lost or stolen. Doesn't that seem incredible to you?"

"Yes, but it's typical of her. That's what she did with us, too, until we began working and there was no longer any need for her help. Her only failing was that she wanted to do everything herself and jealously guarded the details of her life and her savings. For us it was always a mystery how she managed to take care of our grandmother and my mother, from the time when she used to gather almonds in the fields. I know that as an adult she learned to be a good manager, that she was parsimonious, and that she was incredibly fortunate with her investments. My mother used to say that even as a little girl she could make money multiply like the fishes in the Gospels. Just imagine, right after the war, she helped us buy our first house, giving us quite a substantial sum of money."

"Where did she get this money from? Didn't you ever wonder where it came from?" asked Lilla point-blank. She had done some mental calculations: at that time, Mennù was only a maid, working for a miserable wage. Grandmother Lilla was still alive then and managed the Alfallipe properties herself. Could Mennulara have duped her and stolen from the family?

"We certainly did. My father was a carabiniere and a really upright man. He was unwilling to accept her gift and was frankly worried about it. The family discussed it at length. He even went so far as to insinuate that it was money stolen from your family. I recall that he decided to write her to try to find out where it came from. Aunt Rosalia corresponded frequently with us, even though she needed someone to write the letters for her—you, actually, signora Bolla, as you well know, because I still have the letters written in your fine handwriting, dictated by my aunt." Mancuso smiled, then added, "She wrote back right away. It was her money, and that was that. Before the war signora Alfallipe had given her a present that she had been able to invest abroad. She understood her brother-in-law's scruples and wouldn't take offence this time, she said, but she wouldn't tolerate any further doubt about her honesty. She would prefer not helping her beloved sister any more to enduring such a humiliation again. From then on we asked her no more questions. Once, during a visit, she decided to go to talk to the manager of her bank in Varese, and then in Switzerland. My brother took her. I suppose she kept her money there on your family's advice—there's no other explanation. My aunt was a poor peasant woman, and certainly, as managers of the princes of Brogli's estates, you are familiar with such investments. Ask at the bank. I always thought that her savings were invested together with your capital."

Lilla stammered, "I don't know, I married very young, I know little about the family's investments in those days." She didn't want to reveal her family's ignorance and lack of financial know-how to the nephew of their maid.

"Allow me to interrupt you," said Gerlando Mancuso. "I also remember that Aunt Rosalia earned money on the sale of one of your estates, a percentage on the price. She was very pleased with that deal, but I am more than sure that she was accurate and honest in the management of your property. That's the way she was. There's nothing else I can tell you," he added, worried in case he had said too much. "In our eyes she had no faults, except for her touchiness."

Gian Maria Bolla, noticing a certain irritation on Mancuso's part, stepped in. He was afraid that Mancuso might wish to end the meeting too soon. "Fancy that. I never thought she was touchy . . . With my wife, she was affectionate and forthcoming."

"She was touchy all right! Although she was proud of being a servant to a great Sicilian family like your wife's, she was aware that she had, let's admit it, coarse ways and no schooling. She was afraid that people might look down on her, and so she preferred to stay home, cleaning and cooking, rather than take part in our social life. At most, she would venture to the grocery shop on the corner to do the shopping. One day she got it into her head that the grocer was making fun of the way she spoke, and she made us stop going to his shop. She was unshakable in her decisions. We were little, but I can still remember her words: 'You must do as I tell you, because it's for your own good. You must still greet him when you pass the shop, but you must never buy from him again. It's a question of family honour: he has insulted your aunt.' "

Lilla listened carefully. This was the Mennù she knew. Gerlando Mancuso added, "I wouldn't like to give you the impression that she was petty or vindictive. She was generous and altruistic. Surprisingly learned, too, about subjects that interested her. In her last years, I presume when she had more time at her disposal, she read a great deal and was interested in modern literature. You will certainly know about her enthusiasm for Greek pottery, to which she must have been introduced by your father."

"Why didn't you come to the funeral?" asked Lilla, who didn't want to tell him about the Greek vases.

"Aunt Rosalia wouldn't let us visit her in Sicily. We said our good-byes peacefully in August. She made us promise not to go to Roccacolomba even for her funeral. She was sure that you would see to things, as you did, and the Mancuso family is grateful to you for that. The priest who used to write her letters told us of her death.

"I'd like to tell you one last thing, and please be so kind as to repeat it to your brother and sister, if you see fit. My aunt spoke and wrote a lot about you: how you played, what mischief you made, but also serious points about your strengths and weaknesses. She dreamed of your success and complained sometimes when you didn't study as diligently as she would have liked, but she always spoke of you with affection and pride. She did the same with us: she urged us to study and to improve in all things. She was a benevolent tyrant. Then she mentioned you less. We thought you had gone to boarding school, and we continued to ask for news of you, for you had become a part of our unknown Sicilian family. She avoided our questions. One day, I asked her why. She replied that a woman was looking after you; she had gone back to being only a maid, and talking about you made her suffer, but she would always keep you in her heart. I realise that she was a woman without an education, but the advice and the support she gave us from a distance helped us immensely in our adolescence, and I could never understand this change in her work. Could you explain it to me?"

Lilla said that her parents had employed a qualified young lady who spoke good Italian, as was customary when children reached a certain age.

"I see," said Gerlando Mancuso. "It must have been very painful for her. Although I suppose she must have got over it, as she continued to serve you devotedly for many more years."

Monday 30 September 1963

XX

37. The vases return to Roccacolomba

On Monday morning 30 September Gianni and Lilla were travelling towards Roccacolomba. The eight crates with the Greek vases, which they had just taken back from the museum, were stowed carefully in the boot and on the back seat of the car. It had been agreed that they would open the envelope with the certificate of authenticity in Alfallipe House, in the presence of Carmela and Massimo, as well as their mother.

Lilla had rushed from Rome as soon as she heard that the vases were ready, and she was in a good humour. She was telling Gianni, who had picked her up at the airport, about the meeting with Gerlando Mancuso. "You know, perhaps we judged Mennù badly. She loved us, she was a farsighted woman, and she brought up her nephews well. As for the vases, it's incredible that she learned so much about Greek art . . . Papa must have taught her a lot, but that surprises me too—I didn't think he was such a connoisseur, frankly." Gianni agreed.

Lilla went on. "I cannot imagine Papa and Mennù, together, reading in the study, researching, cataloguing finds . . . They were so different. For all his faults, Papa was still an elegant, well-read man, even a bit of a snob, and she, poor

Mennù, was so uncouth, so ungraceful—in speech, dress, everything."

"I don't know if I agree," said Gianni. "After she first met Mennù, Anna told me something about her that stuck in my mind: 'She has a good body and an interesting face. She could pass for a beautiful woman if she looked after herself a bit more, but she doesn't know where to begin.'"

Lilla smiled but chose not to reply. Everything that Anna said was gospel for Gianni, who adored his wife and was under her thumb, the exact opposite of their father. "What shall we do with the vases?" she asked. "There are eight of them. Shall we take two each, Mama included?"

Gianni spoke with a certain embarrassment: "To tell you the truth, it would be a shame to break them up, especially if they make a collection. If you don't mind, I'd like to keep them all. I am the last of the Alfallipes, and we could put them in a glass display cabinet in the new house, in memory of Papa. What do you say?"

Lilla was vexed. Her sister-in-law obviously had had a hand in this. It was better to postpone the discussion. Her husband had said to her that he would be prepared to buy his in-laws' share, at a price to be agreed upon. Greek vases would add the ultimate touch of refinement to their flat. She smiled again, trying to imagine Massimo having a similar conversation with Carmela. "Let's talk about it together at home, with Mama; they might be horrible, or maybe false, who knows?"

"Don't talk nonsense. I have no doubt that they'll be splendid!" exclaimed Gianni. "What bothers me is where they came from. If they belonged to Mennù, she certainly must have bought them from some grave robber and they must be stolen. We'll have to talk to a lawyer."

Lilla did not agree at all. "I cannot believe that Mennù bought anything from thieves. She was honest."

"You weren't talking so well of her last week! You accused her of having robbed us of Papa's estate."

"Shut up. You always talk rubbish. Last week we were all upset, and she certainly didn't leave things the way she should have," replied Lilla, and to avoid a row with her brother, she spoke little for the rest of the journey. Before they got to the turn for Roccacolomba, she said, "I'm sure that Mennù will send us another letter, one that will finally tell us where the money is. Goodness knows how much effort it took to organise this network of letters. It would have been so easy to leave a will or to write everything down in a single letter."

"Anna thinks that she did it to put us to the test, that she didn't trust us."

"What are you getting at?" Lilla had trouble putting up with her conceited sister-in-law.

"I'm saying that we made a lot of mistakes in managing Papa's estate and would have done better to follow Mennù's advice. The funds must be managed by the bank, and this time it would be better to leave them there and draw the interest, just as we have been doing all these years in practice, every month."

"All you care about is your university research and keeping your wife happy," said Lilla crossly, "but I want to manage my affairs by myself." She was bothered by the thought of an indivisible, frozen legacy. In the meantime the car was entering Roccacolomba.

38. *Meanwhile in Catania, Zurich, and Palermo, Mennulara's last wishes are carried out*

As requested by signor Mennulara, Dr. Palmeri had sent a telegram to a Zurich bank. A strange request, this, but one to be respected: after all, signor Mennulara had donated to the museum some Siracusan coins that rounded out its collection, and had also given antiquities to the curator and to Dr. Palmeri himself.

"Certificate delivered. Vases picked up Monday 10:30" said the telegram. Dr. Stutz, a bank official in Zurich, received it that same morning and immediately took from the "Confidential Foreign Investments" file the folder entitled "The Mennulara Estate." It contained the will of Maria Rosalia Inzerillo and five large envelopes, four still sealed, entitled respectively:

A. Complete text of the obituary published the day after death.
B. Modified text of the obituary published within two days of death.
C. Complete text of the obituary published within four days of death, after the funeral.
D. Complete text or modified text of the obituary published later than four days after death.
E. No obituary published.

He took envelope C, the only one open. It contained the obituary page of the Thursday, 26 September 1963, issue of the *Giornale di Sicilia*, in which the obituary of Maria Rosalia Inzerillo had been published. The first letters of the phrase "Almighty Lord, forgiveness and limitless love, in praise eternal" were highlighted, and rewritten in the margin: "Alfallipe."

Dr. Stutz took the page and held it in his hands, his thoughts turning to the client with whom he had communicated for decades through such fake obituaries, a complex but safe system. This was the first time it had been used to check the behaviour of the presumptive heirs and to decide if they deserved the inheritance, using an ingenious scheme that Dr. Stutz had meticulously prepared with the client on the occasion of their customary annual meeting in Catania in August. If only these Alfallipe people, unknown to him, had published the obituary straight away, as per the terms of envelope A, they would have spared him a lot of work and they would have come into possession of the deceased woman's estate immediately.

Now instead, Dr. Stutz and his collaborators had to carry out, with scrupulous attention to the slightest details, the disposition agreed on with the client. He checked the documents once more and telephoned his correspondent in Palermo, a trusted lawyer. The lawyer had a duplicate of envelope C. He opened it and took out a smaller envelope, yellow, on which was written: "Letter to be delivered by hand to the Alfallipe heirs once the museum has issued the certificate." He opened it carefully, to avoid damaging the contents. Inside was a sheet of white paper with a message written in large block letters—the handwriting of someone unable to write any other way. The lawyer added the date and put the letter in an envelope already addressed to the

Alfallipe family. He gave it to a trusted assistant, whose task was to go to Roccacolomba and hand-deliver it to Alfallipe House the following morning.

39. *Don Paolino Annunziata is present, so to speak, when the vases arrive at Alfallipe House*

Towards midday, Lilla telephoned her sister. They were in a bar halfway home and would be there by one o'clock. Massimo was to wait for them in front of the garage to unload the vases from the car, far from curious eyes. She urged Carmela to make sure that Santa wasn't in the house.

Don Paolino Annunziata lived, as we have said, in the two small rooms next to the garage of Alfallipe House, formerly the coachman's lodgings. It was a cool day, and the rheumatism in don Paolino's knees had got worse. He was sitting in an old armchair, a blanket over his legs. The soup pot was simmering merrily, filling the room with a pleasantly warm steam smelling of fresh cabbage, potatoes, onions, and tomatoes. Don Paolino's appetite was whetted by the smell. He thought that donna Mimma would soon be setting the table for lunch.

He was disturbed by shouting and swearing coming from next door. He called his wife and they sat there listening. They heard the voice of Massimo Leone. He was probably trying to open the main door of the garage, which had been hard to open for as long as don Paolino could remember. The old sense of duty prompted him to toss the blanket aside, get up quickly, swearing quietly about old age leaving him in such poor shape, and go into the street to see what was happening and to offer help.

Massimo Leone was standing in front of the garage door, furious. He was shaking the handles, kicking the doors, banging the lock with his fist, turning the iron key this way and that, thrusting it in like a screwdriver, bracing himself against the wooden planks that reinforced the lower part. He pretended not to know don Paolino and refused his offer of help. Don Paolino, undaunted, told him what he had to do to make the lock work, but the advice was not well received: Leone suggested that don Paolino go back home to eat his soup and mind his own business.

"The door opened after a few more shakes," don Paolino later told his brother-in-law, don Vito Militello, in the porter's lodge of Palazzo Ceffalia. "He treated me so badly that I felt duty-bound to see what else he was up to in the garage of Alfallipe House, out of respect for the memory of signor Orazio." Don Paolino was making an effort to disguise his indiscreet curiosity as the devotion of an old retainer in order to justify his behaviour on that fateful afternoon.

In the Annunziata household, husband and wife got along because they saw things eye-to-eye and, after many years of marriage, had no need for long discussions. They understood each other without even having to look each other in the face. As soon as don Paolino told donna Mimma about Massimo Leone's offensive behaviour, without further discussion the couple went into action. Donna Mimma grabbed her sewing basket, took the soup pot off the stove, and told her husband that she was going to sit at the front door to sew—until late at night, if necessary—and that she would take a careful look at every car that passed by. Don Paolino gave up hope of having his soup for lunch.

Instead he began bustling about. He moved the chairs and small table from the wall adjacent to the garage, took down the picture of the Madonna delle Lagrime di Siracusa, with the big heart streaming with drops of blood, and delicately ran his hand over the plaster at the point where the picture had been hanging. In the wall, there was a small hole with a lens inside it: a rudimentary peephole through which one could observe the interior of the garage. It was a system devised by his predecessor the coachman in order to keep an eye on the carriages, the horses, and the stable boy who slept by the trough, before the stable had been transformed into a garage for the master's cars.

Don Paolino had kept this antitheft device open and functioning, even though there were few burglaries in Roccacolomba Alta . . . but one never knew, and at the first sound from the garage, he was always on the alert and watching. He had never seen any burglars, but peeping through that hole years before, he and his wife had witnessed certain encounters between Orazio's father, Ciccio, and Pina Vassallo, the cook, that were enough to make your toes curl: the two were both over forty at the time, but they were going hard at it, thrusting so hard against the bonnet of the car that they nearly damaged it. Now don Paolino wondered what else he was going to see as he quietly prepared what he needed for his lunchtime vigil. He arranged a comfortable chair, raising the seat with cushions and blankets, placed a wooden box beside it as a footrest, filled a glass with cool water and set it next to the chair, along with a piece of bread and some cheese in case he got hungry, and then took up his position, right eye glued to the peephole, nose almost squashed against the cracked plaster of the wall, his stick at hand.

Massimo had closed himself in the garage, pulling the doors to. As soon as he heard the sound of a car in the lane, which didn't happen often, he would stick his head out, looking right and left. When he noticed the vigilant eyes of donna Mimma, who was mending a big basket of things and showed no sign of going back indoors, he decided it was better to stay inside the garage, his ears cocked.

Don Paolino, observing him from indoors, congratulated himself on his wife's idea: good girl, Mimma, you've put a scare into Massimo Leone with a couple of old rags to darn.

Gianni's car was heralded by a roar. Massimo hastened to open the door and the vehicle slowly entered. Donna Mimma slipped into the house, still holding a sock and her needle, to give her husband the high sign, but there was no need of this because he was at the observation post, his eye glued to the peephole.

That evening at dinner, don Paolino recounted the events that followed to his brother- and sister-in-law, don Vito and donna Enza Militello. "As soon as the car was inside, Massimo Leone grabbed the boot and tried to open it, tugging at the handle, twisting it as if he wanted to rip it off and yelling 'Open! Open!' while the professor and signora Lilla got out of the car cool as you please, as if they were doing so just to annoy him. The professor gave him a look, the way the late signora Lilla used to, and said, 'There's no hurry—we're not running away with the treasure. If you keep doing that, you'll knock them about and they'll get broken.' Leone swore and stood aside to leave them room to open the boot and the rear doors. In the meantime signora Adriana and signora Carmela had come down the inner stairs and were asking hundreds of questions: 'What did he tell you?' 'Are they all intact?' 'Were you careful on the road?' The professor said, 'The envelope is in my pocket; we'll read it later.' And the two women shut up.

"They all got to work, making a real mess. There were four big crates stowed in the boot and four on the back seat, covered by blankets. The men took them one by one and carried them into the house, handling them as if they were really fragile. They seemed heavy to me, judging by the faces they made when they lifted them. Well, it looked as if there was treasure in those crates. Signora Lilla said she would go upstairs and open them carefully; the other two stayed in the garage to watch.

"At one point, signora Adriana burst out happily, 'Mennù always thinks of us! Now you will be rewarded!' To which her daughter replied, 'Be quiet, Mama. We still haven't read the appraisal. Let's go up to the study.' But they didn't move.

"There were two crates left to carry away. The professor was heading for the boot when his sister Carmela and his brother-in-law, without so much as a sign of complicity, barred the way, putting themselves in front of him. Massimo Leone told him, 'Open the envelope now, I tell you.' He was sweating and seemed angry, even frightening. His wife, right at his side, looked like his lieutenant. Signora Adriana started screeching, 'Don't squabble. They'll break. They'll break,' and she covered her face with her hands.

"The professor got really angry. He didn't deign so much as to look at his brother-in-law, and he ordered his sister to tell her husband to get out of his way, saying the boxes were Alfallipe property and he didn't like his attitude. He made to brush him aside. Massimo Leone gave him a big shove and yelled, 'Read it, you shit!' I was scared, too—he's an animal, that one. The professor fell silent; he straightened up and took an envelope from his trouser pocket, opened it, and out came a piece of paper, which he read to himself. Then he said, 'They're fake.' He was already pretty pale, and he got even paler. Then all hell broke loose. Signora Carmela started railing against Mennulara—but what did that poor soul have to do with it?—theft, swindling, ignorance, she accused her of everything. She looked like she'd gone mad, and the others stood watching her, still as statues. Well, it really was a circus."

"Didn't you get tired sitting there, watching through that hole?" donna Enza asked her brother-in-law. Her sister answered: "He wanted to see it all, he did. There was no way of getting him away from the wall . . . I wanted to look in the garage, too, but he wouldn't let me, he was enjoying it so much, and the pains in his bones seemed to have vanished."

"Wait, here comes the best bit," said don Paolino. "Massimo Leone grabbed the paper and read it; then he raised his eyes and rolled them around, as if he'd been possessed by some spirit. They got bigger—like octopus eyes, they were. It looked as if they would pop out of his head. Without a word, he started punching himself about the head, but hard—you could hear the sound of the blows—and on he went, still silent. The others told him to stop, but no one had the courage to go near him, and that devil started cursing Mennulara, still punching himself, first his head, then his neck and down his chest.

"Then signora Adriana shouted, 'Stop, you'll hurt yourself!' He looked at her and replied, 'I can't beat my wife, who is the cause of all my troubles, but I can do what I want to myself.' And he carried on, punching himself like a madman. The women started raging against Mennulara, and the professor went up to his mother, not saying a thing. I saw that he was afraid his brother-in-law would take it out on him, and so he kept his mouth shut. Signora Lilla had come down—she must have heard the racket—and she too started cursing poor Mennulara. It was pandemonium. Then she and her brother took the last two crates and the Alfallipes went upstairs, leaving Massimo Leone alone in the garage, still beating himself up. He was swollen all over. In the end, he gave his brother-in-law's car a kick and followed them upstairs. Goodness knows what happened up there . . ."

"Then what?" asked donna Enza.

Her sister replied, "What do we know about it? From the shouting I heard, it seemed as if they were killing each other—there was the sound of things breaking—but we couldn't hear very well. We stayed inside. The shouting was coming from the other side of the building. It didn't seem like a good idea to go out. If you want to know what happened, you'll have to find out from other people. This story won't die down until the whole town knows about it." And she went back to wolfing down the steamed vegetables, her first hot meal of the day.

"I wonder what there could have been in those crates . . . Paolino, what do you say?" Donna Enza wanted to know more about it.

"God only knows. Why did they have it in for poor Mennulara so much? . . . Yesterday they were all praising her to the skies. I'll have to think about it." Don Paolino dunked a big piece of bread into the vegetable broth, popped it into his mouth, and set to chewing slowly, savouring it in silence.

40. The Masculo family eats overcooked pasta

In the Masculo home, no one complained about having eaten overcooked pasta and a cold second dish that Monday 30 September. Angelo Masculo, an agronomist, was the godson of the late counsellor Ciccio Alfallipe, who had helped him buy the house next to his mansion, facing his office balcony. The entire Masculo family had repaid the Alfallipes with gratitude and discretion. They had taken no part in the recent gossip, and parents, children, and grandchildren all lived their own lives and minded their own business.

On this particular day, however, they could not resist being spectators to what was happening next door. They were all standing behind the lace curtains at the living room window, watching and listening to the pandemonium that was being unleashed in Alfallipe House.

Lilla had gone directly to the study, where she threw

open the shutters to let in the fresh air and to see better. She removed the ornaments from the grand piano so she could set the vases on it—the best position from which to admire them. She was looking forward to the pleasure of opening the crates one by one, certain that she would manage to persuade the others to give them all to her: she just had to be patient and not talk too soon.

She opened two crates. Inside were two magnificent amphorae, black and glossy, the red figures detailed and elegant, the leaves decorating the rim delicate and perfect. She opened another two and marvelled again: another two amphorae, similar to the first ones, certainly a really important collection. She drew back the lace curtains to let in even more light, then stood there looking at them, satisfied.

She heard an indistinct clamour coming from the inner staircase and immediately thought that her mother had fallen or, worse, that Gianni or Massimo had dropped a crate and broken the contents. She rushed downstairs. As soon as she got to the garage, she understood. Deeply irritated by Massimo's hysterics, she took a crate and carried it upstairs, and Gianni followed.

They carried the crates as carefully as they had before, even though they now knew the vases were worthless, but they put them on the table in the antechamber rather than taking them into the study. Their mother and Carmela joined them. Carmela threw herself down on the sofa, weeping and calling for help. Massimo would kill her for this last taunt of Mennulara's. Her mother sat at her feet, caressing her absently, repeating that she didn't understand at all, that they must have made a mistake at the museum, or someone had duped Mennulara.

Gianni and Lilla remained standing, reading the letter again in disgust. Not only did it confirm the forgery, but it also authorised the sale and export of the vases, since they were fakes. "What a joke," said Gianni, "they're letting us export fakes."

Lilla said nothing. She was livid. Her brother asked, "Where did you find them?" and she pointed at the big bookcase with a weary gesture. "Who knows if there are others?" He went on. "Let's see." He went up to the long book-lined wall.

Carmela got to her feet and joined them. "After Papa's death, that madwoman started spending our money buying fake vases . . . She didn't understand anything about them. Look, who knows how many others there are around here? She thought she was making a good investment, and instead they're all fakes." She opened the lower cupboards of the bookcase. Without troubling to close them again, she took out boxes containing other pottery, objects of all kinds, Caltagirone majolica ware, stacks of things.

Overwhelmed by her anger, Carmela opened everything, even the drawers containing the coin collection and those in the study tables, pulling out papers, objects, brown wrapping paper, and piling them up on the tables, shelves, floor, and chairs. Lilla stood watching her, then joined in.

This was how Massimo found them. Like two Furies, having emptied the lower shelves, leaving the doors wide open, the Alfallipe sisters set to work on the bookcase. They cleared the shelves by throwing the books to the floor, and discovered other secret shelves, full of vases, some similar to the fakes, others different, as well as lachrymatories, lanterns, figurines, plates, and grave goods, all catalogued and in perfect order.

Gianni stood to one side, next to his mother. She was watching in astonishment.

Massimo, too, was standing speechless, watching them. He looked at the fakes, which were still on the piano—beautiful amid the destruction. He shouted, "There they are, pieces of rubbish, and that whore thought they would be her fortune and the Alfallipes' fortune. You're all fools, and she was a shameless bitch. She let herself be conned by a bunch of crooks, squandering our inheritance. For ten years you have treated me like an idiot. You think you're better than other people, but you're the idiots. Why the hell did I have to marry into this family? You deserve to be known as fools all over Sicily . . . It was you who put the obituary in the paper, and I'm an idiot for going along with you." He grabbed a bronze statuette from a low table nearby and hurled it to the floor, then a couple of ashtrays and a small vase. He stopped, shocked at his own boldness.

The Alfallipes' response to this did not cease to amaze the townspeople, to whom the Masculo family, abandoning its usual reserve, later provided a highly vivid account. Lilla, busy rummaging through a drawer, turned at the thud caused by the falling statuette and, lightning fast, rushed to the piano, took one of the vases, held it out in front of her, and dropped it. The vase shattered. She took another and let it fall onto the first. Carmela followed her lead, and even Gianni joined his sisters in a cathartic orgy of destruction. The sound of smashing pottery clashed with Massimo's ranting against the world and against Mennulara. By now they were all howling obscenities against her. Like a Fury, Lilla climbed the library steps and took out her father's antique books and hurled them to the floor, and as they fell loose pages fluttered to the floor and the bindings were ruined. She found more hidden compartments full of big vases, and these too quickly ended up in pieces among the debris.

Gianni went up to Lilla, who handed him a vase like the ones on the piano and said, "Some connoisseur and art lover . . . Look at this, another fake—just like one of those we took to the museum."

Gianni took it in his hands and murmured, "Mennù hated us so very very much. This explains everything . . ." His eyes filled with tears, he choked back the sobs that were catching in his throat, and he let the vase fall to the floor. Now he was weeping without restraint, standing by the library stepladder. He took and smashed everything that Lilla handed to him. Soon the study carpet was completely covered with the shattered pieces of his father's collection.

Carmela's scream made them turn around. Massimo was clutching her by the throat, howling obscenities and shaking her as if she were a rag doll. Gianni rushed to rescue his sister and the two men began to wrestle with each other. Massimo got the worst of it, a bite on his arm, and Gianni's arms and legs were bruised all over. At this moment, Father Arena rang the doorbell.

41. *Father Arena has an afternoon of many visits*

Father Arena had agreed with signora Alfallipe that he would drop in for coffee after lunch, when there were usually no visitors, for a chat on their own. At precisely two o'clock, he rang the bell at Alfallipe House. After a long wait, Lilla opened the small door cut into a panel of the heavy front door, apparently surprised by his visit. She looked a mess—her clothes dusty, her hair loose and matted; she seemed tired and distraught, and without even inviting him into the porter's lodge she brushed him off, saying that her mother had gone to bed because she wasn't feeling well. It was clear that his visit was unwelcome. She was in such a hurry to send him away and shut the door that she did not notice the piece of folded white paper that had fallen from her hand and landed on the pavement. Father Arena picked it up and put it in his pocket, intending to return it to her the next morning. Bemused, he went on his way back down vicolo dei Gozzi, a lane that skirted Alfallipe House, thinking that he had nearly two hours to kill somehow before going to Fatta House, where he was expected at four o'clock.

"Father Arena, out and about at this hour? Come, come and take coffee with us!" The priest gratefully accepted Angelo Masculo's invitation, certain that he would pass the time pleasantly with such hardworking and unpretentious people. But things did not go as he hoped.

As he was having his coffee the priest listened, at first incredulous, then in consternation, to the Masculos' account of events. He lost all desire to taste the marzipan that signora Masculo offered. As each of the Masculos told Father Arena what had been seen and heard, a tragic and grotesque picture began to take shape. Signora Adriana, all four of them said, had been a silent witness to the destruction of her husband's study.

They all took the priest to the window from which the Masculos had witnessed the scene, so that he could see the study for himself, but the shutters were closed and there was no sign of life inside. It was as if nothing had happened. Father Arena would have liked to go away, to walk alone and think, but he couldn't: signora Masculo needed to unburden herself and needed advice.

Father Arena saw that the agronomist and his wife were distraught. They didn't know whether they ought to warn the Alfallipes' friends or relatives—the trusted and discreet ones—or whether they should go themselves to offer help to signora Alfallipe, or if they should call Dr. Mendicò. Meanwhile their son and daughter-in-law, despite being fine people, probably couldn't resist the temptation to talk about the extraordinary events they had witnessed from the window.

Father Arena was very much afraid that before evening the entire town would be in the know. In a vain attempt to salvage what little credibility and respect the Alfallipes still enjoyed in Roccacolomba, he assured the Masculos that he would immediately inform Chairman Fatta, and he urged them all to maintain their reserve.

Angelo Masculo saw the priest to the door; he wanted to speak to him alone. "Father, I'd like to tell you a few things that only I know and that have given me a great deal to think about. In the last few years of his life, Orazio Alfallipe stayed home a lot and spent the days in his study. By night, certain people would come by in a cart; these weren't faces I recognised. They would stop beneath the balconies and wait. Then Mennulara would open a window and let down a basket at the end of a rope, as if she were doing the shopping. She would haul up these big baskets, full of stuff covered by sacks, and I used to wonder what they contained . . . Now I think it was goods stolen by grave robbers, the very things destroyed this afternoon. Perhaps I should have talked about this with signor Alfallipe, tried to dissuade him from making those purchases. Perhaps the children are being threatened now, or blackmailed, and they smashed it all up in a fit of panic." The priest reassured him, saying that Orazio had been stubborn and wouldn't have followed signor Masculo's advice, so he had done well not to say anything.

"Another thing used to happen then. It's embarrassing to talk about," added Masculo, "and I ask your forgiveness. None of my family knows anything about this; they're good children, but a word can always slip out, and I don't want to harm the Alfallipes. I'll say this only to you, Father. I suffer from insomnia, and at nights I go into the living room to read the paper so as not to disturb my wife. In the summer evenings, signor Alfallipe used to leave the shutters open, and I would stand at the window listening to the beautiful music he always played—he had a marvellous gramophone. I could swear that through the lace curtains I could see a woman on the sofa in front of the fireplace, a woman with very little on, you understand. I don't know how he managed to get her in there, with signora Adriana at home, yet I saw her, always the same one, with long dark hair. Beautiful she was. Right up to his last years he had her in the house. I hadn't thought him capable of such behaviour; perhaps not even his late lamented father would have done this . . . True, even as an old man he still went to the whorehouse, but at least he didn't bring them home!"

Father Arena's reply was prompt and vigorous: "My dear Angelo, you can't say that. Only a priest knows all the weakness of men and the sins of the flesh that they commit. Without betraying the secrets of the confessional, all I can say to you is this: I'm not surprised by what you tell me . . . As the proverb has it, '*Lu piro fa pira*,' the pear tree produces pears, and women of this type, smuggled into private houses by day and by night, are plentiful . . . Fortunately there was no scandal in town, and what you saw was neither unusual nor surprising in Alfallipe House. Priests learn this and other things in the confessional. May God rest the souls of signor Ciccio and his son, Orazio. You would do well to keep silent. If this rumour should reach signora Adriana's ear, she would suffer terribly, not to mention Mennulara, who would be deeply upset if she were alive, for the reputation of the Alfallipes was something she held very dear. I'll talk about this with Chairman Fatta, without mentioning names, and please forget you ever had insomnia."

Father Arena slipped away, leaving Angelo Masculo pleased that he had confided his worries in the priest without mentioning his suspicions about the identity of the woman he had glimpsed in the counsellor's study, suspicions that would have made him look ridiculous. Ashamed of his bad thoughts, he asked Mennulara's forgiveness for his having thought her capable of such impropriety. The priest was right: the Alfallipes, father and son, had loved whores, and heaven help us if signor Orazio had reached the point where he had one of them brought to the study by poor Mennulara!

He went back indoors and said to his wife, "Maria, I've two things to say to you, and you must remember them. The Alfallipes will never appreciate the sacrifices made by their loyal servant Mennulara and the bitter pills they made her swallow, and Father Arena is getting wiser and wiser as he gets older!"

Troubled and dismayed, Father Arena roamed aimlessly through the streets of the town, which were almost deserted at that hour. He felt ill. The dazzling brightness of the sun alternated with dark shadows cast by the buildings. His head was spinning. He bumped into Dr. Mendicò, just back from an urgent call, who invited him to his home. Father Arena accepted and followed him like a lamb through the town, silently, in a state of deep depression.

Sitting in the living room of the Mendicò home and sipping a liqueur, the priest gradually perked up and the two men began to talk.

It was easy for Father Arena to tell the doctor of his worries about the Alfallipes. They were colleagues, in a certain sense. One tended to the soul and the other to the body, and they had often found themselves together, absorbed in their respective duties, at the bedside of the dying. The two men knew the secrets of the town, although they had never discussed them with each other. Now, in their keenness to get to the truth about the Alfallipes and Mennulara, they talked quickly and eagerly, weaving in and out of the story that was unfolding in the comforting half-light of Dr. Mendicò's living room.

The doctor had a clear understanding of what signor Masculo had said. Mennulara received stolen goods from grave robbers, certainly on the orders of Orazio, an avid collector. "Orazio was capricious and wasn't overly nice when he wanted something. He must have used Mennulara as a go-between when buying antiquities—lots of people do that, especially since the Monuments and Fine Arts people began the dig near Casale. I don't think he had many pieces, not valuable ones, anyway—he would have bragged about that around town. But I don't understand why his children wanted to destroy them . . . there were lots of things in his study—some beautiful pieces, too. As for women, he, unlike his father, wasn't interested in that kind of woman; he only liked the married sort. And so I can't fathom who might have gone to his place at night. What do you think, Father?"

At those words, Father Arena almost felt ill again. He said nothing.

The doctor, oblivious of the priest's presence, looked towards the balcony, his eyes following the embroidery on the linen curtains fluttering in the breeze, then murmured very quietly, "Unless that woman was . . ."

"Mennulara," said Father Arena, finishing the sentence. He, too, was murmuring, as if reciting a penance.

"Yes," said the doctor, still talking to himself, his eyes fixed on the fern near the balcony curtains. "Mennulara . . . After so many years, that would surprise me."

"Not me. It wouldn't surprise me," muttered the priest.

Dr. Mendicò raised his eyebrows and straightened in his armchair. He laid his hands on the armrests and looked Father Arena squarely in the face, as if he hadn't expected to find him sitting there slumped in the armchair beside his. He dabbed at his sweaty brow with a handkerchief. The priest's words had shocked him. Now it was he who felt faint, confused thoughts swirling through his mind.

"Doctor, is there something wrong?" asked Father Arena. He, too, was rather shaken at his own words.

"No, thank you. The thing is that I'm getting old and I'm slow to understand certain things. My brain isn't as sharp as it used to be," the doctor replied, adding solemnly and pronouncing each word clearly, "Mennulara never ceases to surprise me." He went back to looking out over the balcony; the curtains had billowed out in the breeze and he could see beyond the plants on the balcony, beyond the wrought-iron balustrade, to the roofs of the town and into the mountains. He stared at the sky, almost white in the strong bright light of the autumn sun.

"Tell me, Doctor, as if you were in the confessional," ventured Father Arena, stammering. He felt in the presence of a soul in torment, like his own.

"No, it's too much," Dr. Mendicò was repeating. Then he looked at the priest again and shot him a question. "Let's forget about the sacraments and remember that we are men: if I tell you about a hypothesis that involves a crime, maybe even two, will you keep the secret?"

"If it's about Mennulara, I certainly will!" came the prompt reply.

With a certain difficulty at first, Dr. Mendicò continued. He was no longer sweating and he seemed calm. "Well, as you know, like Mennulara, Orazio Alfallipe had a tumour. He was going to die soon, in any case. He was afraid of suffering. I couldn't spare him physical pain—morphine has its limitations. And he would have had a long and agonising end had he not been killed first, which is what I believe occurred. I have no proof, for only an autopsy could establish this, and that's out of the question." He looked the priest straight in the eye and went on. "The day Orazio died, Mennulara was in the country—a perfect alibi. She was his nurse; I had given her some phials of morphine and other substances that can be lethal if the wrong dosage is given. She knew all that, and I had complete trust in her. But this was homicide—or euthanasia, as some call it nowadays." He took a sip of water and continued. "It didn't occur to me at the time, believe me. At his death signora Adriana had hysterics, and I had to look after her, and I would never have imagined then that Mennulara's devotion to Orazio Alfallipe might extend to the point of killing him. A devoted servant doesn't go that far. But a woman who loves and is loved in return could even kill the man she loves." He straightened in his armchair. "Father Arena, do you think that Mennulara loved Orazio Alfallipe?"

"I don't know. If you are referring to real love and not to youthful lust, Doctor, I really don't know. In the last years of his life, she stayed holed up in Alfallipe House, so we saw each other only rarely and briefly." Father Arena paused, reflecting. He spoke again, stammering: "But if she loved him, she would have been capable of killing him without guilt or remorse."

"I have another question for you, Father," said the doctor. "What if I told you that she died after poisoning herself with sweets she had made herself with bitter almonds?"

"I wouldn't be surprised. She didn't want to be a burden to signora Alfallipe, and she was afraid she might suddenly get worse. She told me she was ready to die, that she had done her duty towards both the living and the dead. She wasn't a believer—did you know that?"

Dr. Mendicò lowered his eyes in assent; he took the bottle and filled the glasses again. They sat together in silence, each immersed in his own thoughts, drinking the liqueur. The wind had dropped. They stared at the beam of light flooding into the room through the openwork of the embroidered curtains, cutting through the shadows and striking the floor. Imprisoned in that cylinder of light, dust motes fluttered and danced in perpetual motion. A somnolent sensation of peace slowly descended upon Dr. Mendicò and Father Arena.

This is how the doctor's sister found them when she came in to greet the priest. The town was already buzzing with the story about the terrible row among the Alfallipe children caused by a question of money and inheritance; the mystery surrounding Mennulara was steadily thickening. Signora Di Prima was disconcerted by the reaction of the two men, who said almost in unison, in slightly amused tones, that there was no mystery about Mennulara, may God rest her soul. "There's no mystery? Do you want someone to get killed?" she said, irritated.

"Killed? Heaven forbid!" replied the doctor, and he winked at the priest.

Sensing that the doctor and his sister were on the verge of arguing, Father Arena stood up to take his leave: he would be late for his appointment with Pietro Fatta. The doctor saw him to the door; they agreed that they would see each other again to talk some more, and the doctor said, winking again, "Remember, Father, these things come in threes!"

Pietro Fatta had forgotten about Father Arena's visit, so hectic had the last hours been. Margherita Fatta took the priest into her little parlour, apologizing for her husband's delay and saying that he had received an unexpected visitor. She was on tenterhooks, for she had just talked on the telephone to her cousin Adriana, who was heavyhearted about the umpteenth misfortune to befall her children. She herself had even been struck on the arm by a collapsing bookshelf in her husband's study. Father Arena listened to her sympathetically, and they took comfort in bringing each other up to date.

Pietro Fatta joined them, explaining that his lateness was due to a matter in connection with the Alfallipes. He asked the priest to wait another half hour, but, surprised by his own boldness, Father Arena refused. "Chairman Fatta, I would like to speak to you for a few minutes in private."

Margherita excused herself so they could be alone. Pietro Fatta spoke quickly, betraying a certain irritation at the priest's request. "There is a certain Risico, a Communist, who works in the post office. He is married to signora Pecorilla's shop assistant, whom perhaps you know. Well, this Risico has ascertained that on the twenty-fifth of every month Mennulara received money from a Swiss bank, whose clients include certain important mafiosi, and he has a theory: that there exists nothing less than a secret alliance between Massimo Leone and Mennulara under the aegis of the mafia. Today, he found that someone had destroyed the engine of his car, a Fiat Seicento, by pouring cement into it. Neither he nor that spineless boss of his knows which saint to turn to." On hearing this expression, Father Arena could not suppress an ironic smile: perhaps it contained a profound truth. "The manager of the post office tells me that Risico wants to involve the police, and to bring a suit against Carmela for a series of offences committed at the post office. This Risico is even talking about mafia gangs, drug and arms trafficking; in short, he is raving, and so the manager sent him to me to see if I could get him to change his mind. He is in my study now, with his wife. I don't know how to calm him down and persuade him to keep quiet. For Orazio's children, it would be a disaster, and for him, too," added the chairman, who was obviously worried.

Father Arena gave him a brief account of what the Masculos had seen, and of the suspicion that Orazio Alfallipe had purchased items stolen from tombs or archaeological digs. Could it be that Mennulara was in some way involved in smuggling antiquities and that this might explain the connection with the Swiss bank?

"I would rule that out; I would have noticed. Orazio and I were very close, and he couldn't have concealed it from me. I know that he had dealings with certain country folk— he would buy the finds they turned up in their fields when their hoes struck a slab over a tomb. Perhaps he even dealt with a few grave robbers, but I don't think he was involved in the sort of trafficking you describe. I also know that Mennulara used to help him catalogue the finds, and she asked me to write some letters for her, usually to the Regional Museum, to have them identified. Yet, it would be a plausible explanation, and perhaps even acceptable for Risico."

Father Arena recalled the letter Lilla had dropped in the street and he gave it to Pietro. There, this was the second thing he had done that he ought to be ashamed of and maybe ought to confess—both of them attempts to protect

Mennulara. And the Lord God would forgive him for his affection for her; he was sure of that.

Pietro read it and gave it back to him. "This explains a lot, but not everything. Mennulara must have bought some fakes, believing them to be genuine. Orazio used her as a front to conceal direct contacts with certain people on the fringes of the criminal world, grave robbers mostly, I'm sorry to say. Orazio's children need cash, and they must have thought to sell some pieces from the collection and then wisely decided to have them appraised first. Their hopes dashed, they destroyed them, and they must have argued too, don't you think?" With that, Pietro Fatta returned to the Risicos.

Father Arena was soon rejoined by Margherita Fatta. Baroness Ceffalia had just been on the telephone to tell her all the details of the young Alfallipes' furious row, never mind stories about collapsing bookcases. Father Arena was exhausted; he no longer felt up to comforting the lady or even to listening to her. And so he fell back on an expedient that always worked: he suggested that they recite the rosary together.

Margherita Fatta, relieved, set about the task with diligence. Father Arena intoned the Paternoster and the Ave Marias with unusual slowness, long pauses, even stammers, to make it last as long as possible. This was how Pietro Fatta found them when he came back after saying good-bye to the Risicos: Margherita kneeling on a cushion, her eyes fixed on the image of the Virgin above the chest of drawers, Father Arena in an armchair, his gaze sometimes anxious, sometimes blank. They were all tired, and by common consent they decided that the visit should end there. This time, Father Arena gladly accepted Pietro Fatta's invitation to come to lunch the following day.

42. Monday is a heavy day for the Risicos

Signora Pecorilla and her shop assistant, Elvira Risico, were hard at work in the bookshop, crowded with schoolchildren and their parents. There was a lot of shouting—bored children picking up books at random, looking at the covers and putting them back higgledy-piggledy, listlessly answering their parents' questions. They chattered away with their classmates and chewed gum, the latest craze among the young, while their parents brandished the list of textbooks to be bought, shouting and complaining about their prices. They leafed through the pages of secondhand books, pointing out the scribbles made by previous owners, demanding discounts and jostling to get ahead of the other customers. The telephone next to the till rang, but it was drowned out by the noise of the customers. "I'm busy, Gasparu'," said Elvira apologetically.

"Just to tell you that the reply confirms my predictions. See you at lunch."

Under signora Pecorilla's reproving gaze, Elvira returned to the customers with a broad smile on her face.

Elvira was late for lunch, as she had first to get the bookshop ready for the next invasion of children and parents. Gaspare was already home, restlessly pacing up and down in the living room. He gave her a distracted kiss. "We have a really big problem. There's no way I would ever have believed that the note from my colleague in Milan would be intercepted in the post office, but clearly it was. I received it in a sealed envelope—I'm sure of that—and I tore it up into tiny pieces and threw it in the bin. All it said was, 'The answer to your enquiry is affirmative. Watch out.' So whoever read it knew about my conversation with my colleague. Then, late this morning, I went to get the car to go to the office in Roccacolomba Nuova, but it wouldn't start. I opened the bonnet and saw the engine was covered with cement, already hardened. It looked like a modern sculpture."

Elvira listened to him openmouthed. Gaspare noticed her shock but continued: "You have to respond to this kind of intimidation, so I went to the manager. He panicked and begged me not to speak of it to anyone, not to report it. He even asked me, as a personal favour, to discuss the affair with Chairman Fatta."

"What's he got to do with it?" asked Elvira, interrupting him.

"What's he got to do with it? He's one of those capitalists who hasn't done a single day's work in his life, but he was a friend of Orazio Alfallipe and knows everyone. Fatta is a powerful man, and that moron of a manager had already told him about signora Leone and the letters, and so he wanted me to talk to the chairman before doing my duty and reporting the Leone woman and those bastards who ruined my new car! This is intolerable, an infringement of my rights as an employee and a citizen."

Gaspare's eyes were gleaming, his fists thrust deep into his pockets. He would have split the jacket lining had Elvira not gently taken his hands between hers, looking at him straight in the eye, and said with calm determination, "We must give him what he wants. He has always been obliging with you, he respects you, and I think he wishes you well. I'll come with you to the chairman's place; I have to take some books to him." Elvira glimpsed a sign of agreement on Gaspare's lips and she went off to the kitchen, whence she continued: "We can postpone lodging a complaint against signora Leone, but we must report the damage to the car." She reappeared in the doorway, resting her forearm against the doorjamb, and said seriously, "Gasparu', call the manager. Let's make an appointment with Chairman Fatta right away, and then let's eat."

"He's expecting us at four o'clock," murmured Gaspare.

"These things happen, but you've solved the puzzle and I'm proud of you. Chairman Fatta will be surprised about it, too, you'll see," and she added, "Now let's make lunch, and then I'll call signora Pecorilla."

This was one of the rare occasions on which Gaspare Risico helped his wife set the table. He even dressed the green salad, rather than watch her as she busied herself in the kitchen. They left home in the early afternoon, passing by the bookshop to pick up the books to be delivered to Chairman Fatta. On the way, Elvira took her husband's arm, and she didn't let it go until they reached Fatta House—all the way up the steep steps of Roccacolomba, through the winding little streets and the narrow alleyways, chattering all the time to distract him and cheer him up. When she felt

Gaspare's hand pressing against her hip, she knew she had succeeded.

Chairman Fatta welcomed the Risicos in person. He showed them into his study and thanked Elvira for the copies of D'Annunzio she had brought him. Won over by his charm and in no way intimidated, she started to talk about new editions and rare books, giving Pietro Fatta a chance to observe her taciturn and clearly worried husband. They were interrupted by Lucia: signora Fatta needed urgently to talk to her husband. Fatta apologised profusely and went off. On his return, he found them looking out over the balcony, holding each other tightly. He was touched by them. He wanted to talk privately with Gaspare Risico, so he proposed to Elvira, with a courtesy that overwhelmed her, that she take a seat in the drawing room and look at some old books they had talked about before.

"Please tell me, signor Risico, without leaving out any details, about the enquiries you made in the post office about signorina Inzerillo," began Pietro Fatta.

"What enquiries?" replied Gaspare, suspicious of Fatta's studied deference towards his wife and, perhaps, in his heart of hearts, jealous.

"Let's talk frankly about it. We are meeting because your manager has told me about you and the damage done to your car." Pietro Fatta assumed a serious, purposeful tone. "None of us has time to waste. To show my good faith, I shall talk first. I am very worried about the three Alfallipe children. Their father was my best friend and their mother is my wife's first cousin. I'd like to know why they are acting so obtusely after the death of their servant, but I'd also like to know why others, like you, are acting in a way that at the moment is merely annoying the mafia but that soon might very well make them angry." Pietro Fatta stiffened and continued. "In that event, you, signor Risico, would disappear, or you'd end up a corpse in some field. If you want the two of us to try to understand something about this together and to come to a solution, I am at your disposal. My aim is to prevent the children of my best friend from continuing to behave in an indecorous and irrational manner, placing their lives in jeopardy and saddening their mother. What is yours?"

Gaspare appreciated the chairman's frankness. And so he explained his theory about Massimo Leone: that there was a mafia plan, in which Inzerillo and Leone had had precise roles to play, to introduce drug trafficking to Roccacolomba, as had already happened in the cities, and then to control and expand the building business around the town. He wanted to collaborate with the state to upset these plans.

"Can you explain why the mafia is supposed to have such a strong interest in the construction business in Roccacolomba particularly?"

"Chairman, you know that the mafia is under pressure in the big cities, where the law is likely to crack down hard. And so it's fallen back on small towns and will later return to the attack." It was obvious that Gaspare was repeating what he had learned in the Party branch office, but he did so with passion.

"What makes you think that it is under pressure and losing power?"

"You just have to read the papers—read and understand them, obviously. There are people who are rebelling, who don't want to bend the knee to the mafia. And we must support them. At the trial of Tommaso Natale, Pietro Messina's widow offered to testify against her husband's murderers, but then she was forced to retract because they threatened her and her children. But others will succeed. Our members of parliament, the Communist ones, are hammering the government with questions. We in Sicily want work, development—we want a future, Chairman."

Pietro Fatta liked this young idealist. He thought of asking him if he had any children, but he didn't. "I see. You want to change the world," he said. "Good for you."

"Sicily, Chairman. I want to change Sicily. Work, water, development, justice. I believe in justice," said Gaspare with a certain emphasis. But he was careful not to appear too ardent, for he didn't want to turn Pietro Fatta into an adversary. "I believe in the struggle against extortion, against corruption, I am fighting for the right to work, for equality among citizens. For these principles, I am prepared to make sacrifices and even to run risks."

Pietro Fatta thought of his dutiful and reliable son Giacomo. He was a good, conscientious cattle farmer, a shrewd manager and an affectionate son, father, and husband. He was different from this young man standing before him now, reciting his credo so passionately. Chairman Fatta would have liked to know him better, but he knew this was unlikely.

"Allow me to set forth my thoughts about signorina Inzerillo and Leone with you," said the chairman, adopting a calm and serious tone to restrain his new and unexpected emotions, "starting from the premise that signorina Inzerillo enjoyed the protection of the mafia. I will hazard a guess that would explain this messy business. First, she was a customer of their principal Swiss bank, as you discovered. So she was well connected. Second, she received probably large sums of money through the post, which implies that one of your colleagues in Roccacolomba, a mafioso, must have checked to ensure that there was no pilfering and that the postal service was punctual and efficient in the case of signorina Inzerillo. Third, she gave part of her money to the three Alfallipes. Fourth, a famous and powerful mafioso was seen at her funeral. Fifth, a postal employee, you, signor Risico, makes discreet enquiries and finds the engine of his car destroyed."

Chairman Fatta balled the hand on which he had counted out his five key points into a fist and held it that way. "Now I'm going to give you proof of my utmost trust by disclosing information that few others possess. All I ask is that you keep it to yourself, and refrain from talking about it even to your wife." From his balled fist he snapped out his thumb and recommenced: "Sixth, the manager of the post office receives a warning not to take any interest in signorina Inzerillo's correspondence, which is why he came to me last week. Seventh, I learned this afternoon that the garden of a local worthy was destroyed, probably because he had made offensive remarks about the late signorina Inzerillo. Eighth, Massimo Leone's car was damaged after he accused signorina Inzerillo of having been the lover of mafiosi. Ninth, the Alfallipes, in their search for money, convinced themselves that some of the antiquities purchased by signorina Inzerillo were valuable, and they took them to an expert to have their authenticity confirmed. On learning that the vases were fakes, they destroyed everything that my friend Orazio had collected—objects of little value perhaps—and even came to blows among themselves. These events occurred today. This last piece of news has opened up a whole new perspective on the situation. If you wish, call your wife and I shall explain my theory to both of you."

Elvira chose the chair next to her husband, and Pietro Fatta, still standing, began to talk. "Signora Risico, I apologise for my apparent discourtesy towards you, but it was necessary. Now I would like to tell you about signorina Inzerillo, known to us as Mennulara." Elvira settled down to listen, fascinated.

"Left an orphan, she supported her ailing elder sister with her wages as a maid. She went into service at Alfallipe House as a girl, and the late signora Lilla, who took a liking to her, protected her. She had someone give signorina Inze- rillo lessons, and the maid learned to read, although not to write. She was intelligent and willing, and she helped her mistress a great deal, particularly in the administration of the family properties. After signora Lilla's death she became de facto manager of the Alfillipes' estates, a task she performed successfully. She also helped Orazio Alfallipe, my dearest friend, in his hobby of collecting. Orazio was a man of eclec- tic interests, including, for a while, the antiquities that he acquired from grave robbers. I did not approve of his con- duct, but I am not here to pass judgement. Well," he said, taking a breath, "Mennulara therefore assisted my friend in the purchase of stolen antiquities—obtained, as far as I know, from people from Riberese who pretended to be selling vegetables. Perhaps that was how she came into contact with the mafiosi who control that market.

"I imagine that, in exchange for antiquities—or fakes, as they apparently were—she agreed to act as a front on behalf of certain mafiosi. Mennulara received post, cash, and documents intended for others and kept a part as payment for her services. Having become a small cog in the mafia machine, she was an untouchable, like the others. This hypothesis would explain the presence of a mafia boss at her funeral, as a sign not only of respect but of power. It would also explain her evident access to cash and her generosity towards the Alfallipes, whom she treated as if they were her own children.

"The Alfallipes, I hate to admit, are what they are: incompetent, grasping, presumptuous, and ignorant, a sad example of a family that could have made a positive contribution to the life of Roccacolomba but didn't. All they want to do is go on exploiting Mennulara's generosity, and so they sent Carmela, the most brainless of the three, to the post office. Fortunately, the clerks and you, signor Risico, refused to grant her requests."

Elvira took Gaspare's hand and clutched it tightly in her lap, never taking her eyes off Chairman Fatta.

"I have not mentioned Massimo Leone. Believe me, no responsible employer, far less the mafia, would consider him worthy of even the most insignificant position. He is a good-for-nothing who talks too much. He won't beat Carmela to death—I'm sure of that—for he is also a coward. I am amazed"—and he looked young Gaspare straight in the eye—"I am amazed that an intelligent, shrewd person like you could have made a blunder, if I may be permitted to define it as such, so colossal as to demonise Leone."

Gaspare did nothing but nod slightly, as if he had already thought it over and drawn his own conclusions.

"He has nothing to do with Mennulara, whom I knew well and respected. She was coarse and aggressive, perhaps to establish her authority, but with children and invalids she could be patient and delicate. I'll tell you another thing: Mennulara abhorred physical violence. She never wanted to meet Leone because they say that he had once raped a woman." Chairman Fatta waited to let the effect of this revelation sink in.

"If you don't want to withdraw the complaint against Carmela, at least consider the consequences. Signorina Inzerillo was protected by the mafia, and you could end up getting killed, a pawn in a game bigger than you are."

Pietro Fatta opened the French doors that gave on to the terrace and invited the couple to follow him.

"On the other hand, as for the damage to the car," he continued, "it is right to report it to the police. They receive plenty of these complaints against persons unknown, which go to make up the statistics that will be used by all the political parties—including your own, signor Risico—to earmark subsidies and increase public spending in the struggle against crime, funds that will wind up, through channels known to and protected by the system, in the pockets of the people who pour cement into cars owned by young working families, and in the even greedier pockets of their masters.

"I like you, signor Risico, and I would like you to live a long life. Forget the Alfallipe, Leone, and Inzerillo families and carry on with your work. I am referring not only to your job in the post office but also to your well-known political commitment."

Signor Fatta avoided looking Gaspare in the eye, sure that he would betray his affection. He leaned against the balustrade, and all three stood absently contemplating the jasmine clinging to the wisteria branches against the stone walls of the house, but their thoughts were far away.

"I admire your courage," continued signor Fatta, "I who am not courageous. I didn't rebel against the rigid social system I was born into. I didn't even try to persuade my parents to let me pursue the course of studies that would have been congenial to me. Dutifully conformist, I stayed here, in the family home, to look after our property, as my forefathers had. I belong to another world, and you would say I am an exponent of the Right. No matter how I may regret this, I can't be anything else."

The coming sunset made itself felt. The scent of the jasmine grew stronger. A rosy, sensuous light illuminated Roccacolomba, gently touching the cast-iron tables and chairs on the terrace and tracing arabesques of shadow on the blue-and-white majolica floor.

"You see, signor Risico," said Pietro Fatta, turning towards the familiar panorama spread out before him, "I think a change is necessary, and it will come. I don't know when, but it will come. I don't even know if it will be the one you are hoping for. The fact is, it's not simple to know the enemy. Take a little look at this town of ours. The Palazzo Brogli has been a ruin for decades now, an empty shell. Only we notice this, from this terrace, and no one else. It looks solid and imposing. Some people want to take it over and restore it. Some want to make it a centre for cultural services, for the community. But it really doesn't exist any more. Its power is almost a mirage, an illusion. Sometimes I amuse myself by imagining it caving in on itself and disappearing, like the island of Ferdinandea." He smiled. It was a sketchy smile, almost a frown. "The Leones and signorina Inzerillo do not deserve your energies. Think of other things, pursue your convictions, but don't concern yourself with these people."

"But Chairman, you too can do much," said Elvira all in one breath.

"Thank you, signora Risico, but that's not so." Pietro Fatta turned towards her husband. "I have learned to practise the art of the feasible. The feasible, do you see? My goal is a moderate contentment, but one that lasts—my granddaughters, the Farmers' Association meetings, and my study, where I satisfy the mind and the senses with books. And here, from my box at the opera, I have the privilege of this ultimate beauty."

That evening, at dinner, Elvira commented, "But you were afraid. When I came back home, I realised right away that you weren't my usual Gaspare. These are terrible experiences . . . You were brave not to panic. I wouldn't have managed that." Her stomach was still in knots, and she felt slightly nauseous. "We'll get over this nasty experience together."

"Afraid? For me, not in the slightest—for you, yes, a lot, and for our future children, a great deal. For you, sweetness of my life, I was worried." Gaspare was finally pulling himself together, and he gave her the first caress of the day, a chaste pinch on the cheek. Elvira smiled. She got up from the table and gave him a long tomato-flavoured kiss.

Tuesday 1 October 1963

✖✖

43. Another letter from Mennulara arrives at Alfallipe House

Signora Alfallipe and her daughters were in the drawing room. They had awakened at dawn, after a bad night which had left them exhausted. Now they were waiting for Santa to bring their morning coffee. They were drained after the previous day's orgy of destruction, then the laborious task of tidying up the study to some extent, throwing away the broken pieces, covering up the evidence of the quarrel and the ensuing painful arguments.

During the evening, the three children had forced their mother to make some decisions. They had to sort out where she was going to live and how to protect Carmela. It was decided that signora Alfallipe would remain in Roccacolomba, where she would live either in her daughter's home or in Alfallipe House, where Carmela would join her if she separated from Massimo to safeguard herself and her property. Mennulara's flat would be sold and the money would be used to have work done on Alfallipe House. Lilla would return to Rome, taking the two remaining fake amphorae with her, and Gianni would go back to Catania. They would keep in touch by telephone. It was clear that neither of them wanted to continue the strict routine of visits to their mother on which Mennulara had insisted.

There was nothing else to be done, apart from forgetting Mennulara, her nastiness, and the whole ugly business. They would not speak badly of her, for obvious reasons; in any case, the source of her mysterious wealth and the reason for her mafia protection had not been discovered. "We must be careful," said Carmela, looking severely at her mother. "Watch out with my maid, and remember that what happened to us is a just punishment for those who are overly familiar with servants."

Santa came in with the coffee and the post. Lilla opened the letters, mostly condolences, and passed them to Carmela and her mother. There was an envelope with a typewritten address. She opened it absently, assuming it was a bank statement or a bill. Instead, it was another letter from Mennulara:

You did well to do as I said. Now you have a certificate that allows you to take eight Greek vases out of the country. Take them back home, if you haven't already done so, and go into your father's study. Open the shelf facing the one from which you took the eight crates. Behind the fake door are eight vases identical to the fakes. They are authentic. I had copies made in order to get a certificate that would allow you to export and sell them.

Replace the fake vases with the real ones, and take them to Zurich within two weeks of today. Phone the Archaeological Museum in Zurich right away and say that you want to make an appointment and that signor Mennulara has sent you. They are expecting you. You may decide whether to sell or keep them.

The curator of the museum knows my bank manager; you can talk to him about my estate, which you now deserve because you have obeyed. Do as he advises you.

"Here, read this," said Lilla, handing the letter to Carmela, and she burst into tears.

44. Father Arena calls on signora Alfallipe and sees the destruction of Orazio Alfallipe's collection

Father Arena was nervous on his arrival at Alfallipe House late that Tuesday morning. He found signora Adriana alone and dejected. She told him that Lilla and Gianni had left and that she was resigned to living with Carmela, whose marriage was on the rocks. She was disappointed in her children and missed Mennulara. Not knowing how to comfort her, Father Arena thought to reassure her by saying that the volumes of D'Annunzio were finally in Pietro Fatta's hands.

Signora Alfallipe brightened up and she took him to the study right away so that he could choose some other books. The priest reluctantly entered Orazio Alfallipe's study. The signs of destruction were evident, though the room had been tidied up. The upper shelves of the bookcase, where the rows of Orazio's old volumes had once stood, were empty, while those that had escaped the devastation—books that Mennulara had proudly arranged, by author, for literature and by subject for art—were in piles on the lower shelves. The handsome pottery pieces that once stood on the shelves had vanished, as had the objects on the tables and the silverware displayed on the piano. The room had been violated. Behind the piano, a dozen or so jute sacks that were usually used for storing almonds were piled.

Father Arena had the feeling that he had already witnessed this sort of devastation before when, during the war, he had visited a church desecrated by vandals. This study was the chapel that Mennulara had wanted to dedicate to what she believed in—knowledge, beauty, and who knows, perhaps even love—he thought, and now it languished, defiled. Father Arena, ashamed of this blasphemous thought, concentrated on selecting books to take home with him.

Signora Adriana waited, leaning against the sofa in front of the fireplace that faced the balcony looking onto the Masculos' living room. Her image was reflected in the big mirror that hung at a slight tilt over the mantelpiece. Father Arena recalled the description of the naked woman glimpsed in the study, and he felt ill at ease and excited at the same time. He wanted to get out of that room full of shadows and suggestions, and so he grabbed some books at random and went back to the living room.

In the meantime, Dr. Mendicò had come to call, but he didn't stay long. Signora Alfallipe took comfort in discovering hitherto unknown qualities in her Mennù. "That's what she was doing, every afternoon, closed up in Orazio's study, after his death . . . She was studying Greek art, carrying on my husband's work. I wonder why I never noticed this affinity between them; perhaps not even he realised. Mennù was very reserved. You won't find such a devoted person today in all of Roccacolomba. I said as much to my children—'Trust Mennù'—but young people don't listen to their parents the way they used to." Other visitors arrived, and the signora and the priest took leave of each other.

45. Father Arena takes a long walk with Dr. Mendicò

Since their conversation the previous day, Father Arena and Dr. Mendicò had developed that close and complicitous relationship that sharing a secret instinctively creates among men. They decided to take a stroll before lunch.

For a whole day now, Dr. Mendicò had given himself no rest. Having never given thorough consideration to Orazio's death, it was important for him to find out more about Mennulara, and he explained this to the priest: "I knew they had had intimate relations. I thought it had all finished with the abortion, before the war."

Father Arena was surprised. "I'm sorry, poor woman, I didn't know she'd had an abortion too."

"It was the tragedy of her life. She was about twenty-five; she was brimming with energy, and she devoted herself enthusiastically to the three children. Carmela had just been born. As always in these cases, Orazio's name was never mentioned, but it was obvious that he was the father. I imagine that, bored with his wife, he turned with excessive enthusiasm to Mennulara, who I must admit was in the flower of her youth. She wanted to be sterilised, and signora Lilla, who was with her, didn't try to dissuade her." The doctor tried to relate the events as succinctly as possible, aware that he was divulging information that had come to him as a professional confidence.

Father Arena thought he should explain the probable reason that Mennulara had never talked to him about the abortion. "We had a big row, the only one in many years of friendship, and after it we both agreed that we wouldn't talk again of Orazio Alfallipe in this context."

"What row?"

"You see, I met her when she started working at Alfallipe House. I used to give her lessons in Italian and arithmetic. She learned what she needed to know right away, and we spent the rest of the time talking about all the things that interested her—she was extraordinarily intelligent. She felt like a prisoner in Alfallipe House, and she had a lot of anger inside."

"Against whom?"

"First and foremost, God. I encouraged her to read books of prayer, but she refused. One day, she said to me, 'My mother taught me that we are all equal, me, you, and the queen, only you are a priest, the queen is the queen in her palace, and I am a maid in Alfallipe House. If we do our duty, we earn the respect of others. God has His duty like everyone else. He must think of us, help the good and punish the evil. I don't like God. His duty towards my parents, who are dead, and my sister, Addoloratina, who is still unwell, was to ensure that they didn't lack bread and medicine. And He didn't do that. He was unjust to me, and injustices must be paid for sooner or later. If He doesn't do His duty, then He doesn't deserve my prayers.' From this sprang her aversion to our social and economic order, the rich, who inherit money and power without having earned them, and the poor, who have no chance to study and learn.

"In short, she was a true revolutionary as a young woman, an iconoclast. Nonetheless, she accepted her fate, the life that her mother had preordained for her: she had to be a maid to signora Lilla and the other Alfallipes, to watch over the honour of the family until death, so that the lady would pay for the medicine her ailing sister needed. And she had to save her wages for Addoloratina's trousseau, find her a husband, and look after her children. As for herself, she had to be content with the pleasures obtainable within those limits."

"What does this have to do with Orazio?"

"As a girl, Mennulara had a great need of love and was a sensual creature, but always a rational one. Her intimate relationship with Orazio, especially at first, represented something special: it was a weapon with which to oblige signora Lilla to look after her sister, who had been put in the convent orphanage. As you know, signora Lilla forbade Addoloratina to set foot in Alfallipe House, for fear of contagion, and so the two orphan girls saw each other only rarely, when Mennulara visited the convent."

The doctor said, "I told signora Lilla many times that Addoloratina was no longer contagious. I found that prohibition cruel and stupid. I recall a conversation with Mennulara that broke my heart. She was barely fifteen, and one day she asked to speak to me alone. She told me in that solemn tone of hers that she had some savings. She wanted me to promise to warn her if her sister's health declined and if I needed money to buy her medicines; she would pay. But this wasn't necessary, because signora Lilla paid generously for her treatment—which surprised me, too, knowing her stinginess." Then he added, "Father, allow me to say that I don't see how she could have blackmailed her mistress—she, an orphan alone in the world . . . in those days it being almost customary for the young master to take advantage of young serving girls."

"Had it not been for signora Lilla's obsessive fear that Orazio and Vincenzo would come to the same end as their father. Try to see it that way," Father Arena suggested.

The doctor understood. "Venereal diseases, caused by poor, sick prostitutes." They were on the same wavelength once more.

"Precisely. For her elder son and favourite, she found, if I may put it like this, a clean whore there at home, but the whore nevertheless could have denied her services . . . It was in this that Mennulara's power rested," said Father Arena.

"I refused to believe that Mennulara, as I knew her, could have accepted a situation of that kind," said the doctor, resisting Father Arena's laconic portrayal.

"Dr. Mendicò, I too loved Mennulara, and I respected her. Listen. I will repeat her very words, the words that were the reason for our fight."

By now they had left the main street of Roccacolomba and were far from curious ears; the conversation flowed freely. Father Arena spoke vehemently, heedless of the stammering that occasionally slowed him down. "Try to understand. You know about the abortion—of which I was unaware. But I know the tumults of the soul, which are as complex as illnesses in the bodies you treat. I must add another thing: Mennulara had an enquiring mind, though she was shy and reserved and was merely a maid. She felt ill at ease with the other servants and was profoundly alone. Her curiosity could be satisfied only by knowledge obtained through books. For her, Orazio was the sole means of attaining that end. I saw his study today. In that room, she found a world of equals—she, a maid without a family, confined in

Alfallipe House. She was young, too, and had no fear of God. She accepted Orazio's attentions, or she seduced him, or perhaps it was a youthful love requited. I don't know. She knew that for him she was one of many playthings, whereas for her Orazio represented freedom of thought and her only chance to learn. Moreover, we know how weak the flesh can be. And as I said, she had no religious constraints."

"I see," murmured the doctor. "Also, she played a role that was—how can I put it?—prophylactic, and thus certainly welcome to signora Lilla, who was obsessed with health. And that's why she gave Mennulara a purse full of gold coins and didn't oppose the sterilisation."

"Precisely, so long as Orazio's desires continued to be satisfied by her and not by prostitutes, potential carriers of disease," continued Father Arena bitterly. "Our argument occurred because an old cook at Alfallipe House, now dead, had scruples about this and talked to me about it. This woman had known many men. She was one of those with a fire under her skirts, but on the face of things she was God-fearing, and what's more she cooked very well, better than a chef. She had taken Mennulara under her wing and spoke to her freely, even about certain activities that are harmful to the health and about others that are against nature. She regretted this and worried that the girl, sixteen at the time, might end up by doing these things with Orazio. I talked about this with Mennulara because, frankly, I was worried too. She made a terrific scene, one of those that made her many enemies. She told me that her destiny was to stay in Alfallipe House and to serve the masters. She didn't want to moulder away for a lifetime without enjoying what she had at her disposal, and that was precious little. Orazio was kind and he respected her as a lover; if she said no he would accept. That was her job, and she wanted to do it well, and in that, too, she wanted to improve. At the same time, she needed to safeguard her health. If Orazio lost interest in her, he might go off to look for whores and she would run the risk of contagion. And she had to look after her health." Father Arena mumbled, for these were painful memories.

Dr. Mendicò was thinking out loud. "The relationship continued, therefore, during Orazio's marriage, as is proven by the abortion. At the time, I had the courage to talk to her about it as her doctor. I wanted to persuade her not to get sterilised. She might have married and had a family. But she was indignant, almost as if I had suggested adultery. Her behaviour was like that of a loving wife. It was the only way, she said, to keep the relationship alive. But Orazio, at that very time, got involved in one of his most passionate relationships, followed by others, as we know. After that, Mennulara withered like a flower without water"—he looked at the priest—"but you tell me that according to Angelo Masculo, there was an intense relationship between them in the last years of his life."

"Now I understand why Mennulara changed then," said Father Arena. "She worried me. She was closed up in herself, and she had lost her love of life, but not her energy and will. The only thing she kept up was singing in the choir at the church of the Addolorata, to which I had introduced her as a young girl. She was a good singer and would stand with the nuns, far from the eyes of others. Only for brief moments was she serene. Perhaps Orazio would go back to her, in the intervals between one mistress and another, or maybe the cook's teachings held an enduring attraction for him. I really don't know. Or perhaps she had got him out of her head, having finally understood that he was unworthy of her."

"There's no doubt he wasn't in the same class as Mennulara," agreed Dr. Mendicò.

"You know I used to write letters for her," said Father Arena. "We were very close and saw each other often, until I left the parish. Mennulara was grateful to Orazio for having helped her acquire a knowledge of art, letters, and music. She was enthusiastic about his crazes. I don't know if you are aware of this, but she also put his collections in order, learning to catalogue them and reading texts, even abstruse ones, to help him. She was disappointed every time Orazio dropped things half-finished to devote himself to some other interest. I believe she continued to study Greek pottery on her own for years. She was, believe me, the most intelligent person I ever met."

Now they were on a narrow track, almost in open countryside; they took a breather and sat down on a low stone wall.

Father Arena continued: "Mennulara discussed with me whether it would be fitting for her to take on the family's administration, to save them from economic disaster; she felt it was her duty towards signora Lilla and the Alfallipe family. She spoke with detachment and tolerance of Orazio's amours, mentioning the expensive presents he continued to give his lady friends—her behaviour was like that of a tired wife who is no longer hurt by a husband's betrayals. Frankly, I was worried about the burden she was planning to shoulder, apart from her work as a maid, and I was afraid of how people might react, especially on the estates, if a servant became an administrator. I was afraid for her.

"She told me, 'My duty is to serve them, and I can handle it. I wasn't the one who chose masters who are my inferiors. But they're still the masters, and I'm destined to be their servant.' "

Dr. Mendicò said, "We don't know if she loved him like a betrayed and tolerant wife, or like a lover, or like a servant grateful for having gained access to the world of culture. What remains beyond a doubt is her devotion to Orazio and, I believe, the truth of what Angelo Masculo saw. If she killed him, she must have done it thinking of his good."

"May the Lord forgive her," replied Father Arena. On remembering that he was a man and a sinner as well, he thought that he too ought to ask forgiveness for having sullied Orazio's memory when talking with Masculo the day before, trying to protect Mennulara's reputation.

"That leaves the mystery of her money. Sometimes I think it's an exaggeration on the Alfallipes' part and that she had only a little put by," murmured the doctor.

"Given that we're telling each other all the secrets, Doctor, I'll tell you another. She was rich, and had been for some time. I have no idea where her money came from, but I wrote a lot of letters to the bank for her. And she was generous. Just think, she paid for my godson's studies for seven years . . . No one knows that, and she helped other people in secret."

The long walk had led them far away. They returned to

Roccacolomba, each one immersed in his own thoughts, walking in silence.

46. Orazio Alfallipe's letter to Pietro Fatta

Chairman Fatta was sunk in his armchair in the study, his legs spread out, his hands hanging loosely from the armrests. In his right hand he held some sheets of paper covered in minuscule, almost illegible handwriting. He was looking out of the balcony, his gaze lost in the distance. He gave a start when Lucia's voice announced the arrival of Father Arena, and gathered together the pages of Orazio's letter, which had slipped out of one of the copies of D'Annunzio brought to him by signora Risico, and prepared to receive the priest.

Lilla Alfallipe had called to tell him, with a certain embarrassment, that they had received a second letter from Mennulara, in which she said where the authentic amphorae were. They were unfortunately the ones she and her siblings had broken the day before, thinking they were yet more fakes. The tension and recriminations among them had led to renewed bickering, and now Lilla was going back to Rome. She asked him to look after Carmela and her mother.

Pietro Fatta was a calm, dignified man. He now needed to get things off his chest, to ask advice, to talk about Mennulara and Orazio—in short, to understand. He talked at length with Father Arena, discussing his friend's letter as if making a confession. The priest said enough to comfort him, but no more. Father Arena asked only one question: "Tell me, Chairman, do you think that Mennulara was in love with Orazio?"

"I don't know, and, from what Orazio wrote to me, he didn't know, either. I've been racking my brains about that too."

"Don't think about it. We shall never know. What's done is done. May God rest both their souls," concluded the priest, and they went out onto the terrace to wait for lunch to be served.

When Father Arena took his leave, Pietro Fatta reread the letter.

Dearest Pietro,

You will receive this letter after my death and after that of the woman for whose sake I lied to you. With old age almost upon me, I have found happiness in the extraordinary encounter with the woman who has always been with me, the steadfast household god and muse of my long years of indolence. She didn't want me to talk to you about our love, but she has allowed me to write to you about it. I thus revive the intense communion of spirit on which our friendship rested and which made life in Roccacolomba tolerable and even pleasant for us.

I have led an idle life, shunning responsibility, like a provincial lounge lizard, frittering away the family estate due to my neglect and prodigality. I have had numerous lovers, of whom you know. I have cultivated my literary, artistic, and musical interests in a fickle and superficial way, while enjoying an undeserved reputation as a cultured man. I die after having lived a life that one might be content with but not proud of. I was able to do all this thanks to the tireless devotion of the woman I love.

I have described her to you as the adolescent who initiated me into the pleasures of the flesh; after this, she took on the role of the woman with whom I would occasionally resume an exclusively sexual relationship, one that was totally satisfactory for both of us but only when I felt like doing so.

I have also described her to you as the astute and honest administrator of my property, an invaluable assistant who catalogued and organised my collections, my accomplice in engineering lies to cover my extramarital affairs, the only person who never asked me for anything and who pandered to my every wish. You know that I had blind faith in her, and with good reason. For almost thirty years we were in daily contact, in the respective roles of master and servant. But it was only five years ago that I realised that I had always loved her. Other women pale in comparison to her.

In the past, you and I discussed my affairs down to the slightest detail. A woman's seduction and conquest was our complicit pleasure. I dare not profane my true love in such a way. Out of the ties of affection that bind us, I feel duty-bound to describe to you how I fell in love as a youth and rediscovered this love in my later years. I know you will understand the rest.

We were thirteen and seventeen years old, respectively, and the seduction was mutual and gradual. Through the mists of memory, I think that she had already sensed that my attraction to her was ineluctably predestined by circumstances, allied to intellectual curiosity and sensuality, a fundamental part of her nature. At first I considered our encounter as lighthearted, sensual play; then it became love, and then a powerful physical passion.

It was at the beginning of the long school summer holiday; I was the enthusiastic owner of new prismatic binoculars. I would go up onto the terrace of the laundry room, the highest room in the house, and look at the countryside or scan the streets, terraces, and balconies of Roccacolomba. I would get settled in the most hidden corner of the terrace, protected and separated by the rows of sheets hung out to dry by the laundrywomen.

It was a particularly windy day. The washing on the lines bellied out in the wind, curled up when it puffed capriciously, and flipped over with thunderous flaps when it blew. When the wind veered, the strings used to attach the sheets and table napkins to the wires would run from one end of the line to the other, piling the wash up in huge soft tangles of white. I watched enchanted—it was a metamorphosis of nature. The sky seemed like a stormy sea, with ranks of scalloped clouds racing across it at high speed like the angry foam of surging breakers; the sheets looked like the sails of ships in danger, clustering together to protect themselves from the fury of the elements. Then it happened that a gust of wind made a breach between the rows of sheets. I saw her, slender and petite, doing some washing in the wooden washtub. Unaware of my presence and undaunted by the furious blasts, she carried on working. She was kneading the mass of washing immersed in the suds, hands in tight fists. She wrung the articles out one by one, then opened them out again and scrubbed them rhythmically on the sloping washboard, beating them against its corrugated surface, oblivious to the wind that tousled and tossed her curly hair into long tresses that swayed like the tentacles of a sea anemone. I crouched down to avoid being noticed. She was wearing a light-coloured slip, now soaked by the splashes of water. I trained the binoculars on her, bewitched by the rhythmic movements of her body, by her small, pointed breasts, and by her shapely young arms. She was beautiful.

She spotted me and with a cry abandoned the washtub and went back into the laundry. A few moments later she returned wearing her grey maid's uniform, and she set to washing again. I put down the binoculars but couldn't take my eyes off her. She carried on with her work, unperturbed. She moved to an oval washtub, into which she plunged the twisted lengths of wrung-out washing, so as to give them a vigorous rinse. She repeated this operation twice, pouring the water onto the floor and then bending over to pick up the big pitchers full of fresh water to fill the tub and then rinse again, occasionally shooting me long, truculent looks.

The wind dropped. She moved along the rows of sheets, straightening them out. Untangling the knots that had formed, she smoothed them out by flapping them in the air, then reattached them firmly to the wire lines while watching the sky-sea, which was itself once more, an intensely bright azure furrowed by banks of clouds soft as tufts of cotton wool. When she came to the last row, she looked down at me. I was still crouching in the corner. She observed me with circumspection but without fear.

"What's that?" she asked, pointing to the binoculars. I proffered them. She took them in her hands, turning them around and around. She tried to look into the wrong end.

"Teach me how to look into it," she said. She had the guttural voice and thick brogue of country people. I got up and obeyed. I held the binoculars steady in front of her eyes in order to adjust them. She gave off a pungent odour of lye that made me feel drunk, yet I didn't dare touch her. I felt she was tense. I kept my arms extended wide around her shoulders and I didn't brush her even once as I showed her where to point the instrument and turned the focus knobs.

She took the binoculars and moved around the terrace, pointing them from left to right without speaking. When she handed them back to me, she asked, "How do they work?" I explained the movements of the various knobs.

"I understand that, but how do they work? What is there inside, and how do they make things come closer to the eye?" I didn't have an answer ready.

"Read about it in a book and then tell me. I can't read and I have no books." And she went back to rinsing the wash.

I left the terrace before she finished, and as I passed by her, I stopped. She continued to knead the linen in the tub, but she turned her head towards me and waited for me to speak to her. I asked her if my presence disturbed her. All she said was, "You are the master and you can do as you wish. I am the servant here." I headed towards the door again, and as I took the stairs, she yelled after me, "If you have to come back here again, remember to find in the book how that thing works."

I went back there several times. She concentrated on her washing, always with her uniform on, even in hot weather, and she was still wary. Nevertheless, she would allow herself a few breaks to look at Roccacolomba through the binoculars and to observe the rays of light through the prism. One day, I even made an experiment with mirrors and we managed to set fire to some pieces of straw. I had studied the subject well in order to answer her questions.

I had taken to drawing, and one day I asked her if I might sketch her as she was washing. She gave me the usual answer: "You are the master and I am the servant." She looked at my sketches and was critical. She pointed out that I had joined an arm to a shoulder clumsily. I dared to suggest that if she'd worn only her slip, I could have drawn better. "No, I'd have had to stand still, and I'm here to work. Go into the red drawing room: beside the fireplace there is a picture. Look at it. On the left there is a woman in this position. Go to look at her and learn." She was right: the pose in the picture was identical. I took her my revised drawing. She laughed at it: "You're no good. Wait." She closed the laundry room door from the inside, took off her uniform, and assumed the required pose, wearing only her slip. Afterwards she put her clothes back on and carried on working, without taking the padlock off the door.

Our meetings, never planned, became frequent. I don't know how she arranged things in order to be alone, but she managed. I drew her in chaste and conventional poses. I would help her get into the desired position, and little by little I grew bold enough to touch her arms, her neck. I was not rebuffed, but I wasn't encouraged, either.

During the Christmas holiday, I wanted to reorganise one of the bookcases in the study. Two maids were assigned to help me. One day, only Mennulara was available. We worked together in silence, as if there were no other relationship between us apart from work. She climbed up the wooden library steps and I handed her the books to be set on the top shelves. At a certain point, she sat down on the second-last step, waiting for me to hand her the books. I saw her naked legs from below; her skirt had got hitched up at the back when she sat down. I stood there looking at her, stock-still, my trousers beginning to bulge. She noticed this and returned my gaze, but she didn't move. All I had the strength to say was, "Come down." We loved each other for the first time. After that the study continued as the scene of our intimacy.

I discovered the fulfilment of the senses without commitment or guilt, with a woman who asked for no explanations and made no recriminations. Our relationship was based on the equality of man and woman in sexual intercourse whose aim is the pleasure of both. The initiative came solely from me, and she was not always willing, although she seldom denied me. At times, I didn't seek her out for long periods, whole years; other times, we had sex frequently. It was a calm and secret understanding, without overt emotional involvement on either side, I thought. And you knew about it.

Five years ago I invited my mistress of long standing to my home for dinner. Mennulara knew about her, and after serving dinner, she deliberately insulted my wife and my mistress, ruining the evening. It was the first time she had behaved that way. I was furious and decided to go up to her room to reprimand her, which I had never done before. Feeling betrayed and humiliated, I went up the spiral stair to the mezzanine for the first time in my life. I sensed that it was an important moment, and I thought I would fire her, such was my anger. I found myself in a dark corridor. There was a faint sound of music. It was the end of the third act of Aida. The voice of Maria Callas was responding to the oboe in the andantino. "Fuggiam gli ardori inospiti di queste lande ignude." Stunned, I stood motionless, listening. I found myself squatting on the floor, leaning against the wall, down which my back had slid without meeting any resistance. "Là tra foreste vergini." The music continued to swell in sweeping coils, filling the entire corridor, pressing up against the walls, which opened up to transform that cramped space into a nocturnal landscape, damp and velvety, slightly scented. "Io son disonorato." I was seized by a whirl of competing emotions; I felt myself literally swooning. In my breast grew a sense of wonder that annihilated me: I had never thought of her as someone with a soul.

The door of the room at the far end suddenly opened, and the music slipped along the corridor. Another door opened and closed again. I heard water running; she was in the bathroom. Shortly after, she reemerged, and I saw her in her full splendour before she switched off the light and closed herself in her bedroom once more. She was wearing only a bathrobe, open at the front, and she struck me as beautiful, her serene face framed by her long hair hanging free. Feeling a powerful desire to enter, I went to her door, but I didn't have the courage. I was afraid she would send me away. I was the sinner. Radames. "Io son disonorato."

I stayed leaning against the wall. She got up to turn the record over. Her steps made the floorboards creak, and the door swung half open. "Già i sacerdoti adunansi." I feared the door would close again, but perhaps she had fallen asleep. I waited some more; then I gently pushed the door, which opened with a creak. "Discolpati." The leaden light of the moon fell on her bed, where she lay, covered by a light sheet. Standing in the doorway, I listened, my eyes fixed on her. "Discolpati." Her folded arm covered her face. I didn't know if she was awake or asleep. I was weeping without realising it. She noticed this, and she turned her head towards me. "Don't cry, just listen," she said. Then she covered her face again, resuming her previous position. And I listened, I listened until the arm of the gramophone lay motionless on the turntable.

It was as if I were paralysed.

"What do you want?" she asked.

"May I stay here?"

"No, tomorrow I have to get up for work. Get off to bed, because it's late for everyone."

———

That night I sobbed for a long time, lying on the sofa where we'd had our first encounters, in the study. At dawn I wrote a letter of farewell to my mistress.

I saw Mennulara again the following day; she served me my coffee as if nothing had happened. She was wearing her usual grey cotton uniform, her hairdo the same as ever, drawn up in a bun. She seemed devoid of grace and sensitivity. Even like that I loved her. I was confused and timorous as an adolescent in love for the first time, unsure of what moves to make, hopefully waiting for his beloved to encourage him. Presumably she was aware of this, because she said to me laconically, "If you wish, sir, you may come to the study after lunch." Since that day, I have found happiness.

I live for the few hours of intimacy that we are able to share, and for our studies. I would have done anything to be able to live with her, on our own, forever. I would have abandoned my home and my family. She prevented me. At first I feared that my love was unrequited, that the long years in which I neglected her had ruined everything. But she insisted that we were different: that masters see the world in a certain way and servants in another. Her entire existence proves her feelings for me, but she cannot say "I love you." She had the certainty that we would meet again but she didn't know when; for me she had furthered her study of Greek art on her own, even surpassing me. She allowed me to use the pseudonym "signor Mennulara" in our correspondence with experts, whereas I desired ardently that our names be united in public. Only the collection of Greek pottery will bear silent witness to our passion for art and to our love.

I die with the immense regret that people will not know about this woman's extraordinary qualities and my love for her.

Pietro Fatta hauled himself out of his armchair, still holding the sheets of paper. He seemed weighed down by emotion. He looked for some matches in the drawer of his desk; then he crossed the room with measured tread and without making a sound.

That year in Fatta House, they lit the fire earlier than usual.

47. In don Vito Militello's lodge, they analyse the situation

At the market, Lucia had done the Fattas' shopping in great haste in order to be able to drop in on her uncle Paolino and aunt Mimma without arousing the curiosity of Marianna, the other maid. Don Paolino was at home; Mimma had gone to the shoemaker's to pick up some shoes that had been resoled. "She'll have gone to catch up on the gossip. Uncle Giacomo's shop is in vicolo dei Gozzi," said don Paolino. "Don't wait for her. She'll be there for hours, and I won't be getting a hot meal today, either." Uncle and niece brought themselves up to date about the Alfallipes' affairs, and then Lucia went off home feeling satisfied with herself. This story was more gripping than the TV serial she was allowed to watch—from a distance—in Fatta House, her chair next to the wall, while signora Fatta sat in the front row, so to speak, in her comfortable armchair in front of the new television set.

Donna Mimma came back late, without the shoes. "He hasn't had time to work, poor soul, first on account of the ruckus the Alfallipes kicked up, then because he had to tell the story in detail to everyone who flocked to his shop and asked him to repeat what he'd heard."

"And what was that?"

"They had it in for poor Mennulara, and the things they said . . . enough to make your hair stand on end. A dishonest thief, even a whore, they called her, while the Alfallipe children and their brother-in-law called her all sorts of things themselves. Listen, let's go and eat at my sister Enza's place. We'll find out even more!"

In the porter's lodge of Palazzo Ceffalia, the four in-laws were talking fast, taking advantage of the fact that there were no visitors. That morning donna Enza had gone to help the maids tidy up the baroness's pantry, hoping to pick up some gossip. She got her reward, for the mistress had other news: the Parrinos' garden and the car belonging to the post office clerk Gaspare Risico had been vandalised: "a warning," according to the baroness, for those who had talked too much and said bad things about Mennulara.

"She didn't show up in church very often, only for the sung Masses, but she must have had a very special saint who gave her a whole lot of protection," said donna Enza.

"Sure, a saint with trousers, a flat cap, and a sawn-off shotgun," added don Vito, "while the Alfallipes must be under a curse, since nothing goes right for them. Santa dropped by not long ago, and she says that yesterday they broke everything there was to break in the master's study and then laid into one another. Today, a letter arrived that said they had broken the wrong things, and they beat one another up again. The fact is, they're a wretched bunch, and they take it out on Mennulara."

Despite the wealth of details about the Alfallipes' row, there was less talk in town about the broken vases and their origin. But don Paolino was racking his brains over the matter. "If they took those vases to the museum, it means they thought they were genuine and valuable. They must have belonged to Mennulara, so it would have been she who told them to do so. I remember them saying it was a joke at their expense, but that wasn't like Mennulara. She wasn't the kind to play tricks or practical jokes, and she wouldn't have laughed. Not her. Maybe the vases were genuine, and they read things wrong, or the museum people got it wrong in their letter."

"But why take it out on her if she made a mistake about the vases? She wasn't a professor. Even though she knew a lot for a maid," said donna Enza.

"No, you're wrong, Enza," said don Paolino. "At the time of the dig at the villa near Casale, Orazio Alfallipe was young, and he got all enthusiastic about ancient Greek things. He even set to digging near Cannelli, a beautiful property that had been sold, because they said that under the ground there was an entire ancient city. He found some potsherds and took them home. That poor soul Mennulara had to work at nights. The table in the room next to the study looked like a mosaic, for all the pieces had been put there. It was a puzzle, but she had sharp eyes and she managed to glue them together so that they seemed perfect. Then the master was taken by another craze, and the pottery fragments didn't interest him any more. But Mennulara enjoyed fixing them up, and there were plenty of them left. I even saw her looking at books with photographs. She liked them."

"Poor woman, amusing herself with broken pottery.

What a pitiful life," commented don Vito. "By the way, did you know that don Luigi Vicari died this morning?"

Don Paolino started. "Was he still alive, then?"

"Yes, he was ninety something. His grandson told me about it when he dropped in at the lodge on Wednesday. I was telling him about the funeral. He said that his grandfather was still all right in the head but was bedridden, and then he died in his sleep today. A good death!"

"A good death my foot. His daughter was telling me that he had been raving since last Thursday—he was afraid they were going to kill him . . . he died of fright. He was off his head, the poor soul," said donna Enza.

"Oh, that happens . . . But he set up a shop and he got rich," commented don Paolino. "I tell you, from now on there won't be any more talk about Mennulara and the Al-fallipes. What's been said will be forgotten, and in Rocca-colomba the name Alfallipe will disappear. They'll all go away. As long as they don't kick us out of our house, that's fine by me."

Don Vito agreed. "In this lodge, I've heard all kinds of nasty things about that poor woman—there's nothing left to make up about her. People talk far too much and understand little about her." He began his account, spelling out the sto-ries on the fingers of his left hand, one by one. "Starting with her father. They say that she was the illegitimate daughter of a mafioso, who had her raised in Alfallipe House so as to have an informer there. Others say she was a daughter of the prince of Brogli, and the late signor Alfallipe took her in to keep people quiet, and that she had a good dowry of her own given her by the prince. Then there are those who say that she was signor Alfallipe's daughter, and that the late signora Lilla put up with that humiliation and took her into the house. So that would make her the sister of Orazio Alfallipe, which was why he gave her so much power in the household. So she was a daughter to everyone except that poor devil of a real father of hers, Luigi Inzerillo—and no one says that she had protruding teeth like him, and his eyes, too. All you had to do was look at them to see that they were father and daughter. She was the spitting image of her father, she was!

"Then there's Mennulara herself. She was a spinster, but now they've lumbered her with children. Some say that Father Arena's godson isn't his housekeeper's child but Mennulara's and that she paid for his schooling. Others say that her so-called nephews, the ones on the mainland, are her children, fathered by men whose names cannot be mentioned, and that's why they don't set foot in Roccacolomba . . ."

"We know little or nothing about her," concluded don Paolino, "and that's that. The truth is, she was good at her job and liked telling people what to do, and that's where the problems started. The masters like to have good employees, but they don't like to be told what to do. If they'd listened to her, they'd be much richer today, but we remain poor and mistreated, even in death."

Wednesday 23 October 1963

✗✗

48. Don Vincenzo Ancona is rude to his wife

On the morning of Wednesday 23 October don Vincenzo Ancona, seated on a straw chair set obliquely to the kitchen table, ready to go about his business, was drinking his first coffee of the day in silence, served by his wife. It was the moment in which he prepared his work, mentally going over the recent past and the immediate future. Although he was eighty-one years old and rather corpulent, don Vincenzo was in reasonably good health; but above all, he had a tenacious memory, which was essential for him, because he read and wrote with difficulty.

His wife interrupted his train of thought. "They told me that last month you went to the funeral of a certain Inzerillo. Today is the memorial Mass for her. Who was this woman?"

"You've no business asking me questions like that. Mind your own business. See to your wretched children and get out of here!" Don Vincenzo slammed his cup on the table, making the coffee he hadn't drunk splash over the waxed tablecloth, and stamped out of the kitchen. In the entry, two men were waiting for him. At his nod, they hastened to help him put on his jacket, then opened the door, remaining silent. His black Alfa Romeo Giulietta was ready, the driver waiting to start her up for the long journey to Palermo.

Don Vincenzo was taciturn and bad-tempered through-out the trip. He even refused to make a stop at the usual mo-torway café for another coffee, and he ordered the driver to go faster. The car sped along the twisty road, winding down hairpin bends on the mountain, overtaking cars on blind turns, roaring up and down inclines as the driver cleared a path with the horn and ignored the speed limits; he had the assurance of those who know they have every right to do as they please. In that confident progress lay a tradition of power and violence with which roads, towns, and people have a sort of unwilling familiarity, a consciously vague intimacy that unceasingly opens and closes like a stage curtain. They crossed the mountains that had been the im-mense fief of the princes of Brogli, where the Anconas had been mafia bosses for generations. This route was full of nostalgic memories for don Vincenzo. It reminded him of his youth, when his father, don Giovanni Ancona, taught him the job that he later handed down to him, from father to son: like aristocratic titles, always to the firstborn son.

Only don Vincenzo lacked this joy, denied him, thanks to the imbecility of his only son, who had betrayed the rules of the honoured society out of a carnal weakness that was in-tolerable in a mafioso. True, his son had gone places and was still a man of honour, but he had had to make his way out-side Sicily, and his father had been deprived of the comfort and satisfaction of having him near and seeing him take over from him. A weak man, that's what he was, and his own flesh and blood! They passed the Cannelli estate, where Giovan-nino had committed the act that had changed his life.

Don Vincenzo let slip a blasphemous oath: "Accursed be the hands of God." His travelling companions started and looked at him; the driver slowed down nervously. "Keep going," ordered don Vincenzo. "I was thinking about my own affairs." He thrust himself backwards, leaning against the seat. He let his head fall back, put on his dark glasses, and stared at the road ahead.

His memories assaulted him. The event that had changed his son's life and had caused him and his wife immense pain had happened more than forty years earlier, but it was as if it had happened yesterday. Don Vincenzo's father had died when he was still a boy, but he had learned a lot and was well able to take his place: under the cover of being overseer for the princes of Brogli, he was the unchallenged mafia chieftain of their lands and of the adjoining estates, which belonged to bourgeois families and petty aristocrats. With good reason he was respected and feared, even outside the province. He was known to be an irreproachable man of honour, farsighted and willing to encourage new business ventures.

Fond of his family and totally faithful to his wife, don Vincenzo doted on his Giovannino, so intelligent and bright, a worthy successor. He was proud of him as only a father can be: he found him handsome and strong, he sensed his burgeoning masculinity, and even more deeply he was aware of a shrewdness, an awareness of his own worth, a determination and also an arrogance that, allied to a vague business sense, would allow his son to tackle what he intuited was the modern world. Don Vincenzo knew that times had changed for everyone and that the mafia had to adapt to these changes in order to penetrate the new social and political order. He knew that these changes would have profound repercussions, some of them drastic, and that certain aspects of the code handed down from father to son, a code to which he was nostalgically attached, would become dated and finally sink into oblivion. This pained don Vincenzo, because it was precisely the honoured society's insistence on a severe, strict, and therefore predictable code of conduct that had proved one of the foundations of its success: united by the terror of a sure revenge against anyone who failed to respect the code of honour or dared to rebel against wrongs, both mafiosi and "the others" saw this behaviour as a sign of integrity and even-handedness on the part of the mafia. Don Vincenzo genuinely enjoyed this dual role of judge and executioner, although he was fully aware of its hypocrisy. It was up to him, and to him alone, to be his son's teacher, convinced as he was that he could bequeath him a fitting education.

His son's initiation called for don Vincenzo to take him into the estates at harvest time, so that everyone, master and peasant alike, would come to know him, and in turn Giovannino would learn to treat people the right way. That May morning they went down on horseback to the prince's big almond grove, which lay all around the farm. The beaters were lashing the boughs of the almond trees with supple canes, implacable with the fruit but careful with the trees. A hail of fleshy green almonds whose shells had barely hardened, like gigantic olives, was falling to the ground. At a distance, they were followed by teams of almond pickers, women and young men on all fours, like ants. The males were supervised by a man and the females by the overseer, an old woman who had the right and the duty to scold the beaters if they dared add bold or seductive words to the verses of the *stornelli*, the time-honoured folk songs. Almonds were seldom picked in silence. They all sang call and response; this serene and ordered activity marked the transition from late spring to summer, when food was most abundant for everyone.

That day, don Vincenzo had the ill-fated idea of leaving his son with the almond pickers who were working around the farm while he went to the water trough on the other side of the almond grove. A mafia boss must be seen but especially must see and listen himself, be always on the alert. Keeping an eye on the traffic around the water trough, listening to the conversations of the peasants and young men filling water jars to take to their homes, was an agreeable and necessary surveillance. He would eat bread and cheese with them before returning in the afternoon to go back to town with his son.

At around two o'clock, he was joined by a countryman from the farm, Luigi Vicari, who was on the back of his mule. They spoke briefly and immediately went off together, keeping the animals at a walk as long as they were in sight of the people around the water trough, then at a trot as they neared the farm. Don Vincenzo felt like spurring his horse to a gallop but he didn't want to attract attention—even clods of earth have eyes and ears. He arrived at the farm, which seemed deserted and tranquil, as if nothing had been happening. The almond pickers were still toiling industriously away, the beaters were singing, the peasants were in the fields, and the day was warm and bright.

They went into Vicari's home, and only then was he told

in a low voice what had happened. Refusing the glass of water offered him, don Vincenzo listened. About an hour earlier, Luigi Vicari's wife had gone to clean out the hen house next to the barn. From there she heard a woman screaming very loudly: "He's killing me. Help!" Then silence. Shortly afterwards the screams began again. She had no idea of who it could be, as no strangers had come to the farm. She called Luigi, and together they rushed to the barn, which served as a dormitory for the female almond pickers. They saw a tangle of arms and legs. His trousers around his ankles, Giovannino Ancona had thrown himself onto the hay, on top of the girl, and she was kicking and struggling. Such was the young man's ardour that he didn't notice their arrival. But that she-devil noticed, and she bit the hand covering her mouth and started screaming again. They were separated. Luigi Vicari had the boy adjust his clothing and sent him into the cowshed, where there was a hiding place, and there he remained. "I took him a little water, but he doesn't want to eat, and the wound isn't serious," said the countryman, fearful of the wrath of don Vincenzo, who was listening to him with an impassive stare.

"Where's the girl?" he asked.

"She's here, in my place. My wife stayed with her." He nodded in the direction of the other room. "She hasn't screamed any more, and no one knows anything. They're still working, all of them."

"Call your wife," ordered don Vincenzo. The woman was agitated. She tried to affect composure before such an important and feared personage, but you could see that she had just stopped weeping. "Tell me what happened," he commanded, and turning towards her husband he added, "Luigi, I thank you both for your presence of mind, and I shall remember it. Now go tell my son to clean himself up. Get the mares and give them both water, because we'll be returning to town straight away."

Left alone with the woman, he asked her to tell him every detail of what she had seen, who the girl was and what state she was in, without embarrassment and with all the particulars. She couldn't manage this. She spoke in sobs, calling on all the saints and her husband, who could explain everything better than she, she who was only a country-woman and had never seen such things. Don Vincenzo understood right away that this was a clear case of rape. He knew Mennulara, and he knew his son, too.

"Do you know her well?" he asked. The woman over-came her embarrassment and assured him, swearing on the souls of all the saints, on her father's grave, and on the lives of her own children, that Mennulara was a virgin and her behaviour was proof of this: since they had dragged his son off her, she had managed to get the girl to go into her bedroom, where she threw herself on the floor and did nothing but moan. She still had bloodstains on her clothes and between her thighs; she had even refused a drink of water. She was a virgin.

"I know Mennulara better than the others, because she's been coming here for many years. They are poor as poor can be—she doesn't even eat her ration, so she can take it home—they're starving. We all love her, and every so often we leave her a couple of eggs, some greens or a piece of cheese hidden in the barn for her to take home. If we offer her anything face-to-face in front of the others, she is ashamed and refuses, so we do it like this: we leave the food in a hole in the wall in the barn where she hides her provisions, and she knows and she takes it. Just this morning while she was gathering almonds, my husband told her there was something in the barn for her, and she was so happy . . . but you can see that she's proud and never asks for anything.

"I don't know why she went into the barn at lunchtime. I think she probably went back to fill the jug with fresh water, for I saw it in the corner. Nor do I know why your son showed up there." The poor woman was terrified and didn't want to blame the son of a mafia boss for an act as vile as it was unusual for a mafioso to commit.

Don Vincenzo said, "According to you, was it rape or not?"

The woman began to weep again softly and didn't reply.

"Talk. Was it rape or not?" repeated don Vincenzo imperiously but without raising his voice.

"You are a father, and I too have grown-up children, and I swear to you on my mother's grave that the screams of that little girl, and the state I found her in, leave me in no doubt that it was as you say, but only God knows the truth."

"Open the door and let me see her," he ordered. The woman didn't want to obey; she told him that the girl was semiconscious and would certainly die on the spot if she saw him. That was all they needed! He couldn't question her in the state she was in.

Don Vincenzo lost his composure and raised his voice. "Listen to me. I know how to behave. I only want to see her.

It's not for me to talk to her." He got up and opened the door.

The room was immersed in shadow; the only window was in the centre of the wall, almost beneath the roof beams, the shutters half-closed. The stench of poverty, the smell of mildew, manure, and hay took him by the throat. On the floor lay boxes, baskets, piles of blankets, tools. The bed was actually just a mattress thrown on the floor, covered by a grey cloth; a small crucifix over the mattress identified it as a sleeping place.

At first he didn't see her. In a corner stood the only piece of furniture in the room, a chair. Mennulara was lying near it, looking like another pile of rags. Huddled on the floor like a newborn baby, her back was curved in a virtual circle, with her legs drawn up and her head, bent over her breast, touching her knees; whining like an injured dog, she was shuddering rhythmically. She didn't notice his presence. The red bloodstains were visible on the back of her slip. One leg was uncovered, and its pale flesh was streaked with blood that had run down to the foot.

Don Vincenzo closed the door again, thanked the woman, and went into the barn. His son was standing waiting for him, he too with bloodstains on his trousers and shirt. Don Vincenzo said, "Come." In silence they mounted their horses and trotted off as if nothing had happened. Passing the almond pickers at a distance, they called out the usual greeting, "*Salutàmu*," and did the same with the beaters. The journey back to town took about three hours. Don Vincenzo didn't look at his son, but rode ahead of him, making his way through the woods, avoiding the most frequented tracks and paths. His wife and daughters were waiting for them; the little girls were cheerful. Don Vincenzo was heartbroken at the tragedy that had befallen his family. He told them that Giovannino had fallen and hurt himself, nothing serious, and he sent them off to the pharmacy to buy medicines.

When they were alone in the stables, he asked his son, "Did you start it?"

"Yes. I don't know what came over me."

Then don Vincenzo waded into his beloved son, punching and kicking him repeatedly in the belly and the testicles, weeping and cursing the misfortune that had befallen his house. Giovannino had to stay in bed for a few days after that.

In the meantime don Vincenzo arranged for his son's departure. It was said that he was going to live in the north of Italy, at a cousin's place, to pursue his studies. He was so intelligent that his life would be wasted in Sicily, and he would learn far more things at school on the mainland. The honoured society was informed about the real situation and approved don Vincenzo's wise decision. Giovannino behaved like a man: he acknowledged his guilt and promised his mother, who was distraught at his departure, that he would uphold the family honour, that one day she would be proud of him.

At a meeting of the men of honour, Giovannino Ancona humbly admitted his sins, exhibiting surprising dignity for a sixteen-year-old. Not only had he done something that could not be tolerated by the ethical code of the mafia—allowing himself to be overcome by carnal lust in the course of his duties (whether he had had his way with a consenting female, man, or beast, it didn't matter, for a mafioso must never lose control)—but the fact that he had raped a virgin, and a child at that, cast doubt on his judgement. He had broken the rule that other people's women were not to be touched. Even if they silenced the girl and the witnesses, there was a risk that someone might talk in the future, and that remote possibility made it impossible for him to be a worthy and respected heir to his father and forefathers on those estates. Contrite, Giovannino Ancona promised to exploit the opportunities that the modern world could offer in the service of the honoured society, like a true Ancona, as all the others of his family had done before him.

In reality, despite his burning humiliation and the sorrow at leaving his family and Sicily, Giovannino Ancona knew that he was able and eager to learn. The prospect of devoting himself to study and working in business fascinated him; moreover, he realised that he liked a less austere life than that imposed by the code of the country mafia. He seldom returned to Sicily; he lived and got married in Lombardy. For don Vincenzo and his wife, he was a lost son.

Don Vincenzo Ancona had to refer the matter to Ciccio Alfallipe, the princes of Brogli's estate manager, but he played down the occurrence, as if it were merely an error on the part of two hot-blooded youngsters. He had him understand that he would appreciate it if Mennulara were found another job, one in town. Thus it happened that signora Lilla Alfallipe met with no objections on her husband's part when she told him she was thinking of taking another maid into service, Nuruzza Inzerillo's daughter.

Don Vincenzo then bought the silence of the Vicaris,

who left the farm and opened up a greengrocer's shop. They were always watched, and knew it. He kept tabs on the Inzerillo family and Mennulara, too, ready to kill anyone he suspected of talking or merely wanting to.

49. Don Vincenzo Ancona relives his only encounter with Mennulara

Almost twenty years later, before the war broke out, through a man from Enna word reached don Vincenzo that Mennulara wanted to talk to him when it was convenient. He was amazed and perturbed: blackmail or a request for compensation after all that time was the fruit of an unstable mind, whereas he knew that she was anything but that. He had always kept up to date about Mennulara's life, and had been told that she had a name for being a well-balanced person, cautious and of few words, who treated no one with familiarity. In short, she kept her lip buttoned like a true *fimmina di panza*.

This request for a meeting surprised him very much. Don Vincenzo decided to put the matter off for two weeks; besides, she had indicated no urgency. But the thought of Mennulara became a pall of gloom hanging over his head, and it worried him more than anything else.

A few days later don Vincenzo and his wife had reason to be justly proud of their Giovannino; they learned that, thanks to the honoured society, he had obtained a high-ranking position with the bank that managed a large chunk of the Family's money. Now he was destined to become one of the mafia's most important financiers abroad. Giovannino, who had attended a prestigious university in Milan, now spoke fluent French, was unrecognisable as a southerner, was a trusted member of the mafia, and would surpass even his father in the hierarchy of the honoured society.

It struck don Vincenzo as ironic that his son's success should coincide with Mennulara's request. Then he began to suspect a nefarious connection between the two events, a link he was unable to imagine, and he was very worried by this. He considered silencing her; she would become one of the many people who disappeared without a trace, never to be found again. As a young man he had killed several men, and as a mafia boss he had ordered dozens of deaths. It was easy. Yet in the end he decided to let her talk, perhaps out of curiosity—he needed to verify what had really happened in the past. He would decide about the rest afterwards. And so he gave her an appointment in the office of a trusted notary. It seemed clear that she wanted to blackmail him.

It was two o'clock on a Thursday afternoon—he remembered this perfectly—when there were few people on the streets. Nervously, Mennulara came into the office, where the notary and don Vincenzo were waiting for her. Thin, her face pale and bony, her hair pulled back into a chignon, and dressed in a simple, austere grey dress, she looked older than she was. The notary stood up to receive her, but don Vincenzo remained seated, his head lowered, one hand on his leg and the other resting on the desk.

Mennulara sat down in the chair opposite and greeted

don Vincenzo. "I thank you for giving me this appointment," she began.

Don Vincenzo had to look up. He stared at her intensely; he had a way of doing this so that the other person never noticed. Earlier, he had tried to recall what she looked like, but he hadn't been able to remember her features. All he could remember was that her singing was beautiful, strong and melodious; now that she was in his presence, the image of a nimble little girl singing folk songs at the top of her voice under the trees flashed through his mind.

Mennulara met his gaze without shyness, and she said simply, "Don Vincenzo, afterwards, I never sang again for my own pleasure."

"You must believe me. I'm very sorry."

The notary interrupted this cryptic conversation and explained, as agreed beforehand with don Vincenzo, that the reason for his presence was that if there were any need to talk concretely, he was at their service to draw up an agreement. Then he became aware that not only Mennulara but also don Vincenzo were looking at him as if he had spoken out of turn. He had interrupted an intimate, solemn conversation.

In a low but authoritative voice, Mennulara said to the notary, "Sir, I don't need money, and it would be better if you left. Don Vincenzo can call you if he needs you." Don Vincenzo lowered his head in assent.

They were left alone, seated facing each other at the imposing solid-wood desk. On the opposite side stood the notary's empty chair, an equally imposing piece whose tall back was framed by a broad carved wooden moulding. It seemed like the chair reserved for the missing character, his Giovan-nino, whose name was never uttered but whose presence was almost palpable in the dense, heavy air of the office, as if he were a ghost.

Don Vincenzo was breathing with difficulty; he moved his hands and then returned them to the same position as before. Then he raised his completely bald, ruddy head and asked her point-blank, "What did he do to you?"

"I've never told anyone," replied Mennulara, looking him straight in the eye. "Must you hear it now?"

Don Vincenzo nodded: it was an order.

She talked in a monotone without interruption, reliving in clear and exact detail the trauma suffered at the age of thirteen, her gaze empty, devoid of emotion, as if she were recounting events that had happened to another person. "You know who I am and you also know that I worked to provide for my late mother and my sister. I liked the open-air life and I was happy in my work. The country folk at Can-nelli took pity on us three poor women and they left me gifts of cheese and other things to eat—hidden behind a stone in the hole beneath the little window of the barn—which I would then take home. That day, don Luigi Vicari told me there were two eggs for me, and your son must have heard. It was a hot day and there were many trees to shake, but the beaters were slow and lazy, and they left lots of good almonds on the trees. I would climb up to pick them all. I liked climb-ing trees, I was still a child.

"He must have noticed me as I was working. I don't know, all I know is that when we stopped for the lunch break, I got really hungry, and I ate all the cheese and the olives they gave us. Normally I would nibble a little and keep the rest to take home—my sister had little appetite but those things tempted her. He was doing the rounds of all of us workers, the way you used to. I told the other girls I shouldn't have eaten it all, that cheese with pepper, which was marvellous. He heard me and he came up and said he had a half round of that cheese and could give me a big slice of it. I would find it in the barn if I went there right away, because it wouldn't last long.

"You had already gone, don Vincenzo, and so I believed him. I and another almond picker took away two empty jugs to change for two with fresh water. We carried them held upright on our heads, the way we unmarried girls were entitled to. Afterwards, I wasn't entitled to do that any more, I couldn't even carry them flat on my head." She fell silent. She looked at him and then her eyes seemed to glaze over, seeing again, reliving again, her old desperation.

Then Mennulara continued in the same tone. "I went for the last time in my life to fill the water jugs at the farmhouse well, and then I made a beeline for the barn. He was hiding behind the door. As soon as I went in, he pounced on me like an animal in heat. I couldn't defend myself. He tore at my clothes and my flesh. He was stronger than I was, and he had his hand over my mouth. I bit him twice to call for help, and that was that. He punched me on the mouth and on the breast so hard, I can still feel the pain. He penetrated me all the way up to my innards; I felt I was dying. Luckily, don Luigi Vicari and his wife came. But before they helped me, they saw to him. He's your son; I was only an orphan girl, hungry and shamed. And so I was left in zi' Maria Vicari's place. I wanted the ground to swallow me up, I was so ashamed. I was aching all over, inside and out. Zi' Maria washed me a bit and gave me some eggs, greens, and lots of bread, and I made my way home alone, without even saying good-bye to the others. Every step was a torment, so badly had I been mauled.

"My mother, God rest her soul, had already been told that I had compromised myself with a man and that it was my fault. She would have beaten me to death if she hadn't been so weak, but when she saw me, she understood that it wasn't true and she asked no questions. She had great respect for you, don Vincenzo. She said that you could have sent my father away when he was working as a field hand and was too weak to hoe because he was dying, but you didn't have him fired, and maybe that's why I believed in your son's goodness when he offered me the cheese. Deep down, it has always rankled that you, don Vincenzo, like the others, perhaps believed me to be at fault for what happened, because it's not true. Until now, the truth was known only to me and him.

"I stayed home for a few days, I couldn't think. There was no future for my family. The food ran out, and my mother and sister were very ill. My mother put me into service at Alfallipe House, even though she had never wanted me to do that, for she said that there was no trusting the masters—the menfolk, I mean—and she was right, because I am now a prisoner there, and there I'll die, without ever being able to have a family and children of my own.

"I got pregnant by counsellor Orazio Alfallipe, but he mustn't know that, and you are the only one who does, apart from Dr. Mendicò and signora Lilla. I got rid of it; this is how it had to be. While I was in hospital, I learned that there is a test to discover people's blood type and fingerprints so you can know who they belong to. I had these tests made on the handkerchief that boy had used to clean himself with—not only of the blood, which was plentiful, but also of his shame—and fingerprints were left in the bloodstains. I kept it. You can know the person they belong to. I know, and I have no need of proof, but if you don't believe me, I'll give it to you, along with the tests I had done. I'm not here to blackmail anyone or to get money from you, far less from him. I'm here to tell you that the truth is known, and I'll give you the only proof I possess, which I never want to see again."

She opened her bag and took out an envelope, which she laid on the desk.

"All I ask of you is three favours, which you can refuse me. You know I can never harm either you or him, nor do I wish to. Signora Lilla Alfallipe took pity on me, and she gave me fifty gold coins to make amends for what her son Orazio had done. Perhaps it was too much, for I had already been shamed, and he was never violent with me, unlike the other one. I go on living in their home. If I had left them then, all I could have done was whore for other swine, and my sister wouldn't have had any medicine and would have died." She paused. "I am not ashamed, because I managed to have my sister, Addoloratina, treated and I managed to marry her, still a virgin, to a good man. She has two fine sons and is happy, as my late mother wished." She stopped and looked don Vincenzo in the eye.

"What can I do for you?" he asked hoarsely.

"The first is immediate: I need help in order to invest those coins. I can read a little and I understand a lot. I don't want anyone to know that I got this gift, and I already have some small savings. You are powerful, and I know that the Family has investments abroad: I think it wise to invest this money well and in secret, which is, after all, what you do. It doesn't matter how, but I want this money to grow, because I am afraid of one thing only: of being poor again.

"The second is for the future: if ever I need your protection and I ask you for help, give it to me, with all your power.

"The third is for the respect I deserve: if I should die before you—and I feel inside that I have suffered too much to live for long, and we Inzerillos all die young—promise to come to my funeral, because in this way, a man of honour pays his debt to a poor almond picker who was dishonoured by his flesh and blood."

Don Vincenzo stared at her fixedly, motionless. He leaned over and took her hands. He held them fast in his and dropped his eyes. Mennulara did the same. Then he said, "Word of honour."

They stood up. Don Vincenzo took the envelope and left.

Don Vincenzo Ancona didn't see Mennulara again, and he kept his word. He had her money invested in Switzerland, and he saw to it that she received the same deferential treatment reserved for the honoured society. The bank official would meet her in Sicily, when he came to keep up contacts with his clients during his "archaeological holidays," and with her he used the discreet, tried-and-tested channels of communication.

Don Vincenzo had the lab tests on the handkerchief done again. He then spoke to his son. It was not a difficult discussion. He told him that he owed all his fortune to Mennulara, because otherwise he would never have been exiled from his home and his town. Now that he was rich and safe, he would have to think about paying the moral debt he owed her: he was to add a considerable sum to the gold coins immediately and to keep an eye on her account, but without her noticing anything. Giovannino, still afraid of his father and wanting to show him that he was contrite and a man of honour, did his duty. This was the origin of Mennulara's wealth, but she remained in ignorance of the means by which her investments continuously increased.

Satisfying the second request was more difficult. The Puleri estate, which the Alfallipes had bought cheaply from the princes of Brogli, was not very profitable, but it bordered on Roccacolomba Bassa. Mennulara sent don Vincenzo a message, saying that she knew there was talk of building a new school in Roccacolomba Bassa and of the rebirth of the town. If it was possible to declare Puleri as building land and to construct the school on it, she would be happy, because the estate had to be sold. Don Vincenzo had to pull strings to arrange this, but in the end he managed. There they built not only schools but also public housing and a cement works, thus making the Alfallipes rich.

The third and final request was satisfied on Tuesday 24 September 1963. Mennulara deserved all his respect and he would watch over her reputation. God help anyone who spoke ill of her.

50. The thirtieth day after Mennulara's death

Not only the folk of Roccacolomba but also the Alfallipes were surprised by the notice in the *Giornale di Sicilia* that reminded friends of the date and hour of the memorial Mass for signorina Maria Rosalia Inzerillo in the church of the Addolorata.

Father Arena officiated, speedy as ever. This time he didn't preach a sermon. He could have said whatever came into his head, since hardly anyone was there, thought don Paolino Annunziata. He was one of the few people who was present. Signora Adriana Alfallipe and Carmela Leone were beside Chairman Fatta and his wife. Vazzano, the notary, was behind them, next to Dr. Mendicò and his sister. There were few other people, about ten in all. "I told you so," murmured don Paolino to his wife on the way back home. "People forget, and I've no complaint about that. It's right. The very word *mennulara* is on the point of disappearing from our language, for nowadays there are no almond pickers on the estates any more. Men collect the almonds with big tarpaulins, and the Tunisian workers are coming here to our mountains . . . and that's the end of the women fruit pickers."

After the Mass Pietro Fatta insisted on inviting Father Arena to lunch. He wanted to discuss something important with the priest and with Gianni Alfallipe, who was coming specially from Catania and would join them around one o'clock. When they rose from the table, Pietro invited Gianni and the priest into his study. He was particularly formal and seemed rather embarrassed.

"Gianni, I have some good news for the Alfallipe family, and I want to discuss it first with you and Father Arena, so that you might tell me how best to convey it to your mother and your sisters, and give me some idea of the role that I hope you will wish to play."

"Be more explicit, Uncle Pietro. What is this role you're talking about?" asked Gianni moodily. He had been awakened that morning by a friend who had read in the newspaper about the Mass, a service in which the Alfallipes had no hand this time. He talked to his sisters and his mother, all three of whom were in the dark about both the announcement and the Mass. Seized by panic, he feared that yet again Mennulara wanted to set a trap or play another bitter trick, and he didn't know whether to go straight to Roccacolomba or to stay in Catania. He even telephoned Father Arena, who told him that celebrating Mass on the thirtieth day after death was customary; he had agreed on this with Mennulara herself and was surprised that Gianni didn't know. Then came the invitation to lunch at Fatta House because the chairman had important news that he wished to give him urgently.

"A well-known and respected lawyer in Zurich, about whom I have made discreet enquiries, wrote to me and the prefect last week. An old client of his, an art connoisseur, died recently, leaving part of his considerable estate for a philanthropical purpose in connection with your father."

"My father? I don't believe it," said Gianni.

"That was my first reaction, too, but on thinking it over, I have reached another conclusion. Orazio was a learned and charming man . . . this benefactor, unknown to us, must have met and admired him," said Pietro Fatta. "Now he wants to establish a musical event devoted to opera. It would take place in the month of May, in memory of your father, in the provincial capital. In addition, he has set aside funds for a scholarship reserved for a destitute young person, to study singing at the conservatory in Catania."

"Anything else?" asked Gianni, incredulous and sarcastic.

"I am the president of the foundation, and it is my task to nominate the members of the various committees, and I'd like to know if you're interested. The benefactor's conditions are few and clear. He demands that they play pieces chosen by him at the first and last performances—all of Verdi's operas, beginning with *Aida*. He wishes that you or another representative of the Alfallipe family be invited to award the prize to the winner of the singing competition, and that the event, called 'La Mennulara,' be dedicated 'to the memory of counsellor Orazio Alfallipe, man of culture and collector.' "

"Fuck!" Gianni was stunned.

"Congratulations, Professor. Your father would be happy," said Father Arena with an ironic little smile.

"What will people say?" said Gianni, worried. "What if it's a trick, and the mafia takes it out on us? We still don't know where the money is coming from. I'm afraid Mennù has a hand in this; she'll be the ruination of us all."

"Take it easy, Gianni. You don't have to do anything. I have accepted the appointment; I simply wanted to know if you want to take part. It could be interesting; this is going to be a serious affair and an important one for the province, and maybe even beyond. Your wife could sit on the artistic committee. Perhaps Lilla will want to take part, maybe even Carmela. For the Alfallipe family, it is an honour. But what I'd like to know is what your mother will think of it."

"I don't know. She still adores her Mennù, despite everything, so I'm sure that she'll be happy about it."

Pietro Fatta and the priest exchanged a knowing look: this was good news; they had feared worse.

Gianni found his courage again and went on angrily, "Let's talk plainly about this. Who this benefactor may be, I don't know, but I have the feeling that this is money Mennulara stole from us, and now she's tossing it in our face. It's disgusting. Mama will never understand, but it's a shameful business, not to mention my father's memory: he would have been mortified by the idea of finding his name linked with that of a servant. It certainly isn't what he would have wanted. After all, nothing prevented him from doing the same thing himself." He glanced around. Pietro Fatta and Father Arena looked impassive—examples of that ability to dissimulate thoughts and feelings that Sicilians imbibe with their mother's milk.

"Do as you wish, Uncle Pietro. I didn't expect this from you. I thought you were my father's best friend," said Gianni coldly.

"And I still am." There was a note of tension in Pietro Fatta's voice.

Gianni raised his voice. "People will say that there was goodness knows what kind of improper relationship between my father and Mennù, a love affair. Do you understand? That's what she wanted. She didn't manage it in life, and that's why she's got it in for us now. We'll have to explain around town that their relationship was completely different."

"Your father loved her, you know," replied Pietro Fatta firmly.

Gianni was dumbfounded. "I don't believe you, Uncle. The honour of the appointment has you confused. Now you're going to tell me that she too loved my father, loved us children, and wanted the best for us. And that we would have done better to obey her," he added sarcastically.

Father Arena stepped in. "Calm yourself, Professor. I cannot betray the secrets of the confessional, but I can assure you that there will be no disagreeable repercussions from the mafia or anyone else, as long as you don't criticise Mennulara in public. You have already found this out at your own expense. You will not receive letters or other missives from her. All we are talking about is a musical event. It's a fine thing and it will add lustre to the family name."

Pietro Fatta added, "Don't be afraid of looking ridiculous, Gianni. Quite the contrary; this will redeem your family's conduct in the past. You were the ones who published the obituary—twice. I shall moreover give an explanation of the chosen title, as the benefactor requires. A member of the household staff who became an administrator and who served you honestly—they are your own words. I will add that your benevolence permitted her to study, and thus she also became Orazio's assistant in his artistic and musical researches. And what's more, thanks to her work as administrator, she gave him the time to devote himself to art. I'm not exaggerating; it all corresponds to the plain truth."

Pietro Fatta spoke well and Gianni calmed down, even though he was thinking of their immense loss . . . If only they hadn't smashed those Greek vases!

Father Arena left Fatta House in the afternoon and went straight to the Mendicò home before taking the bus back to the country. The doctor was sitting in the parlour with his sister, reading the newspaper.

"All I have to do is give you a brief reply, Doctor," said Father Arena, refusing the invitation to sit down and take coffee with them. "Last month, you asked me a difficult question, to which I was unable to reply. Now I know the answer is yes."

Her brother's exaggerated and unpredictable reaction gave signora Di Prima occasion to note that, sadly, he was becoming really odd, perhaps on the verge of senility. In fact, on hearing those words, Dr. Mendicò, who had got up from his armchair to welcome the priest and was still standing in front of him, grabbed the priest's arm, forcing him to stoop while he threw his short arms around him and gave him two loud kisses on the cheeks . . . and he didn't let the priest go, but hung on to him in a long embrace. For his part, Father Arena made no attempt to break free and seemed to accept this behaviour as normal. Finally the two old men separated and looked at signora Di Prima like two schoolboys taken by surprise.

Father Arena took his leave in some embarrassment and with much stammering. The doctor saw him to the door and at the moment of farewell said quietly, "Good for Mennulara. It's true what they say. Love is ageless!" And he embraced Father Arena again before returning to rejoin his sister in the parlour.

Signora Di Prima immediately asked him, "Mimmo, what did Father Arena mean by that answer?" She was ready to bombard her brother with questions.

"Concetta, some things are private and are no business of yours. That's enough now, please," said the doctor, who went back to his reading. Offended, signora Di Prima retired to her room, leaving Dr. Mendicò alone to read the paper, happier than he had been in a long time.

Epilogue

Gaspare Risico was transferred to Palermo and given a small promotion.

Massimo Leone and Carmela Alfallipe moved into Alfallipe House to keep signora Adriana company, and there they stayed until her death in 1967. Carmela and Massimo separated shortly after, following another violent row.

Carmela decided to open a clothes shop in Roccacolomba, a business venture that enjoyed a remarkable success. She lived in a flat in Alfallipe House and often spent the evenings at home, seated at the table, playing with the jigsaw puzzles that she had become keen on after trying to glue together the vases that she and her brother and sister had broken on 30 September 1963. In fact, she did this so well that the three Alfallipe children decided to take Dr. Palmeri, of the Regional Museum, the fragments of their father's collection (which were then restored and are now on display at the museum)—an act of contrition to placate the spirit of Mennulara, who in their minds had assumed omnipotent and demonic dimensions.

The puzzles became the comfort and the obsession of Carmela's evenings, almost a nightly ritual, from which she was sidetracked four times a year, at the turn of the seasons, when a good-looking representative of a ladies' knitwear manufacturer came to Sicily from Naples to take orders from his clients. Then Carmela would abandon herself in the arms of the representative, engaging in a passionate but tranquil seasonal love affair. When the Neapolitan left her to go around the other provinces, Carmela serenely fell back into the lethargy of the senses, comforted by the pieces of her puzzles, until the next visit.

Massimo Leone went to live in his sister's house and continued to live by his wits. At fifty years of age, he got a girl from Catania pregnant. Her brothers threatened him, and it looked as if they were not joking. Encouraged by his brother-in-law, Massimo moved to another town to flee his persecutors, and nothing more was heard of him in Roccacolomba.

Lilla became a much-valued habitué of Rome's most refined salons; she entertained in style in her beautiful home, where a place of honour was reserved for two Greek amphorae, hugely admired by the cognoscenti of the capital as splendid examples of the art of Magna Graecia. In addition, Lilla was one of the judges in the annual competition entitled La Mennulara, which, together with the musical performances, became known and appreciated throughout Sicily.

Gianni lived a fulfilling, serene life with his wife and son, Orazio, in Catania, and his university career was a reasonable success. He never suspected that Orazio was not his son but that of a very dear family friend, a colleague of his wife's. Alfallipe House remained intact, only a little run-down. Gianni and his wife stayed on the main floor when they came to Roccacolomba for holidays and for the musical performances, often inviting friends. Young Orazio was conceived in signor Alfallipe's study, on the sofa in front of the fireplace.

The folk of Roccacolomba soon forgot Maria Rosalia Inzerillo, known as Mennulara, but they remember with pride their illustrious fellow citizen, Orazio Alfallipe, a great scholar and collector, whose memory lends prestige to their small Sicilian town.

Acknowledgements

I wish to thank two people for their help in the making of this novel: Giovanna Salvia, first reader, enthusiastic intermediary, unstinting and discreet dispenser of suggestions, and now friend; and my editor at Feltrinelli, Alberto Rollo, whose constant support and patience proved invaluable, as did his impeccable professional judgement. Working with him was a pleasure as well as a constant lesson. Not only did he give me a memorable master class in writing, his scholarship went beyond that to reveal the meaning of some Sicilian and English words hitherto unknown to me.